A DABHAND

4·C

IMPRESSION
II

ANNE ROONEY

DABS
PRESS

©Anne Rooney 1993
ISBN 1 870336 10 0
First Edition January 1993
First printed in the UK January 1993

Editor: Roger Amos
Typesetting: Mark Nuttall
Cover Design: Mark Nuttall

Published by: Dabs Press Publishing, PO Box 48, Prestwich, Manchester. M25 7HN

Printed and bound in the UK by Ashford Colour Press, Gosport, Hampshire, PO12 4DT.

Contents

Preface: Versions of Impression

Computer Concepts frequently issues upgrades to Impression and Impression Business Supplement. You can get an upgrade free by returning your Impression disc 1 or Business Supplement disc. Upgrades often have new features and fix bugs in earlier versions. It is worth phoning Computer Concepts occasionally to find out whether there is a new version you should have.

This book was written using Impression version 2.17. If you find that Impression does not behave as described here (for example, if you can't put a picture into an embedded frame simply by dragging its file icon into the Impression document window) you probably have an earlier version of Impression. Contact Computer Concepts for an upgrade. Of course, newer versions of Impression will supersede 2.17 and Impression may have more features than are described here. To find out what version of Impression you have, you need to load Impression and then use **Info** from the icon bar menu; the version number is shown in the bottom line of the dialogue box. Chapter 2: *Getting ready to use Impression* explains how to install and load Impression.

1 What is Impression?

You probably bought Impression because you wanted to produce nicely laid out documents, or perhaps because you wanted a word-processor and realised that Impression offers more than the others on the market for the Acorn RISC OS range of computers. Perhaps you knew that you didn't want to have to use a separate word-processor and desktop publishing program and that Impression performs both functions in a single program. Impression will certainly fulfil any of these needs, and it may do even more than you had realised it could. Impression is a fully-featured desktop publishing program, but it also has many word-processing features — more than Acorn Desktop Publisher, which is its closest rival.

With many desktop publishing programs, on Archimedes and PC-clone machines, routine desktop publishing is difficult and restricted. It is assumed that you will prepare your text with a word-processing program and then lay it out with a desktop publishing program. Impression aims to combine the stages: it is not just a word-processor or desktop publishing program, but a document processor. You can compose your text directly in Impression, either adding styling features as you go or putting them in afterwards. You can design each page separately, or use the same basic design for each. You can include pictures in your document. You can add running headers and footers to each page. You can create an index and contents page automatically. You can divide a single document into several chapters. And, as well as printing your document on your own printer, you can produce files you can take to an imagesetting bureau to generate really professional-looking output.

Impression as a word-processor

You can compose all your text directly in Impression. This is possible not only because it has full word-processing capabilities, but because it automatically generates new pages with text flowing from one to another as you need them.

As a word-processor, Impression lets you do any of these:

• type text that flows continuously from one page to the next automatically

- import files you have created using another text editor, such as 1st Word Plus or Edit

- add text files into the middle of a document you are already using

- cut, paste and copy text within a document

- find and replace text

- check your spelling

- expand abbreviations

- compile an index

- compile a table of contents.

As Impression is a word-processor you can type your text directly onto an Impression page. However, if you have text you have already prepared with 1st Word Plus, Edit or another text editing system, you can import it into an Impression document to lay it out.

Impression as a desktop publishing package

Impression uses a frame-based system for page design. This means that all text and graphics must be contained within a frame, a box on the page that is not printed out but is used as a guide for layout. Impression allows you to flow text from one page to the next through linked frames, to add extra frames to a page to hold graphics or additional text, and to create master pages which will be used as templates for the basic initial design of all new pages. The position of the frames will determine the margins. You can layer frames, change the order in which they are stacked and control their colour. Frames can also have a border that is printed. Impression is supplied with a selection of borders and you can buy extra borders or design your own. Don't worry if any of these terms are unfamiliar; they are all explained later on.

Pages can have one or more columns of text. You can also add headers and footers, including page numbers, that will be repeated on each page. You can style your text, using different sizes and fonts, and using special effects such as italic, bold and underlined text. You can control the colour of text, the space between lines, whether to add rules above or below text, and where to place tab stops. You can choose the justification of text (that is, its arrangement between the margins) and set indents. You can insist that some pieces of text are kept together (items in a list, for example). On a smaller scale, you can control the kerning (space between letters) to fine-tune your documents so that they look precisely as you want them to.

You can include pictures in your document, whether they are pictures you have created yourself with an art package or with Draw, clip art you have bought, scanned images, or even pictures captured from video. You can overlay pictures and text, too.

Impression gives you complete control over the design of every page of your document. Whether you choose to model all your pages on a single master page or design each page differently — as you may if you are producing a newsletter, for example — there is a great deal of scope for imaginative design.

You can send your documents to a printer or take files to an imagesetting bureau. If you have a colour printer, you will be able to print your document using colours for text or graphics. With the Business

Supplement, you can also produce colour separations for four-colour printing at a bureau.

Impression as a document processor

Impression claims to be a document processor; this means that it is both a word-processor and desktop publishing system, and also allows you to process long documents using some relatively sophisticated techniques such as building up a table of contents and an index, and handling multiple chapters within the same document. Features of this type are generally only offered by expensive and memory-hungry programs on more expensive computers and personal workstations. Impression is unique (so far!) in bringing these advanced facilities to the Archimedes range. It makes the Archimedes a better bet for desktop publishing than PC-type computers of equivalent price.

Using Impression

You can use Impression to create any type of document you like from business cards to complete books. While you work, you can see on screen exactly what will appear on the page when you print your document. This feature is called WYSIWYG — What You See Is What You Get. Impression also allows you to choose the scale at which you view your document, so you can zoom in for fine, detailed work and zoom out to look at several pages at once to get an idea of how your layout looks overall.

Impression uses *master pages* as templates for all new pages. For example, you might have a master page with two columns for text; all new pages you create using this master page will automatically have two columns to hold your text. You can create new pages explicitly or automatically — Impression will create a new page if the text you are typing or import from another file spills over from the current page. This feature makes it easy to maintain a consistent layout within each document and to build up a whole series of documents keeping a consistent style. You can use more than one master page in each document, too. This makes it especially easy to use complex layouts but give your document a consistent look. For example, you might choose to use one master page for the main text of your document and a different master page for all the pages of the index. Master pages not only save you time as you don't have to create the columns and frames for each page, they also make it easy to make sure each page of the same type has exactly the same layout; this is very difficult if you are laying out each page from scratch every time. Impression comes with a selection of pre-prepared master pages, and you can also create your own or alter those supplied.

If you have already used some other desktop publishing programs, on a RISC OS computer or another computer, you may be surprised to find that Impression is quite different in style from most other desktop publishing applications. It does not follow the common Ventura-style model of different modes for typing text, styling paragraphs, creating text frames and drawing graphics. It is rather closer to some of the Macintosh-based systems. Impression handles all types of task from the menus, and does not have any tools visible on screen as you work. It has only one main window, which shows your document (though you can open several windows at once to look at more than one document or to see the master pages of a document or other areas of the same document). Even if you are used to a different type of desktop publishing program, you will find Impression quite easy to use once you get used to the differences. If you have not used any other desktop publishing programs, you're in luck because Impression is easier to learn than many others!

What next?

The next chapter explains how to make copies of the Impression discs and install Impression on floppy or hard disc to use with your computer. If Impression is already installed, you can skip the next chapter and go to chapter 3, which tells you how to begin using Impression.

2 Getting ready to use Impression

Before you use Impression, you need to make working copies of the discs. You can make copies on floppy discs, or install Impression onto the hard disc of your computer. If you are going to run Impression from floppy discs, don't use the distribution discs, but make and use working copies, keeping the original discs as back-up copies.

Impression comes with a special copy-protection device which is officially called a 'hardware key'. It is commonly known as a 'dongle'. Impression won't run unless the dongle is fitted to the parallel printer port on the back of your computer. This is to protect Computer Concepts (who manufacture and distribute Impression) from software piracy; the need for the dongle means that you can't make multiple copies of the Impression discs and distribute them free (or even for a price!) amongst your friends; Impression won't run if there isn't a dongle on the machine, and you obviously can't make copies of that.

The licensing agreement document distributed with Impression explains how you are allowed to use the program. For example, if you have two computers, you can only run Impression on one of them at once — but you are limited to this by only having one dongle, anyway.

This chapter explains how to:

- make copies of the Impression discs on floppy discs
- install Impression on floppy disc
- copy or install Impression onto your hard disc
- fit the dongle to the printer port so that Impression will run on your computer.

Making working copies of the discs

Impression is supplied on five discs, but you don't need most of the information on them just to run Impression; there are a lot of examples, clip art and borders.

Disc 1 contains:

- !Impress: the Impression program

- !Install: a program you can run to install Impression (but you don't need to use this)

- Extensions: special modules to read text in several formats in case you want to import text you have prepared with a different program into an Impression document.

Disc 2 contains:

some example documents and useful utility programs. You don't need these to start with.

Disc 3 contains:

a set of clip art and some border patterns. You don't need these to start with, either.

Disc 4 contains:

!Fonts, which is a selection of outline fonts you can use with Impression. You will already have a !Fonts directory and may want to add some of the fonts supplied with Impression to it. There is information on doing this later in this chapter.

Disc 5 contains:

more clip art and some printer drivers. You may well already have the printer drivers as they are the standard RISC OS 2 Acorn printer drivers; there is a section later in this chapter that tells you how to check whether the printer drivers on the Impression disc are a more recent version than the ones you already have.

The licensing agreement provided with Impression allows you to make copies of the program and utilities discs for your own use. You should do this immediately. You can then keep the originals as back-up copies. A back-up is a copy of a disc that you keep safely in case you lose or damage your working copy of the program. As long as you have a back-up copy, you will be able to re-copy the program and continue using it if anything happens to your working copy.

Although you are encouraged to make a copy of the Impression discs for your own use on one computer, you are not allowed to make copies to give or sell to other people, or to use on several computers. In fact, you won't be able to do this anyway because Impression won't run if the dongle is not attached to the parallel printer port on the computer. However, if you want to run several copies of Impression at once — perhaps in your school or business — you should contact Computer Concepts and ask whether they can supply you with a site license.

You can make your working copy of Impression on a floppy or hard disc. The instructions that follow tell you how to make a copy on floppy disc, and how to install Impression on a hard disc. Read the section that is appropriate to your computer.

Copying Impression onto floppy discs

To make a copy of each of the Impression discs, you need to:

- format a new floppy disc

- copy the necessary files and directories onto it,

- name and label the new copy.

Before you can make a copy, you need an empty, formatted disc. You can use a brand new disc, or a disc you have used before for information you have finished with. Remember that **all** the information on a disc will be lost when you format it, so make absolutely sure there is nothing on the disc that you want to keep before you format an old disc. To format a disc, follow these steps.

1. Put the disc into the floppy drive of your computer and display the icon bar menu for that drive by moving the pointer over the disc drive icon and pressing the middle mouse button.

2. Move the pointer over the menu option Format and onto the submenu that appears. Select the E-format option. If you are using RISC OS 3, the menu looks like this:

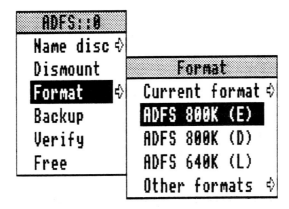

3. If you are using RISC OS 2, a window appears with a prompt asking you to confirm that you want to format the disc; click the lefthand mouse button or press the Y key on the keyboard to continue. The disc will be formatted and verified. If you are using RISC OS 3, a dialogue box will appear instead of a window. Click on **Format** to confirm that you want to format the disc. Whichever version of RISC OS you are using, the window or dialogue box will report the progress of the disc formatting.

4. If you are using RISC OS 2, you will need to press the space bar or click the lefthand mouse button when formatting has finished to dismiss the new window. If you are using RISC OS 3,

you will need to click on OK in the dialogue box to remove it.

The following instructions are divided into two sections, one for computers with a single floppy disc drive, and one for computers with two floppy disc drives. Read the section that is appropriate to your computer.

Copying discs using a single floppy drive

The computer will refer to the disc you are copying from as the source disc. It will call the disc you are copying to (which you have just formatted) the destination disc. You need to write-protect the source disc, but leave the destination disc unprotected so that the computer can write to it. Follow these steps to make a copy of Disc1.

1. Put Disc1 in the floppy drive. Display the icon bar menu for the floppy drive and select the option **Backup**.

2. If you are using RISC OS 2, a window appears with a prompt asking you to confirm that you want to make a back-up of the disc; click the lefthand mouse button or press the Y key on the keyboard to continue. If you are using RISC OS 3, a dialogue box appears reporting the name of the disc in the drive and asking you to insert the source disc:

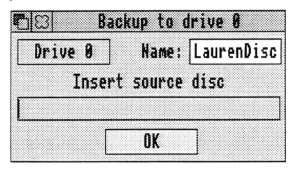

3. If you are using RISC OS 2, a message asks you to write protect the source disc; if you haven't done this already, do it now. Put the disc into the drive and press the space bar when you are ready. If you are using RISC OS 3, you don't get this message; click on OK to start copying. The computer will copy information from the disc into its own memory. If you have a lot of free memory available, it will be able to copy all the contents of the disc. If you don't have enough, it will do the back-up in stages.

4. When the computer has copied as much of the information on the disc as it can store, a prompt will appear asking you to put the destination disc in the floppy drive. Do this and press the space bar (RISC OS 2) or click on Continue (RISC OS 3). The computer will copy the information it has stored in its memory from the source disc onto the disc in the drive.

5. If the computer didn't have space to copy all the information in one go, it will prompt you to put the source disc back in the drive. It will copy more information from it, and then ask you to put the destination disc back. This will continue for as long as it takes to copy all the information from the source disc to the destination disc. When the computer has finished the copying, you will have to press the space bar or click the mouse to dismiss the prompt window if you are using RISC OS 2, and click on OK if you are using RISC OS 3.

6. Clearly label the copy of the disc you have made and use this as your working copy. Keep the original disc safely as a back-up copy.

Make a copy of the other discs in exactly the same way, using more formatted floppy discs. Even though you may not want to use all the examples and clip art on some of the discs immediately, it is best to make back-up copies now in case you forget and later lose a disc with valuable information on it. You may need the printer drivers and fonts immediately, anyway.

Copying discs using two floppy drives

If you have two floppy drives on your computer, making copies of discs is quicker and easier than if you have only one floppy drive. Follow these steps to copy Disc1.

1. Put Disc1 into floppy drive :1 and a newly-formatted floppy into drive :0.

2. Display the icon bar menu for floppy drive :1 and select the option **Backup**. It is important that you use the icon bar menu of drive :1; you don't want to back-up the empty floppy onto your original disc or you will lose all the information on it! (As long as you have write-protected Disc1, you won't be able to do this.)

3. If you are using RISC OS 2, a window appears with a prompt asking you to confirm that you want to make a back-up of the disc in drive :1 onto the disc in drive :0; click the lefthand mouse button or press the Y key on the keyboard to continue. If you are using RISC OS 3, a dialogue box appears reporting

the name of the disc in drive :1 and asking you to insert the source disc.

4. With RISC OS 2, a message asks you to write protect the source disc; if you haven't done this already, do it now. Put the disc into the disc drive and press the space bar when you are ready. With RISC OS 3, you don't get this message. Click on Copy in the dialogue box when you are ready to begin. The computer will copy information from the source disc (drive :1) onto the destination disc (drive :0). Both disc drives will operate in turn until all the information has been copied. When the copying is complete, you will have to press the space bar or click the mouse to dismiss the prompt window if you are using RISC OS 2, or click on OK if you are using RISC OS 3.

5. Clearly label the copy of the disc you have made and use this as your working copy. Keep the original disc safely as a back-up copy.

Make copies of the other discs in exactly the same way. Even though you may not want to use all the examples and clip art on some of the discs immediately, it is best to make back-up copies now in case you forget and later lose a disc with valuable information on it. You may need the printer drivers and fonts immediately, anyway.

Hard discs and floppy copies

If you have a hard disc, your working copy of Impression will be on your hard disc. The section *Installing Impression* below explains how to install Impression onto your hard disc. However, you might still want to make an extra back-up copy of Impression on floppy discs. The licensing agreement allows you to do this.

Before installing Impression

There are some issues you will need to consider before you start the installation process so that you can make appropriate choices. You will need to decide:

• whether you want to use the additional fonts supplied with Impression

• whether you want to install a printer driver and, if so, which one

• whether you want to install modules used for draft printing

• whether you want to install modules that will enable you to import text from other programs

• whether you want to install the additional screen modes Impression offers.

The following subsections will help you make these choices. If you later change your mind about the choices you have made, it is easy to install extra bits or remove bits you have installed. Chapter 20: *Making your own settings and customising Impression* tells you how to do this.

Fonts

Your computer is supplied with some fonts already present. Where they are will depend on the type of computer you have and whether it is running RISC OS 2 or RISC OS 3.

If you have a RISC OS 3 computer, there will be three fonts resident in the ROM (read-only memory). These are Trinity, Corpus and Homerton. In addition, disc App1 (or the root directory on the hard disc) has a directory called !Fonts which holds four more fonts. These are Porterhouse, Selwyn, Sidney and the System font. The only one of these that you might want to use in your documents is Selwyn. This is a symbol font; it contains useful characters such as bullets, telephone symbols, stars and so on. The other fonts in !Fonts are not outline fonts and so aren't useful for desktop publishing. (There is an explanation of what an outline font is in chapter 5: *Some typographical terms.*)

If you have a RISC OS 2 computer, there aren't any fonts in ROM. The fonts will all be in !Fonts on the disc App1 or the root directory on the hard disc. The outline fonts are the same as those available on RISC OS 3 computers: Trinity, Corpus, Homerton and Selwyn.

Impression disc 4 holds some extra fonts you might want to use. At release 2.17, the fonts included are:

Character

Dingbats

Greek

Pembroke

Corpus, Homerton and Trinity are provided, too.

Your immediate inclination may be that if the fonts are available you might as well have them. However, it's worth pausing to think about memory. The fonts will take up space on your floppy or hard disc. It will also use RAM (random access memory) to make the fonts available to you while you run Impression, and Impression will take extra time to process and display more fonts. If you want to run other applications at the same time, and you don't want the overhead in processing time that extra fonts can cost, think carefully before indiscriminately installing all the fonts. The illustration below shows what all the fonts look like so that you can choose those which you think you are likely to use. You can always install more later if you decide you do want some you had left out. (You can also remove some if you install them but find you never use them.)

This text is in Trinity

This text is in Homerton

This text is in Corpus

This text is in Character

✳✳✳▲ ▼✳ǀ▼ ✳▲ ✳❍◗▼▲ (Dingbats)

Τηισ τεξτ ισ ιν Γρεεκ (Greek)

This text is in Pembroke.

Printer drivers

Before you can print any text from any RISC OS application, you need to install a printer driver. Impression uses the standard RISC OS printer drivers supplied with your computer. The procedure for installing and using these will depend on whether you are running RISC OS 2 or RISC OS 3. Both are covered in chapter 16: *Printing Impression documents*. If your computer uses RISC OS 3, you won't need the printer drivers supplied with Impression.

The printer drivers supplied on disc 5 are the versions of the Acorn RISC OS 2 printer drivers that were current when you bought Impression. They may be newer than the printer drivers you have. To find out whether they are, you need to load your copy of the printer driver(s) you are likely to use and look at the version number, then load the printer driver(s) you are likely to use from Impression disc 5 and look at the version number. The printer drivers supplied inside the directory Pdrivers are:

- !Printer DM for dot-matrix printers

- !PrinterIx for the Integrex colour printer

- !PrinterLJ for Hewlett-Packard LaserJet printers, and

- !PrinterPS for PostScript laser printers.

To install a printer driver on a RISC OS 2 computer, open the directory in which the printer drivers are stored (Pdrivers on disc 5) and double-click on the icon for the printer driver. You can only have one printer driver loaded at a time, so if you have another one loaded and you click on the icon of a printer driver, the first one will be removed from the icon bar. When the printer driver has loaded, move the pointer over its icon on the icon bar and press the Menu button on the mouse. Move the pointer over **Info** and across to the right to display information about the printer driver, including its version number. Then load your original copy of the printer driver and see which version number that is. The higher the number, the more recent the version of the printer driver. You only need to use the printer driver supplied with Impression if its version number is higher than the version number of your existing printer driver. In this case, replace your original with the new version and use it for all your applications. If the number is the same or lower, don't load the Impression printer driver.

If you are using RISC OS 3, don't use the printer drivers supplied with Impression: these are only for use with RISC OS 2 and won't work with RISC OS 3. Use the RISC OS 3 printer drivers supplied with your computer instead.

Draft printing

If you have a dot matrix or LaserJet-type laser printer, you can use a special draft printing mode to print simple pages of text quickly. The printout won't have the quality that the normal printer drivers give, and the output will only match the fonts and font sizes as well as the printer can manage with its own resident fonts. It can be useful, though, if you have a large volume of text you want to print out to check before you print it nicely styled (and more slowly) with the proper printer drivers. If you have a PostScript laser printer, you can't save any time by using draft print modules, but pages will probably print quite quickly anyway.

If you think you are likely to want to print using draft mode, install the draft print module appropriate for your printer(s) when you install Impression. The draft print modules are:

- PrintLX for Epson LX80

- Print LQ for Epson LQ800

- PrintLC10 for Star LC10

- PrintKX for Panasonic KXP1124 and Swift 24

- PrintKAGA for Kaga Taxan KP810 and Canon PW1080A

- PrintDJ for Hewlett-Packard Deskjet

- PrintDJ500 for Hewlett-Packard Deskjet DJ500

- PrintLJ for Hewlett-Packard LaserJet

Modules for importing text

Although you can type the text of new documents directly into Impression, you might sometimes want to use Impression to lay out a document you have already produced using another word processing program (such as 1st Word Plus), a text editor (such as Edit) or even a spreadsheet (such as Schema or Pipedream). Impression has several modules which enable it to read text from other programs and interpret some of the control codes used, for example, to indicate special text styles such as bold and underline. There are modules to allow you to load:

- 1st Word Plus files

- Inter-Word files

- Acorn Desktop Publisher files

- BASIC files

- Wordwise Plus files

- View files

- CSV files (comma-separated-value files).

If you think you are likely to use one of these frequently, install it when you install Impression. If you think you may need one or more of them only occasionally, you can save memory and disc space by loading one only when you need it from your copies of the Impression discs.

Screen modes

Impression offers several extra screen modes which you might find useful, particularly if you don't have a VGA or multisync monitor. There is a technical description of the different modes, with their resolutions, number of colours, bits per pixel, memory requirements and frequencies in the Impression *User Guide* and there is a brief description of them in chapter 19: *Getting the most from Impression*. The best way to see whether you think any of the modes will be useful to you is to experiment with them. You can try them out before deciding whether to include them in your installation by double-clicking on the !NewModes icon on disc 2. You can then change the mode by displaying the icon bar menu for the palette icon (on the right of the icon bar, next to the system icon) and using the **Mode** option. Move the pointer onto **Mode** and off to the right to display a selection of modes. You can type the number of a mode that is not shown if you move the pointer to the bottom of the list so that the text caret appears. When you have typed a number, press Return. The extra modes you can use if you have loaded !NewModes are:

With an ordinary monitor: 66, 67, 88, 89, 90, 91

With a multisync monitor: 66, 67, 72-95.

The modes differ in how large everything on the desktop looks (and so how much can be fitted on); screen refresh rate; processing speed; pixel resolution; number of colours; and the amount of memory needed to run the screen mode. Look at chapter 19 for guidance or experiment with them to find the compromise between all these factors that suits you best. You don't need to decide whether to install the screen modes when you first start using Impression; you can load them at any point.

Installing Impression

If your computer has a hard disc, it is best to install Impression to run from it. If your computer doesn't have a hard disc, you will need to install Impression to run from floppy disc.

You can make up a couple of floppy discs or a directory on your hard disc with all you need to run Impression by copying files and directories from the distribution discs, or you can run the Impression !Install program. This program gives you guidance to help you copy the bits you need. The following text explains how to install Impression to run from a hard disc, and how to install it to run from floppy disc. Read the section that is appropriate for your computer.

Installing Impression using !Install

If you want to install Impression to run from floppy discs, you will need two formatted floppy discs to hold Impression and the other bits and pieces you may need to run it. If you want to install Impression on your hard disc, you will need to have 1.8Mbyte free on your hard disc. Impression may not use up all this space once it is installed (depending on which bits you choose to install) but it will be needed temporarily as work space while you run the !Install program. If any of it is left afterwards, you can use it then to store other programs and files.

To install Impression using the !Install program, follow these steps:

1. Put Disc1 into the floppy drive on your computer and open a directory display for it. Double-click on !Install to load it; its icon appears on the icon bar:

2. Click on the icon on the icon bar to begin the installation process. The first dialogue box that appears tells you that you are about to begin installing Impression and gives you the chance to cancel.

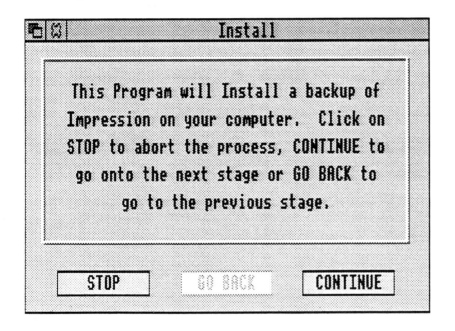

Click on Continue to go on. You can cancel at any stage, but if Impression is not fully installed when you do it will not run properly.

3. The next dialogue box asks you to choose the filing system and medium you want to use.

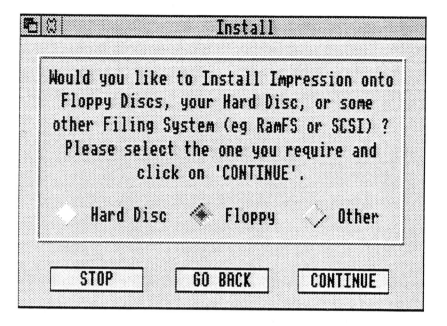

If your computer has an ADFS hard disc, the hard disc option will be available. Otherwise, Floppy disc and Other filing system will be the only options. If your computer has a hard disc but this option is not available, your disc is a SCSI disc. Use the option Other filing systems to display another dialogue box:

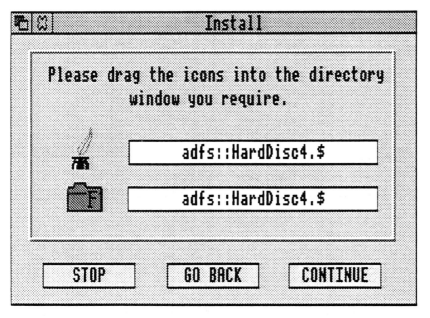

This dialogue box is also displayed if you choose the hard disc option. Open a directory display for the directory where you want to store Impression, and one for the directory you want to use to store !Fonts (if this is different). Then drag each of the Impression and !Fonts icons from the dialogue box into the directory displays. The names of the directories will appear in the writable icons on the dialogue box. (If you just type the pathname of the directories you want to use, you may find that the Install program doesn't register the names and won't work properly; follow the proper procedure of dragging the icons into directory displays.)

If you are installing Impression on your hard disc, it is not a good idea to install !Fonts in the same directory as your existing !Fonts. Your existing copy will be overwritten. It is best to install !Fonts elsewhere and then copy the fonts you want to use into your existing !Fonts directory. Similarly, if you install Impression to run from floppy discs, you should later make up a composite !Fonts directory that you use for all your applications rather than keeping one specially for Impression.

4. The next dialogue box asks you to choose the fonts you want to install. You can install all the fonts (but don't do this if you are running RISC OS 3) or choose the fonts you want.

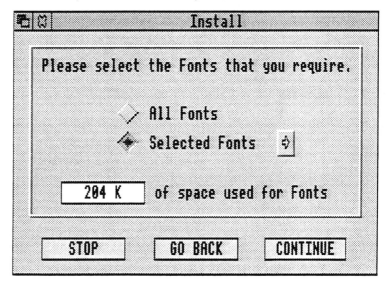

To choose fonts, click on the menu arrow button to the right of the Selected Fonts option. This displays a list of fonts available. Many of the fonts in the menu have submenus offering additional alternatives. For example, Homerton offers Homerton medium, bold, italic and bold italic. Click on the names of all the fonts you want to install; if you use Adjust to click on them, the menu will stay on the screen for you to make extra choices. If your computer uses RISC OS 3, you may not need to install Corpus, Homerton and Trinity as they are permanently available from the computer's memory. But if you use Laser Direct or some other printer for which RISC

OS 3 does not provide a driver, you should install them, as the driver will not be able to use the ROM-based fonts. Ask computer concepts for the latest advice concerning use of the Laser Direct Printer. A report of how much memory will be needed to hold your selection is shown in the icon at the bottom left of the window. Even if you choose to install no fonts at all, the !Fonts directory will be created and this will use some memory. There is not an option to allow you to skip creating !Fonts; you will have to create it and then delete it later if you don't want any of the fonts.

5. The next dialogue box lets you choose the loader modules and draft printing modules you want to install, and say whether you want to install new modes.

Install

Please select the modules you require.

LoadBASIC	LoadFWP	LoadView
LoadCSV	LoadIWord	LoadWW+
LoadDTP	LoadReturn	

PrintBJ	PrintKAGA	PrintLJ
PrintDJ	PrintKX	■ PrintLQ
PrintDJ500	PrintLC10	PrintLX

■ !NewModes

[STOP]   [GO BACK]   [CONTINUE]

Click to turn on the buttons beside any modules you want to use. The modules are described above in the section *Before installing Impression*.

6. The next dialogue box is the last one that allows you to choose options for installation. It allows you to pick the printer driver(s) you want to install. If you are using RISC OS 3, don't choose any of these as they won't work with your computer.

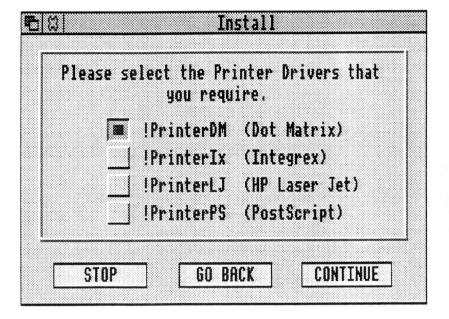

7. The final dialogue box tells you that installation is about to begin and reports the destination you have chosen. If you choose to continue, Impression will be installed. You will be prompted to change the floppy discs as required. When this happens will depend on which items you have chosen to install and whether you are installing Impression to run from floppy discs or some other medium.

Copying Impression to install it

You don't need to use !Install to install Impression on your computer. You can instead copy the items you want. You can also use the procedure described below, or parts of it, to make changes to your installation later whether or not you originally used !Install.

If you want to install Impression to run from floppy disc, you will need at least one and possibly two formatted floppy discs. Follow these steps to copy the bits you need from the Impression discs.

1. Open a directory display for the disc and directory where you want to store Impression. This may be the root directory of a hard or floppy disc, or a directory on a hard or floppy disc. Put Impression Disc1 into the floppy disc drive of your computer and open a directory display for it. Copy !Impress from Disc1 to the directory you want to store it in. If you are using a computer with a single floppy drive and are installing Impression to run from floppy disc, the computer will prompt you to change the discs as necessary.

2. Open a directory display for your copy of !Fonts. This may be in the root directory of your hard disc, or on a floppy disc. Open a directory display for !Fonts by holding down the Shift key and then double-clicking on the directory icon. Now put Impression Disc4 into the floppy drive and open a directory display for it. Again, open !Fonts. Now copy the directories for any fonts you want to use from !Fonts on Disc4 into your own !Fonts

directory. Inside some directories there are further directories to hold the variations on a font. For example, the Homerton directory includes directories for the bold and oblique versions of the font.

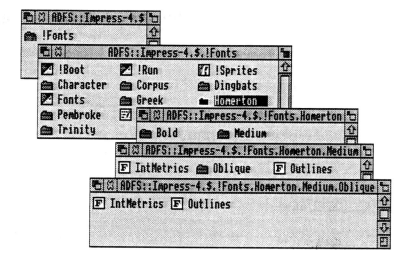

Look inside a directory before copying it to make sure you want everything that is inside it. The IntMetrics and Outlines files are the files that actually define a font. Make sure that you copy a definition within its directory; spare IntMetrics and Outlines files floating around without a home will confuse the computer. You may need to copy a directory and then delete any fonts inside your copy that you don't want to use. If you are using RISC OS 3, don't copy Corpus, Homerton or Trinity to your !Fonts directory as these are permanently

available from the computer's memory. If you
are using RISC OS 2, you will need the outline
font manager, version 2.44 or later. If you
don't already have that, copy the !Fonts
directory supplied with Impression and use that
instead of your old, out-of-date fonts. (If you
don't know whether you have a suitable version
of the outline font manager, you can leave it
and see whether Impression will run; if it issues
a message saying you need the outline font
manager, you haven't got it and can then copy
!Fonts and try again.)

3.   If you want to copy any loader modules or
draft printing modules, you will find these on
Impression Disc1; new screen modes are on
Disc2. Put Disc1 into the floppy drive and
open a directory display for it; then open a
display for the directory Extensions. The loader
modules have names beginning Load and the
draft printing modules have names beginning
Print. If you think you will want to use them
occasionally, copy any of them you want to a
directory on your hard or floppy disc. When
you want to use them, you will need to click on
the icons of the modules you want to load;
they won't be loaded automatically with
Impression. If you want them to be loaded
automatically copy them into the directory
called Auto inside Impression application
directory, hold down the shift key and double
click on the Impression icon. The directory
display that opens will include a directory called
Auto. Open this and copy the modules you
want onto it. If you want to use or copy the
new screen modes, these are kept in a directory
called Utils on Disc2. The file called

!NewModes contains all the new screen modes. When you want to use any of the new modes, you will need to click on !NewModes and then use the palette icon to change screen mode. Again, you can copy them into Auto if you want them into Auto if you want them to be available each time you start Impression.

4. Finally, you may want to copy a printer driver to use with Impression. Printer drivers are on Disc5, in a directory called PDrivers. Don't copy and use any of these printer drivers if your computer uses RISC OS 3 — they won't work. You need to load a printer driver before you can print anything from Impression (or any other application). The procedure is described in chapter 16: *Printing Impression documents.*

!System

The computer needs some shared resources that are used by several programs and applications. Acorn issues updated versions of these resources from time to time, and it is always best to have the most up-to-date versions. These resources are kept in a directory called !System. You should only ever have one copy of !System, which you use for all your applications. If your computer has a hard disc, !System should be in the root directory. Some applications need a fairly recent version of some of the resources in !System in order to run. Impression comes with a !System directory and a utility called !SysMerge to help you update your existing !System. These two are supplied by Acorn and are compatible with your existing !System directory.

To update your !System, open a directory display for it, and for Disc5. Open the directory PDrivers on Disc5, then double-click on !SysMerge in the directory display to open this window:

```
┌──────────────────────────────────────┐
│ ▣ ▣      !System Merge Utility        │
│ Master !System: ┌──────────────────┐  │
│                 └──────────────────┘  │
│   New !System:  ┌──────────────────┐  │
│                 └──────────────────┘  │
│                                       │
│    Drag the original !System into     │
│            this window.               │
│                                       │
└──────────────────────────────────────┘
```

Drag the icon for your original !System directory to the first writable field. The pathname for it will appear in the field. Drag !System from Disc5 to the second writable field. Your original copy of !System will be updated. !SysMerge copies any newer versions of modules and any modules that you don't have in your original !System; it doesn't overwrite your versions if they are newer or the same version as those in the new !System, and it doesn't delete any modules that you have in your original !System that aren't in the new one. You can use !SysMerge each time you get a new copy of !System and you should do this to keep !System up to date.

Using the dongle

You won't be able to run Impression on your computer unless you have fitted the hardware key (dongle). This plugs into the parallel printer port on the back of the computer. It has a socket on it just the same as the printer port socket, so you can still plug your printer into the parallel port. You don't need to unplug the dongle when you want to print from any other applications; the dongle is invisible to all programs except Impression. The only disadvantage is that it sticks out of the back of the computer quite a long way so you can't push your computer to the back of your desk against the wall!

To fit the dongle, follow these steps:

1. Find the parallel port on the back of your computer. It is labelled.

2. If you have a printer connected to this port, unplug it by unscrewing the little screws on either end of the socket and pulling out the plug.

3. Plug in the dongle and tighten the screws. It will only fit one way round and the right way up; don't try to force it.

4. If you have a printer with a parallel interface, plug the printer plug into the back of the dongle and tighten the screws on the dongle.

Whenever you try to start up Impression, it will check that the dongle is in place. If you have removed it (or have knocked it loose) Impression won't start.

What next?

The next chapter explains how to begin working with Impression. First you need to load Impression, then you can open a window for a new document. There is some advice on typing in Impression which will be particularly useful if you are not used to using a word processor.

3 | Starting work

Once you have installed Impression and fitted the dongle to your computer, you can begin to use it. You don't need to attach a printer until you are ready to print something. If your computer doesn't have a hard disc, it will be useful to format at least one floppy disc to save your work onto before you begin. When you are ready to begin using Impression, you need to:

- make sure there is enough memory available for it to run

- load Impression

- open a window for a new document.

This chapter explains how to do these and then gives you a quick guided tour around the window and menus, explains how to type and select text and explains the pointer shapes used in Impression.

Memory requirements

Impression needs 512k to start up. You can check that this is available using the Task Manager. To do this, move the pointer over the system icon at the extreme right of the icon bar and press the Menu button on the mouse to display the menu. Click on **Task display** to open a window showing how the computer is using its memory. In RISC OS 3, Simply click select over the Acorn icon at the righthand end of the icon bar.

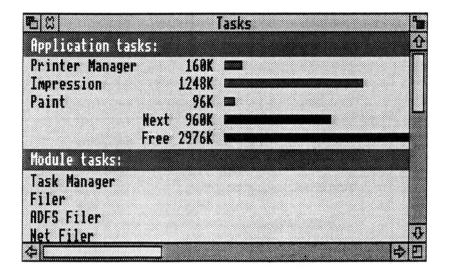

There will be a bar for each application you have loaded, and then two labelled Next and Free. There must be 512k available in the Next slot for you to load Impression. The Next slot shows the memory that has been allocated to the next application you install. If there is less than this, but quite a bit in the Free slot, you can drag the Next slot with the Select button on the mouse to make it longer until it shows 512k as its size. Don't reduce the Free slot to zero, though, as you will need odd bits of memory for saving files, disc access and so on. Try to leave about 80k. If you can't find enough memory in this way, you will need to quit some of the applications you already have loaded. You can do this using Quit from their icon bar menus. If you do it while the Task Manager display is on screen, you will see the Next or Free slot growing as you quit each one and will be able to tell when you have freed enough memory.

Once you have enough memory in the Next slot, you can load Impression. It doesn't matter if there is more than 512k in the Next slot; Impression will only use 512k to start up.

There are some more advanced settings you can make to optimise the screen display and speed of Impression. These deal with special areas of memory and are covered in chapter 19: *Getting the most from Impression*. You can make these settings at any point; you don't need to do them before you start using Impression for the first time, so begin with the default settings (which means don't change anything) and see how you get on.

Loading Impression

When you are ready to load Impression and have checked that there is enough memory to run it, open a directory display for !Impress this will be on the floppy disc Wrk1 created during the installation process if you are running Impression from floppies,.or otherwise on your hard disc It will look something like this:

Double-click on the icon !Impress. After a moment or so, Impression loads. A window appears telling you that it is loading. At this point, it checks whether the dongle is attached to your computer. If it isn't, Impression aborts. If it is, the Impression icon appears on the icon bar. It looks like this:

You can now open a window onto a new Impression document. Click once on the Impression icon on the icon bar to open a new document. It looks like this:

The Impression document window

Many of the features of this window are the same as the features of most other RISC OS windows. The window has:

• a title bar

• back, close, toggle size and adjust size icons

• scroll bars

• scroll arrows.

The *title bar* shows the name of your document. If it is a new document, and is the first new document you have opened, it will have 'Untitled1' as its name. You can open more new documents by clicking repeatedly on the Impression icon. The title bar will show the number of each (Untitled2, Untitled3, and so on). As soon as you make any changes to the document a star (*) appears at the end of the document name. This lets you see at a glance whether you need to save the document if you are going to stop working or turn off the computer. The title bar may also show some extra information, such as the scale at which you are viewing the document and, if you have more than one window open onto the same document, the number of the window is shown. There is more information on viewing options at the end of this chapter. You can move the document window around the desktop by dragging the title bar.

The *back icon* lets you send this window to the back of a stack of windows on the screen. If you have several windows open at once, you can use this to help you reorder them and reveal the one you want to work on. Sending a window to the back doesn't close the window or the document.

Click on the *close icon* to close down the window onto the document. This doesn't close the document; Impression keeps it in memory, with any changes you have made. Your changes aren't lost just because you close the window. Impression calls the window a 'view' of the document. You can view the document again by using *New view* in the Impression icon bar menu. This is described at the end of this chapter. However, you will lose your unsaved work if you quit from Impression or turn the computer off without saving any unsaved work in documents, whether or not they are visible on the screen. If you have unsaved work in documents that are not displayed (because you have clicked on their close icons), it is easy to switch off the computer without remembering to save them first. However, if you quit Impression, or use the Shutdown option (in RISC OS 3), you will get a warning dialogue box telling you that you have unsaved work and giving you the chance to save it. It is a good idea to get into the habit of always using **Quit** to close down any applications before switching off the computer so that you have the chance to save any work you had forgotten about. If you don't save your work, your changes will be lost. Saving files is described in chapter 15: *Saving your work*.

The *toggle size icon* allows you to switch quickly between two window sizes. Click on it to increase the window to its full size. It will occupy most or all of the desktop depending on the screen mode, viewscale and page size you are using. Click on it again and the window will revert to its previous size. You can toggle between these two sizes using the toggle size icon. For full control of the window size you need to use the *adjust size icon* in the bottom righthand corner of the window. Drag this with the Select button to change the size and shape of the window.

The *scroll bars* along the bottom and the righthand edge of the window show how much of the document is visible on screen. If the document is too long (or too wide) for you to see all of it at once, you can drag the scroll bar, or click in the dark area outside the scroll bar to make another part of the document visible. If you want to move the document through the window in small steps, you can click on one of the arrows at either end of the scroll bars.

In the Impression window you will see two sides of a large rectangle with a dotted outline. This is the *frame* in which you can type text. Position the pointer inside the frame and click the Select button on the mouse; the frame outline will turn green and the titlebar will turn yellow (if you have a colour monitor) and the text cursor will appear. The cursor is a vertical red bar. It appears in the top lefthand corner of the window. The document is now active and you can begin typing. You will probably want to adjust the size of the window first so that you can see both edges of the page. Drag the adjust size icon to do this.

Typing text

If you are used to using a word processing program on your RISC OS computer you won't have any problems typing text in Impression. The following guidelines will help you if you are not used to using a word processor. However, they include some useful information on using !Chars to get non-

English characters and symbols which you might like to read even if you are an old hand at word processing.

Text wrap and Return

When you use a typewriter, you need to use Carriage Return each time you want to start a new line. You use it not only to start a new paragraph, but when you have reached the end of the line you are typing and are about to run out of paper.

With a word-processor, you don't need to use Return except when you want to start a new paragraph or add a fixed line break. You can carry on typing after the cursor has reached the righthand edge of the text area, and the cursor will automatically jump to the start of the next line, taking the first part of the word with it if you are in the middle of a word. This feature is called text wrap.

L and One, O and Zero

When you use a typewriter, you can often get away with using lower-case L (l) in place of one (1). A few typewriters don't have a one key at all, forcing you to use lower-case L. Similarly, you can often use capital O in place of zero (0). You shouldn't do this when you use Impression (or any word processor). This is partly because l and 1, O and 0 are actually quite different in many fonts and your documents will look untidy and unprofessional if you have used the wrong ones, and partly because you won't be able to use Impression's search and replace facility properly if you have mixed up l and 1, O and 0.

Typing numbers

You can type numbers in an Impression document either by using the number keys in the top row of the typewriter keys, or using the numeric keypad with Num Lock set on. It makes no difference which you use.

Deleting letters

Every now and then, you will make a mistake while you are typing. If you spot this immediately, and it is only a letter or two, there are three keys you can use to delete the letters.

The Backspace key (to the right of the pound-sign) deletes the key to the left of the cursor and moves the cursor back a space. Any text in front of the cursor moves back one space.

The Delete key in the block above the cursor keys has the same action as the Backspace key.

The Copy key, next to the Delete key, deletes the character in front of the cursor. Any text in front of that moves back a space.

You can also use these Control-key combinations:

- Ctrl-D to delete the word the cursor is positioned in or before. The word is added to the clipboard so that you can paste it back in again if you want to by pressing the Insert key. (The clipboard is described in chapter 10: *Word-processing with Impression*. This explains how to cut larger chunks of text, how to copy text and how to paste text back into a document.)

- Ctrl-L to delete the line the cursor is in. The line is added to the clipboard; paste it back in by pressing Insert.

To use these combinations, press and hold down the Control key and then press the D or L key. (You don't need to hold down Shift; the letters are shown in upper-case simply by convention.)

Transposing letters

If you type two letters in the wrong order — teh for the, for example — you can transpose them quickly using the keyboard shortcut Ctrl-Shift-Q. Put the cursor between the two characters you want to switch round, then hold down Control and Shift and press Q.

Special characters

Sometimes, particularly if you ever type text in a language other than English, you may need to use some characters and symbols which are not on the standard typewriter keyboard. Examples are: é, ß, æ, ¥ and ©. You can include characters such as these in your documents using !Chars. !Chars is supplied with Impression but produced by Acorn, so you may already have it. If you are using RISC OS 3, !Chars is in ROM which means that it is permanently available from the computer's memory and you don't need to access a hard or floppy disc to use it.

When you want to use a character that is not available from the keyboard, open a directory display for !Chars. If you are using RISC OS 3, click on the Apps directory on the icon bar to do this. If you are using RISC OS 2, !Chars is in the directory called Utils on Impression Disc2. !Chars doesn't load onto the icon bar but appears as a window on the desktop. The window shows the full character set available:

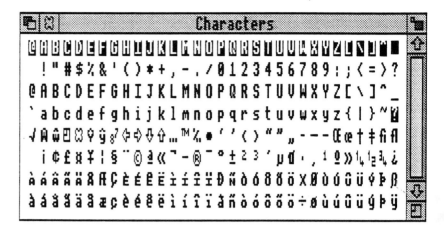

By default, !Chars shows the characters in system font. It has a menu offering all the other fonts on your system. Move the pointer over the !Chars window and press the Menu button on the mouse to display the menu. Some of the fonts have further options (such as medium, which is regular weight, and italic). Click on the font you want to display and the window will be redrawn to show the characters available in that font. It will include all the characters you can get from the keyboard.

When you want to include a special character, click on it in the !Chars window and it will appear at the cursor position in your Impression document.

You can also include a !Chars character by positioning the cursor in the Impression document and then pressing the Shift key. This method allows you to include special characters in the text you type in a dialogue box — clicking in another window would make the dialogue box disappear. You can use this method when you want to search for text containing special characters, for example, and need to show characters from !Chars in the Find dialogue box.

All the characters available from !Chars are in fact available from the keyboard even though they may not be on the typewriter keys. Every character can be obtained by pressing the Alt key (there's one either side of the space bar) and the appropriate combination of numbers on the numeric keypad (not the number/symbol keys of the typewriter). The Alt key enables you to specify the characters by giving their decimal character code. This is a number the computer uses to identify each character. For example, the code for A is 065, so if you press and hold down the Alt key and then type 65 (you don't need the zero at the start): the letter A will appear in your document. If there is a character you use very frequently from !Chars, it might be worth learning the Alt sequence to obtain it as it is quicker than displaying !Chars every time. For example, if your name is Héloése, you might find it easier to remember that é is Alt-233 and Ô is Alt-239 than to display !Chars every time you want to type your name (or leave !Chars on screen all the time). It also saves memory if you use the Alt sequence, as !Chars takes up 32k when its window is displayed. There is a full list of the decimal character codes you might want to use with the Alt key in Appendix 1.

You can also obtain the superscript characters [1], [2] and [3] by pressing Alt-1, Alt-2 and Alt 3, using the numbers on the typewriter keys. This doesn't work using the figures on the numeric keypad.

Selecting text

Many operations work on a selected block of text. Once you have selected some text you can, for example, delete it, copy it, add a new style to it or use a text effect on it. You can select a block of text by positioning the pointer at the start of the text you want to select, pressing and holding down the Select button on the mouse and dragging to the end of the text you want to select. The selected text will be highlighted in reverse colour (usually white text on a black background).

You can select across more than one frame or page. If some of the text you want to select isn't visible, keep Select held down and move the pointer down (or to the right) out of the edge of the window. The window contents will scroll, and everything that passes through the window will be selected. When the end of the block you want to select is visible, move the pointer so that the highlighting stops where you want the selection to end and then release Select. The selected text remains highlighted.

To deselect text, just click anywhere in the window with Select.

There are some keyboard shortcuts you can use for selecting text and changing the selection:

*   double-click on a word to select it

*   triple-click on a line to select it

*   quadruple-click on a paragraph to select it

*   with text selected, position the cursor after the selected text and click with Adjust to select text up to the cursor position from the start of the original selection

- with text selected, position the cursor before the selected text and click with Adjust to select text from the cursor position to the start of the original selection, but deselect the original selection.

The pointer

You will notice when you move the mouse pointer over an Impression document window that it changes shape to a text caret the same colour as the pointer was.

This shows that you can type text in the area the pointer is over.

There are a few other forms the pointer takes in Impression. If you move it over an area of the page that contains frames or text from the master page, the pointer has this shape:

This shows you that you can only change the material in this area by altering the master page.

If you move the pointer outside the frame, it changes to a hand shape. This shows you that you can move the document around in the window.

If you have displayed a dialogue box and move the pointer over a button that gives access to a menu, the pointer changes to a menu shape. If you click any mouse button, a menu will appear.

If you move the pointer over the edge of a selected frame that you can move (one that it isn't locked in its position) the pointer changes to an eight-pointed snowflake showing that you can change the shape of the frame.

If you try to move a frame that is locked in place, the pointer changes to a key.

Impression menus

Nearly all of the facilities offered by Impression are available from the menus, though many are also available by keyboard shortcuts. The main Impression menu, which appears when you press the Menu button on the mouse while the pointer is inside an Impression document window, looks like this:

As with other RISC OS applications, the arrows indicate that there are submenus.

The submenus cover these areas of Impression:

- Document offers tasks relating to the whole document or to whole text stories, including printing, and saving. It also lets you autosave the document, specifying the interval at which the document will be saved, and it lets you set the view scale for the window.

- Edit offers cutting and pasting operations for frames, text and graphics, and has tasks relating to chapters and pages. The menu options in this submenu vary according to what you are doing. For example, if you have text selected and display this menu, the first option will be Cut text. If you don't have text selected, the first option is Cut frame.

- Effect offers text effects (attributes) that you can set singly for selected text or text you are going to type.

- Style offers tasks related to styles and rulers, and styles you can apply to your text.

- Frame offers tasks relating to creating frames and controlling their settings. If you add graphics to a frame and then select it, an Alter graphic option is also available from this menu.

- Misc offers a variety of tasks not covered elsewhere in the menu structure. These include Find (which has a submenu including some Goto options), spelling and abbreviation control, options to hide or display graphics, compile an index or table of contents, insert the current date, time, chapter or page number and control kerning (the space between two letters).

All these tasks are described in more detail elsewhere in this book. If you want to find the function of a particular menu option, look in the index at the end of the book or in chapter 23: *Impression menu checklist*.

As with other applications, you can choose an item from a menu by clicking on it with Select or Adjust. If you click with Adjust, the menu will remain on screen for you to make further choices. The menu will vanish if you click outside the menus with the Select or Adjust button.

Impression also has an icon bar menu. To display this, move the pointer over the Impression icon on the icon bar and press the Menu button.

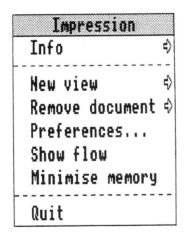

Info displays copyright information about Impression. The other options are described elsewhere in this book. Again, look in the index or menu checklist if you want to find the function of a particular menu option. The option **New view** is described below.

Viewing your document

When you look at your document in an Impression window, you are looking through a window at a file. Often, the whole file won't be visible in the window. This depends on the size of the window and the size of the document. You can move through the document (effectively moving the window over the document so that you can see different areas of it) and change the size at which the document is displayed in the window. You can also open more than one window onto a document, or open a window onto one or more additional documents.

When you open an Impression document it will be displayed at a scale of 100% unless you have changed the default scale setting. Depending on the margins you have set, your monitor and the screen mode you are using, the full width of text on an A4 page may not be visible at a view size of 100%. To change the view size, use **Scale view** in the Document menu. It displays a dialogue box for you to choose the view size:

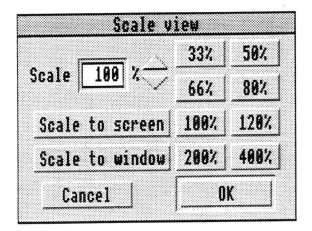

You can pick a scale from the buttons on the right, or type a scale in the writable icon, or use the arrow buttons beside the icon to increase or decrease the scale value shown. Alternatively, you can scale the view so that it fills the screen or fills the window size you are using. If you want to experiment with view sizes, click on OK with the Adjust button so that the dialogue box stays on screen for you to make further changes. The view scale is always reported as a percentage of the actual full size of the view (100%). This means that if you set the scale to 200% and then to 50%, it will finally be 50% of the real scale (half-size), not 50% of 200%. You can alter the default view size using the option **Preferences** in the Impression icon bar menu. This is described in chapter 20: *Making your own settings and customising Impression.*

You may want to open windows onto more than one Impression document at a time, or open two or more windows onto the same document. To do this, display the icon bar menu for Impression and move the pointer across **New view** to display a submenu listing all the documents loaded. Click on the name of a document to open a new window for it. You can copy and move text, frames and graphics between different documents or the same document in different windows. Opening two windows onto a document is useful if you are editing a document and want to work in two different areas of the document at the same time (moving bits and pieces from one chapter to another, for example). There will only be one copy of the document open, irrespective of how many windows you have open onto a document. If you try to load a document that is already loaded, Impression will tell you to use New view to open a window onto the document. As you can't have more than one copy of the same document loaded at once, you can't make conflicting changes; changes you make in one window will affect the other window immediately (if any affected areas of the document are visible). If you have more than one window open onto the same document, the title bar reports the number of the window immediately after the name of the file.

Saving your work

It is a good idea to save your work frequently to prevent losing a lot of it if you make a serious mistake or if there is a power failure or computer failure. When you are ready to save your document for the first time, open a directory display to hold it and then display the Impression menu. Use **Save document** in the Document menu. Move the pointer across this option and off to the right to display a Save as icon. Remove the default name with the Delete or Backspace key, or by pressing Ctrl-U, and then type the name you want to use. This can be up to nine characters long; Impression will add a ! in front of the name when it creates the directory holding your document. Drag the icon to the directory display.

If you want to save an existing document with the same name after you have altered it, use **Save document** and just click on OK to save it with the same name.

When you want to open an existing document, double-click on its icon in the directory display or drag its icon onto the Impression icon on the icon bar to load the document and open a window for it. If the document is already loaded in Impression,

Impression will issue an error message telling you to use New view from the icon bar menu instead.

There is more about saving your documents in chapter 15: *Saving your work*.

What next?

The next chapter briefly outlines some of the basic concepts of Impression. These are all dealt with in more detail in later chapters, but it's helpful to know some of the terms in advance.

4 How Impression works

Before we go on to look in detail at how to use Impression, it will help to look briefly at all the main concepts in outline. Having an idea of how the pieces fit together makes it much easier to read about each element on its own. This chapter introduces the following:

- frames
- styles
- effects
- master pages
- files and directories
- text flow and chapters.

Frames

A frame is a rectangular box on a page that can hold text or graphics. Unless you choose to use a printing border, you won't see the outline of the frames when you print your document. They are shown on screen with a green outline when a frame is active (if you have a colour monitor and are using an appropriate screen mode) and with a dotted grey outline when not active. You can type in an active frame. To make a frame active, click in it with the pointer. When you first open an Impression document, the frame shown has a grey outline. When you click in it to place the cursor the outline changes to green and you can begin typing.

Generally, one or more frames on a page are drawn automatically when the page is created. These are copied from a master page (described below). You can add extra frames which appear just on that page. These are called *local frames*. You can move them around and alter their size and shape.

As well as frames copied from the master page and frames created locally, you may create *repeating frames* and *guide frames*. Repeating frames are copied over several pages of a document. You can delete the repeating frame from any page on which you don't want it to appear. A repeating frame is copied from its first use on a page of a document; it is not kept on and copied from the master page. A guide frame is not a real frame because you can't add text or graphics to it. It acts as a guide for you to position text and graphics frames, helping you to keep your columns at the same position on the page even if your frames are different heights. Guide frames are particularly useful for magazine layouts, where you can use them to show the areas the frames must fall in, even though you want all the frames to be different sizes.

You can give a frame a printing border and set its background colour.

Chapter 8: *Frames* explains fully how to use the different types of frames. You can begin using Impression without detailed knowledge of frames because each new Impression document opens with a frame ready for you to type in. However, when you want to design your own page layouts and add pictures to your documents, you will need to know how to use frames.

Styles and effects

Any piece of text has various attributes which control its appearance. These include the text font and size. Impression refers to some of these attributes as *effects*. Font and size are examples of effects. A combination of effects is called a *style*. A style is a complete description of a piece of text in terms of its attributes. Impression has several styles already set up as defaults, but you can change these and create your own styles. When you apply a style to a piece of text, all the attributes defined for that style are applied to the text in a single operation.

When you create a document, you are likely to want to use the same text style for all the main body text, and another style for headings. You will probably use headings at several different levels and use a different style for each level. For example, you might choose to display the main body of the text in Homerton 10 point, and have headings in Trinity 14 point italic. You would then define the attributes of the BaseStyle used for your main body text, including setting the font to Homerton medium and the size to 10pt, and define another style with the attributes you want for the headings, including setting the font to Trinity italic and the size to 14pt. You would be able to select the text that you wanted to use as a heading and click on the name of the heading style in the Style submenu to change all the attributes of the text to the heading style.

Effects can be used singly if you want to change just one attribute of a piece of text. For example, if you wanted to add emphasis to a word, you might like to set it in bold or italic text. This involves changing only one characteristic of the text — its font. To do this, you would select the piece of text and choose the effect you wanted from the Effect submenu.

A style or an effect can be applied to any size chunk of text, from a single letter to all the text in a document. Many other desktop publishing systems restrict text styles to whole paragraphs though they will allow you to change effects locally within paragraphs. Try not to think of Impression's styles as paragraph styles because this is very limiting; they can be applied to portions of paragraphs, to whole single paragraphs, or to groups of paragraphs.

Styles are described fully in chapter 6: *Using styles*; effects are described fully in chapter 7: *Using effects*.

Master pages

We have already mentioned master pages briefly. A master page is a template from which new pages are copied. It can hold frames for text and graphics, guide frames that help you to position frames for text and graphics, and pieces of text or graphics that you want repeated on every page that uses that master page. You can have more than one master page in a document and use different master pages for different chapters. You can also use a pair of master pages if you want different left and right pages in a document. You may want to do this if you are going to print your document on two sides of the paper and then put it in a binder, as you will need a larger margin on the side that goes into the binding (the left on odd-numbered pages and the right on even-numbered pages).

If at any point you change something on a master page, all the pages that use that master page as their template will be updated to reflect the change. You can also change things locally on just one page, but you have to make the frame you want to change local first. It won't then be updated with the master page. This is explained fully in chapter 8: *Frames.*

A new Impression document has seventeen master pages present already. You can alter these, or create your own new master pages. It doesn't matter if a document has master pages that aren't used.

Master pages are described fully in chapter 9: *Master pages.*

Text flow and chapters

When you type in an Impression document, or when you import text from an existing file, you create a *text story.* You can have many text stories in a single document and if you use Impression to create magazines or newsletters you will routinely do this. A text story can 'flow' across several frames and pages. This means that as you change the story or alter the size and shape of the frames, the text will flow so that it continues to run correctly through the sequence of frames: if you make one frame shorter, the bit of text that is forced out will appear at the top of the next frame in the sequence.

Similarly, if you delete some text, the text below will move up through the sequence of frames to maintain the flow.

If you are laying out a newsletter or magazine, you may have several stories on the same page. You can link frames to define how the stories flow on a page and between pages. If you are laying out books, essays and articles, though, you will probably have longer stories that make up a whole chapter each. There will generally only be one story per page, and each will continue over several pages. When one story ends, you will begin a new chapter to hold the next story. The text flow operates in basically the same way whether you use long or short stories. However, if you have long stories that make up chapters, you may find that editing a story requires a new page (or the loss of a page). When necessary, Impression automatically creates new pages in the middle of the document or removes pages without disrupting the flow of the stories.

There is more on text flow through short stories in chapter 8: *Frames*. Chapter 13: *Multi-chapter documents* explains how to use long stories as chapters.

Files and directories

You are probably familiar with the usual RISC OS process of saving your work as a file by dragging a file icon into a directory display. Impression operates slightly differently in that instead of saving a file, you save an application directory. Each Impression document consists of a directory that contains the text stories, all the styling information associated with the text, and any graphics you have used in the document. An Impression document name always starts with the character ! (usually pronounced 'pling') as it is an application directory. If you want to, you can open the directory and see how your document is built up, but don't change anything or you may not be able to open the document again later.

What next?

The next chapter explains some of the typographical terms and techniques you will need to be familiar with to get the most from Impression and to understand text layout and desktop publishing. The material is not specific to Impression, and may help you with other applications. It covers text fonts, point sizes, units of measurement used for type, text justification, indents, leading, kerning and some other special terms. If you are already familiar with the jargon of typesetting and publishing, you can skip the next chapter and go on to chapter 6 which explains how to use styles in Impression documents.

5 Some typographical terms

Before you can use Impression's styles and effects, you need to know a little about typography. At the simplest level, you need to know what a font is and what the different fonts and sizes available look like, but as you get more practiced you will want to control more and more features of your text. At first, you might be happy to set the space above and below paragraphs, but later you will find that being able to set the space between lines in a paragraph gives you greater control of your document's appearance. This chapter introduces:

- fonts

- points and picas (units used to measure type and elements of the page)

- tracking and kerning

- superscript and subscript

- text justification

- tabs.

Font

A font is the name given to a design of typeface. Fonts are commonly grouped in families which have similar basic appearance but differ in details such as the width of the strokes and the slant of the letters. Some of the Acorn fonts offer a family of four variations on a font. For example, Trinity is available in medium, italic, bold and bold italic. Trinity medium is equivalent to Times Roman. An italic font differs from the upright (medium) version in that it slopes, and it has strokes of different weights. A bold font differs from a medium font in that all the strokes are drawn in a heavier line, giving a dense, black, heavy appearance to the letters. A bold italic font is a bold version of the slanted italic font.

This text is in Trinity medium

This text is in Trinity medium italic

This text is in Trinity bold

This text is in Trinity bold italic.

You will notice as you look at the fonts offered in Impression menus and other RISC OS application menus that Trinity has an italic version but Corpus and Homerton have oblique versions instead. An oblique font is the upright font slanted; no other changes are made to the font, so the width of each stroke is the same as in the upright font. The italic font has a very different design. If you compare the letter f in Trinity medium and Trinity italic, you will see that it is certainly not the same letter slanted:

f (medium) *f* (italic)

Now if you compare f in Homerton medium and Homerton oblique you will see that the oblique font is not really a font in its own right, just a slanted version of the upright font:

f (medium) *f* (italic)

You may see other distinctions between fonts mentioned in books on layout and style. Fonts may be serif or sans serif — with or without serifs, or finishing strokes. They may also be proportionally spaced or fixed pitch.

A serif font has finishing strokes that lead the eye from one letter to the next. Trinity is a serif font; Homerton is not.

A proportionally spaced font is one in which the letters are of different widths and are set close to each other. In a proportionally spaced font, thin letters such as l and i take up much less space than wide letters such as m and w.

Thin letters: litjf

Wide letters: wm

In a fixed pitch font, all letters are given the same amount of space. Old-fashioned typewriters use fixed pitch fonts, such as Courier (equivalent to Acorn's Corpus). The serifs on thin letters such as i and l are disproportionately large so that the letters take up a full character width. By contrast, wide letters such as m and w look rather squashed in a fixed pitch font.

Thin letters: litjf

Wide letters: wm

Most printed material uses proportionally spaced fonts as they are more attractive and easier to read than fixed pitch fonts.

Compare the spacing of these two fonts.

Compare the spacing of these two fonts.

Size: points and picas

Text size is conventionally measured in points. A point is approximately $1/72$ of an inch. You may also meet picas. There are twelve points to a pica, so a pica is about a sixth of an inch. If you work with designers and typesetters, they are likely to use picas and points in specifying the sizes of text columns, margins and so on. You can instruct Impression to display measurements in picas or points if you want to. However, if you aren't familiar with them, and won't be liaising with anyone who will expect you to be using them, you will probably be better off sticking with inches or centimetres, whichever you find more familiar.

You will need to use points to specify the size of type you want to use, though. Font size is always measured in points, as is leading — the space between lines. Typically, the body text of books, reports and other documents is 10, 11 or 12 point. Point size measures the distance between the baseline of one line of type and the baseline of the next when there is no extra space between the lines.

This text shows how text size is measured.

space between baselines

When the lines appear with no extra space between them as in the illustration above, the text is said to be 'set solid'. It is quite difficult to read. It is usual to leave a little extra space between the lines to aid legibility. The space between lines within a paragraph is called leading. This is a relic from the days when typesetters used metal blocks of type and used lead strips to separate the lines of letters. Leading is also measured in points. The figure quoted for leading is the total distance between the baselines of the lines of text, so it includes the height of the text itself. It is usual to allow some extra space between lines of 10pt or 12pt text. This means that 10 point text may be set with 12 or 13 point leading. If you see text referred to as '10 on 12 point'. or even just '10 on 12', this means that 10 point text is set with two extra points between the lines, giving 12 point leading. Impression allows you to control the leading used for each style and has a default setting which calculates and uses leading that is 120% of the font size.

Tracking and kerning

Impression allows you control over another aspect of spacing, too, with its kerning option. This lets you set the space between a pair of letters. Some letters look ugly set side by side and using the usual space between letters. Pairs such as WA, particularly in large point sizes, can look as though they are too far apart, even if their spacing is the same as the spacing between other letter pairs in the line. Impression's kerning facility allows you to alter the spacing between a pair of letters to improve the appearance of your text. Look at the letter pairs below, first with the default kerning, and then kerned to improve their appearance.

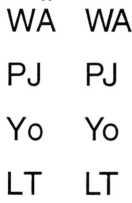

With kerning, Impression allows you to control the horizontal space between adjacent letters (as in the examples above) and the vertical space, so you can move one character up or down slightly to improve the appearance. Be careful with the second of these options, as it is easy to make the line of text look uneven if you alter the vertical spacing of letters.

In books about design and typography you may also see reference to tracking, which is the regular (default) space left between all letters. You can't control the tracking in Impression.

Superscript and subscript text

Two of the effects Impression offers that you may not be familiar with are superscript and subscript text. Superscript text appears above the baseline of the body text. It is often used to give numbers referring to footnotes and to show powers in mathematics. For example, $2^2 = 4$; footnote one refers to this text [1]. Subscript text appears below the baseline of the body text. It is used in chemical formulae. For example, H_2O is water. Superscripted and subscripted text is smaller than the main body text. When you use superscript or subscript in Impression, the point size of the letters will be changed automatically.

Text justification

Text justification is the way the text is laid out between the left- and righthand margins of the page or column. The main body text of most documents is either left-aligned or fully justified. Left-aligned text is aligned with the lefthand margin but ragged along the righthand margin. This means that the start of the lines line up vertically, but the ends of the lines do not. Fully justified text is aligned with the margin at both the left and right hand sides, so the text presents a rectangular block across the page. To make the text line up properly between both margins, Impression often has to add extra space between the words on a line. Unless you are using very long words or narrow columns, you probably won't notice the extra space. However, in narrow text columns, ugly rivers of white space appear to run down through the text. If this happens, it is better to switch to left-aligned text.

This text is left-aligned; the lines are vertically aligned at the lefthand margin but ragged at the righthand margin. This is the default justification used by Impression. You can choose to have your text fully justified if you prefer.

This text is fully justified. Impression adds extra space between words to make the text fit exactly between the left- and righthand margins. Most books use fully justified text as it gives a neat appearance on the page.

Sometimes you might want to use centred or right-aligned text to give emphasis to a heading, achieve a special effect, or set a caption to a picture or table apart from the rest of the text. Centred text is centred between the two margins. Right-aligned text is vertically aligned at the righthand margin (the ends of the lines) but ragged at the lefthand margin.

This is a centred heading

This is a right-aligned caption

Tabs

If you are used to using a typewriter or word processor you will know that the Tab key moves the cursor (or printhead or typewriter carriage) so that the next characters appear at a pre-set tab position. Tabs are useful if you want to line up material in columns in a table, for example. The text below uses tab positions to line up the columns of figures:

Component	Code	Price	VAT	Price inc VAT
A	ABC1	£100.00	£17.50	£117.50
B	ABC2	£200.00	£35.00	£235.00

Tabs can be of several types. The most common — and the type you will find on a typewriter — is a left tab. When you press the Tab key, the cursor moves to the tab position, and as you type the first character appears at the tab position and the following characters to the right of it. However, tabs may also be centre, right or decimal. A centre tab puts the middle of the text you type before next pressing the Tab key at the tab position. A right tab puts the last character of the piece of text at the tab position. In both these cases, the cursor jumps to the next tab position when you press the Tab key, but as you type the characters each appear at the tab position, pushing the text you have already typed to the left. A decimal tab puts the full stop in the text at the tab position. If there is no full stop, the text is right-aligned at the tab. This is particularly useful for aligning columns of figures, such as prices, so that they look neat. In the example below, the figures are lined up with a decimal tab:

A	0.23
B	79.41
C	1053.50
D	7.89

Tabs may have leader characters separating the text at different tab positions, or may have space between the tab positions. Impression allows you the choice, and lets you choose the character you want to use as a leader character.

What next?

The next chapter explains how to use Impression's styles to control the appearance of your text. You can control a large number of features with the Style dialogue box, so it is quite a long chapter. Styles are the most important feature of Impression; if you master styles and using frames, you can do a lot of layout work.

6 Using styles

Styles are the single most important feature of Impression and, because they give you such a large degree of control, are the feature that many people find most difficult to master. This chapter takes you through the items you can set with a style step by step and explains when to use a style rather than an effect, and how to copy styles from one document to another.

This chapter covers:

- when to use styles

- default styles

- BaseStyle

- applying styles

- changing and creating styles

- combining and merging styles

- deleting styles

- controlling the ruler

- clearing styles

- refining headlines and section headings.

The important information on how to use the Style dialogue box is in the subsection *Changing and creating styles.*

When to use styles

A style is a collection of text attributes such as font, point size, space allowed above and below a paragraph and between lines, tab positions, justification and the position of rules. You should create a style for each combination of text effects you want to use. This is likely to cover all the levels of heading and title you want, and perhaps some other items such as captions and text you want to emphasise.

If you just want to use a simple effect, such as bold to emphasise an important word in a sentence, you may prefer to use the Effect submenu. If you want to use more than one effect at once, always use a style. However, you may want to create a style to set just one effect. If you think you may forget whether you are using bold or italic for emphasis, or you think someone else may work on your document and not know what you have used, it may be helpful to create a style called Emphasis setting the font you have chosen to use.

Using styles is quicker than piling up effects and helps you to maintain a consistent appearance throughout your documents. Styles also give you a greater degree of control than effects, as you can set some attributes with the Style dialogue box that you can't set with effects. Junior Impression uses only effects and has no styles facility.

Default styles

A new Impression document has several default styles set up already. This means that you can begin typing and using styles immediately, without knowing how to create your own styles or edit the default styles. The range of default styles may be enough to get you started and help you discover how to apply styles to a piece of text, but you will soon find that they don't cover your needs and you will have to begin editing them and creating your own new styles. This isn't difficult, and you don't need to make any settings that you don't understand. However, if you take it slowly you will soon learn how to make use of all the features you can control from the style dialogue box and become accomplished at styling your text.

The default styles are:

*   BaseStyle: described below

*   Main Heading: a heading style using 24pt Homerton bold

*   Sub-Heading: a heading style using 18pt Homerton medium

*   Italic: Trinity medium italic (no size set)

*   Bold: Trinity bold (no size set)

*   1in Indent: a ruler setting the first line left margin and the left margin one inch from the lefthand frame edge so that all text is indented one inch. No font or size details are set.

- Hanging Indent: a ruler setting the left margin one inch from the frame edge and the first line left margin two thirds of an inch from the frame edge. A tab is set at one inch to line up with the start of subsequent lines. This style can be used for creating numbered lists, for example. There is more about this type of style in chapter 12: *Some special effects.*

- Table: sets rules above and below, plus vertical rules, and tabs for aligning columns of text. This creates rules to make up a table around the text. There is more about this type of style in chapter 12: *Some special effects.*

These styles have keyboard shortcuts set. You may want to remove the shortcuts to use them for something else. This is described later in this chapter.

BaseStyle

Any text you type or import into an Impression document must have some style attributes set — you obviously can't type text that has no font or no size. For this reason a default style, called BaseStyle, is set up automatically and used for any text you import or type without setting a style. It has all the necessary attributes set. It is 14pt Trinity medium on 16.8 point leading with no space above or below the paragraph. It has a font aspect ratio of 100% and is displayed in black on a white background. It is left justified and has the special attributes of underline, strike through, superscript, subscript and hyphenation all set off. The first line and left margins are both set to 0.635mm. There is no leading character, rule-off lines are set to zero thickness and the style has no style labels set. The keyboard shortcut is Ctrl-B.

BaseStyle is a special style in many respects. There are several attributes that you can't turn off, though you can turn them off for any other style. You can't delete BaseStyle and you can't select it from the menu. You can't overlay it over other styles, or remove it from a piece of text. It is generally a background style on which you overlay other styles. You should edit BaseStyle to be your main body text style. Otherwise, you will have to change explicitly any text that you import. You can edit BaseStyle in the same way as any other style, with the exception of the attributes you can't turn off completely. If you edit BaseStyle to set all the attributes you want to use for your main body text, you will have less styling to do after importing or typing text.

Applying styles

You can learn how to apply styles to a piece of text using just the default styles. When you open a new Impression document and begin typing or import a text file, the text will appear in BaseStyle — because it has to appear in some form or another. If you are importing text, you can add styles to it after you have imported it. If you are typing, you can either apply styles as you go along or wait until you have finished and then apply styles.

To apply a style to an existing piece of text, you need to select it. Select text by putting the pointer at the start of the text you want to select and dragging with the lefthand mouse button to the end of the passage you want to select. The text will be highlighted in reverse colour (white text on a black background). Now display the menu and move the pointer across Style to display a submenu. This offers some tasks to do with styles and, in the bottom portion, a list of the styles available. If there are any styles already applied to the text you have chosen, these will be shown as a list of ticked styles above the main list. BaseStyle is not included in the list because you can't remove it from a piece of text and you don't need to apply it as it is always present.

```
╔═══════════════════════════╗
║          Style            ║
╟───────────────────────────╢
║  New style...      ^F5    ║
║  Edit style...     ^F6    ║
║  Clear all styles  ^B     ║
║ ─ ─ ─ ─ ─ ─ ─ ─ ─ ─ ─ ─ ─ ║
║  New ruler...      ⇧^N    ║
║  Edit ruler...     ⇧^E    ║
║ ─ ─ ─ ─ ─ ─ ─ ─ ─ ─ ─ ─ ─ ║
║ ✓Main Heading             ║
║ ─ ─ ─ ─ ─ ─ ─ ─ ─ ─ ─ ─ ─ ║
║  Main Heading             ║
║  Sub-Heading              ║
║  Italic                   ║
║  Bold                     ║
║  1in indent               ║
║  Hanging indent           ║
║  Table                    ║
╚═══════════════════════════╝
```

To apply a style to the selected text, click on its name. The text will acquire the style you have chosen, and next time you display the menu for the same piece of text the style will be in the list of ticked styles.

One very important way in which Impression's styles differ from the paragraph styles used in other desktop publishing programs is that you are not restricted to using only one style at a time on a piece of text. An Impression style may set only some — or only one — text attribute. You can then use it in combination with other styles that set different attributes. For example, you might use a style called Example for examples in your document. If you wanted to include, say, some computer commands within an example using a different typeface and perhaps a different colour, you could use another style, perhaps called Command, which just sets the font and the colour. When you use this style on a piece of example text, all the other attributes will be taken from the Example style, but Command will set the font and colour.

The ability to use styles in combination like this makes it easier to keep consistency throughout your document. A major problem that many users have with the exclusive, one-at-a-time paragraph styles other systems use is that if they make a change to one style, they then have to remember to make the change to many related styles. For example, if your main text, lists, captions and references are all in Trinity 10 point on 12 and you decide to switch the leading to 13 point, you will have to change the leading in all four styles. In Impression, though, you would set common elements such as font and leading in BaseStyle, and only define the different features (perhaps space above paragraph, or indents) in the other four styles. To change the leading to 13 point in all styles then requires a change only in BaseStyle.

When you apply more than one style to a piece of text, there may be elements of the styles that conflict. These will be the bits that you wanted to change. For example, if your BaseStyle sets the font to Trinity, but your heading style sets it to Homerton, this conflict will be the change that you want to make. Impression applies the styles in the order in which you specify them, so any settings in the next style you apply that conflict with settings made in styles already applying to the text will take precedence. This means that you always need to use the style you want to be dominant last.

To remove a style from a piece of text, select the text and click on the style in the list of ticked styles. The text will revert to the characteristics of the other style(s) applied to it, or to the BaseStyle if there are no other styles applied. If you remove a style by mistake, you can reapply it again by clicking on its name in the usual way. However, this is the point at which you are likely to get into difficulties with the order of styles. Here's an example.

Suppose you have applied four styles in the order Style1, Style2, Style3 and Style4. Amongst other attributes, Style3 sets font size to 13pt, and Style4 sets it to 15pt. Your text is 15pt, the size set by the last style you applied. You decide to remove Style2 but click by mistake on Style3 and remove that. If you apply Style3 again, it will be the dominant style, and the text will appear in 13pt, not 15pt. You would have to remove Style4 as well and then reapply Style4 after Style3 to get them in the right order.

Changing and creating styles

Although you may begin to become familiar with styles by using the styles provided in a new Impression document, you will very quickly want to make your own styles, either by modifying those supplied or by creating new styles of your own. The same dialogue box is used to edit an existing style or to create a new style. It is a long and complex dialogue box, but you don't need to use all of it; you can set only the attributes you want to change, and ignore anything you don't want or don't understand. However, with a bit of practice you will soon learn what all the different bits control and how to use them; it's just a matter of being patient and persevering.

To display the dialogue box that allows you to edit and create styles, display the Style menu and click on either **New style** or **Edit style**. If you want to edit a style, first select some text in the style you want to edit. If you are creating a new style, you can select some text you want the style to apply to, but you don't have to do this. When you first display the dialogue box, this is the segment of it that appears on screen:

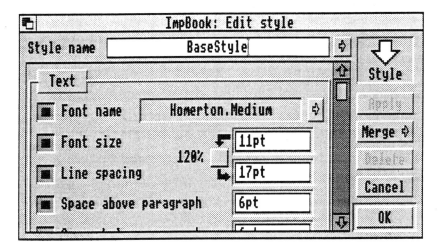

If you used **Edit style** to display the dialogue box, details of the current or selected style will be shown. The arrow to the side of the field for style name shows that if you click on that button a menu will be displayed listing the styles available on your system. If the name in the field isn't the the name of the style you want to edit, as it may not be if there are several styles applied to the selected text, click on this menu arrow to display the menu and choose the style you want to alter. Its name will appear in the field and the dialogue box will show details of this style. If you used **New style** to display the dialogue box, the style name will be Untitled and all the attributes will be turned off.

To move down through the dialogue box to see other settings you can make, use the scroll bar or scroll arrow. Let's look at what the dialogue box allows you to control.

The first segment of the dialogue box allows you to set the style name, choose the font and font size, and set the line spacing and the space inserted above the paragraph.

To the left of each of the settings you can make is a button. If the button is pressed in it is turned on. A red square will be visible. If the button is turned off, it is just grey. You can only change a setting if its button is turned on. To turn a button on or off, just click on it.

None of the changes you make to a style using this dialogue box will take place until you click on the Apply or OK button on the right of the dialogue box. These buttons are described at the end of this section.

Name

A new style that you are creating will have 'Untitled' in the name field; a style you are editing will have the current name in the field. You can change the style name by deleting the name in the field using the Delete or Backspace key, or by pressing Ctrl-U, and then typing the name you want to use. This should not be the same as an existing style name, but Impression distinguishes between upper and lower case in style names so you could have styles called bullet and Bullet (though it isn't a good idea as it would be confusing for you). If you don't give a name, Impression will use a default, descriptive name for the style; for example, a style which uses 16pt Trinity may be called Trinity.Medium/16pt if you don't give it a name of your own. You can change the name of an existing style if you want to. Its original name will be removed from the list of styles in the style menu and replaced with the new name. (You can't make a copy of a style by changing its name as the original is removed.)

Font

To set the font for a style, make sure the button beside Font name is turned on and then move the pointer over the menu arrow and click a mouse button to display the menu offering the fonts available. There is an arrow to the right of each font name indicating that there is a submenu for that font. The arrow is present even if there is only one option for a font. Click on the name of the font you want to use in the submenu.

Font size and line spacing

The next two settings are linked. When you turn on the button for font size, the button for line spacing comes on at the same time, and also a button beside the input fields labelled 120%. This is because the default line spacing is 120% of the font size, and Impression calculates and uses this figure automatically. If you want to use a different line spacing, though, you can change the figure in the field. If you don't want Impression to calculate and use the 120% figure, click on the button to turn it off. Next time you edit the same style, the line spacing won't be updated automatically if you change the font size. You can turn the button back on to display the default spacing (120%) again. Line spacing is leading; it is the font size, plus 20% which will appear between the bottom of one line of text and the top of the next line.

Space above and below paragraph

The next two settings allow you to choose how much space will be inserted above and below a paragraph in the style you are working on. This will only be used when you press the Return key. The space between paragraphs has two components: the Space below setting for the preceding paragraph, and the Space above setting for the following paragraph. For example, if you have a paragraph in style Heading, with space below set to 10pt followed by a paragraph in BaseStyle, with space above set to 6pt, there will be 16pt space left between the two paragraphs. The space below setting is not visible when you first display the Style dialogue box. Click in the scroll bar or scroll arrow on the right of the dialogue box to move down and show this setting. The next segment of the dialogue box looks like this:

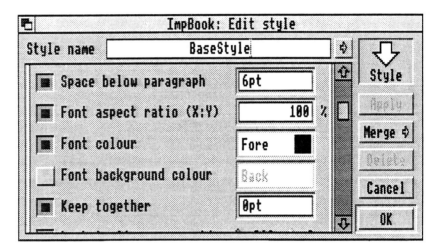

By default, space above and below is measured in points and displayed in points in the dialogue box. However, you can give the figure you want to use for space in any of the units that Impression recognises, using the appropriate abbreviation. The most useful and likely units are:

• millimetres: mm

• centimetres: cm

• inches: in

• points: pt

• picas: pi

You can also set dimensions in feet (ft), yards (yd) and metres (m), though it's difficult to imagine why you might want to.

Impression will automatically convert the dimension you give to points, unless you change the default setting for the units. The original default settings are points for measurements related to fonts, millimetres for measurements related to the page and centimetres for the ruler. (The ruler is described later in this chapter.) You can change the defaults using the Preferences option in the Impression icon bar menu. The procedure is described in chapter 20: *Making your own settings and customising Impression.*

Font aspect ratio

The Font aspect ratio allows you to distort the normal x:y (width:height) ratio of the font. It sets the x measurement (the width) as a percentage of the y distance (the height). The height of the characters remains the same if you change this, but the width changes. For example, if you set the font aspect ratio to 50%, the width of the characters will be halved, so they will be tall and narrow. The default value is 100%; this gives characters their 'normal' width for their height.

Font colour

Font colour is quite a complex setting, although it sounds simple enough and does what it suggests: sets the colour for the text. Beside the Font colour button is a field reading 'Fore' because this sets the foreground colour (the colour used for the text characters) and a block of colour showing the current colour. To change the colour, click in the field. Another dialogue box appears with the title Colour picker.

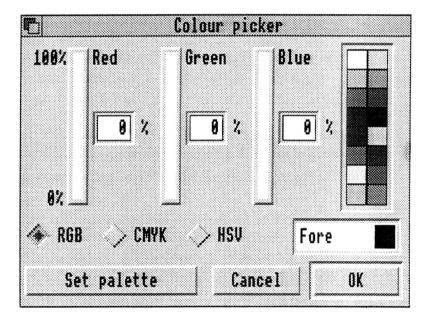

This allows you to define fully the colour that you want to use for the text using one of three methods: RGB, CMYK or HSV. The default method is RGB, or red-green-blue, and this is the one shown on the screen when you display the Colour picker dialogue box. This is the method that most people like to use, as it follows the computer's own method of building up and displaying colours; it will probably already be familiar to you from other RISC OS applications. CMYK, or cyan-magenta-yellow-key (black) is a method of defining colours that printers use. If you are planning to produce colour separations for professional printing you will probably want to use this method. HSV, or hue, saturation and value, is a method of colour definition used by artists. If the method is already familiar to you, you might want to use this one. We will look at each method in turn.

The first screen lets you select the RGB, or red-green-blue, combination that makes up the colour. You can pick a colour by clicking on the palette displayed on the right of the dialogue box. The sliders for the red, green and blue components will show how the colour is made up. You can then modify the colour by dragging the sliders or typing a value in the % fields beside each colour slider. The current value of the colour as you modify it is shown in the block marked 'Fore' beneath the colour picker. When you are happy with the colour, click on Set palette to save it. The palette, which is used to display the colours in the colour picker, will be modified so that the existing colour closest to the new colour you have defined is replaced by the new colour. This will not necessarily be the colour you chose and altered. Other elements of the screen display that use the changed colour will also alter. You can change back the screen display, but retain the definition of the colour in the Impression file, by using the option **Default** on the palette menu from the icon bar. If you do this, the text will not be displayed in exactly the colour you have defined, but in the nearest match available for the screen mode you are using. However, the information about the colour will be saved with the file and if you use a suitable printer to print your document the colour you have defined will be matched.

If you want to use the cyan-magenta-yellow-key method of defining a colour, click on the button marked CMYK to display a different set of sliders. Because these colours cannot all be represented well on the screen using most screen modes, the sliders show blocks of grey rather than blocks of the appropriate colours. Black is the key colour, used to darken combinations built up with the others. CMYK colour definitions describe colours in terms of the proportions of cyan, magenta, yellow and black inks used in four-colour printing. Magenta is a lurid pink, cyan a vibrant turquoise-blue. These colours are not easily represented using the computer's RGB colour models, and in most screen modes the block of colour in the Fore field will often not be a very close match to the colour you are defining. To see the colour properly, click on Set palette. This will replace the colour in the existing palette that is closest to your new colour with the colour you have just defined. Other elements of the screen display will change to the new colour, too. Again, use **Default** in the palette menu to restore the screen display but keep the colour definition for the style.

If you are used to using the Hue, Saturation, Value method of defining colours, you can use this. If you are not used to it, it is not a particularly easy method to use. It depends on a hexagonal cone of colour. The tip of the cone is black and the centre of the hexagonal face is white, with shades of grey appearing between these along the vertical axis. Different colours (hues), from red at 0 degrees through yellow, green, cyan, blue and magenta at 300 degrees are ranged around the hexagonal face. The saturation of colour is most intense at the perimeter and zero in the middle of the face, which is white. This means that value is measured vertically, from black (0%) to white (100%); hue is measured around the face of the cone, through 360 degrees; saturation is measured from the middle of the cone (0%) to the perimeter, where there is pure saturated colour (100%).

When saturation is set to 0%, no colour is added so the value determines the level of grey shown and the figure for hue is irrelevant. When saturation and value are set to 100%, pure colour is given, determined by the hue. If saturation is 100% but value is less than 100%, the colour will be darker the lower you set the figure for value. If value is 0%, hue and saturation are irrelevant and black is defined.

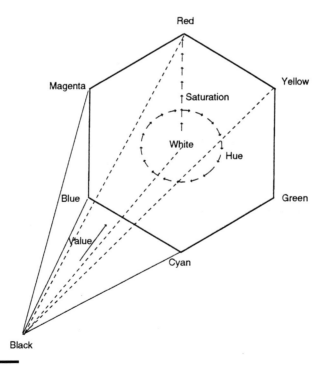

Set the hue, value and saturation figures on the dialogue box by typing in the fields or dragging the sliders. An approximation of the colour you have defined, using the colours in the current palette, is shown in the block on the right of the dialogue box. Again, you can click on Set palette to replace a colour in the existing palette with the colour you have just defined. The existing colour that is closest to the new colour is replaced. This allows you to see the colour clearly. Use Default in the palette menu to restore the screen display but keep the colour definition for the style.

When you have picked the colour you want to use, click on OK to return to the main part of the Style dialogue box.

Font background colour

The font colour will be used for the text characters themselves. You can also pick a colour to be used for the page background behind the text. Turn on Font background colour and then click beside Back in the field. There is a square of white here, though you can't see it as the field background is also white. The method for defining the background colour is exactly the same as that for defining font colour.

Keep together

This setting allows you to control the grouping of paragraphs so that headings are not split from their following body text over page breaks. The Keep together value sets the amount of space there must be between the paragraph and the end of the frame for the text to appear in that frame. For example, if you set the keep together value to 15pt, there must be 15pt of space below the paragraph and within the frame for the text to be allowed to remain in the frame. If there is less space, the text will be moved to the next frame in the flow. You should set the keep together figure to an appropriate value so that there is space to put one or more lines of text. For instance, if your body text has space above the paragraph of 6pt and is 10pt on 12pt leading, your heading has space below the paragraph of 7pt and you want to be able to get at least two lines of text after a heading at the foot of the page, set the keep together value for the heading at 6+7+(2x12) = 37pt. If you want only one line of text after the heading and before the end of a frame, set the value to 6+7+12 = 25pt.

Lock to linespace grid

The next section of the dialogue box looks like this:

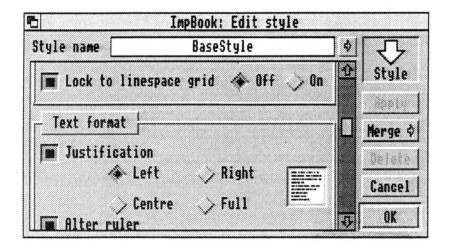

If you have several columns of text on a page, you will probably want the lines of text in the different columns to line up across the page. Unless you control the spacing using Lock to interspace grid the lines are unlikely to line up properly. This is because the vertical positioning of the lines becomes disrupted when different styles introduce different amounts of spacing between lines and paragraphs, when frames start and end at different heights on the page and when pictures interrupt the flow of the text. The linespace grid is an invisible grid that controls the position of lines. As long as lines are locked to the linespace grid, they will line up across columns. This means that the spacing won't be taken entirely from the styles you have defined, but will be modified by reference to the grid spacing so that the lines always line up properly. It gives a much better appearance to multicolumn text than allowing the lines to have the spacing set by their styles. You don't need to lock all styles to the linespace grid, but locking the body text and any other styles you use a lot to the grid will greatly improve the appearance of multi-column text. You don't need to use this feature at all if you are using only one column of text on a page.

Text format

The text format area of the dialogue box allows you to choose the justification and control the ruler. The justification lets you set the text to be left- or right-aligned, fully justified or centred. The illustration to the right of the buttons shows you the appearance on the page of the justification option you have chosen. You can only click on a justification type when justification is turned on. The ruler button allows you to display the ruler and so control the placing of tabs, the position of the start of lines and the position of the end of lines. The ruler is described later in this chapter.

Text effects

The next section of the dialogue box offers text effects.

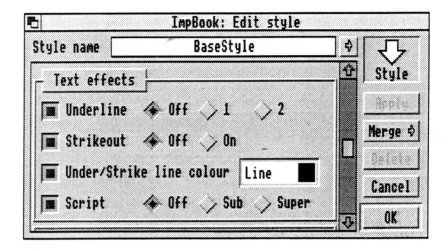

Four text effects are offered:

- underline
- strikeout
- superscript
- subscript.

Text may be underlined with a single or double underline. Text with strikeout has a line going through the body of the text, like this:

~~this text has strikeout set on.~~

It is useful if you are modifying a document and want to indicate that some text is to be removed, but you don't actually want to delete it yet. This might be because you have to have your modifications approved by someone, for example, or you want to keep the text available in case you want to use it elsewhere, or when you need a record of the changes you have made to a document. You can choose a colour for the line used to strikeout or underline text, following the same procedure for defining the colour as for setting font colour and background colour. Both underline and strikeout options have a button marked Off. You don't need to use these to prevent text having either of these attributes unless some other style applying to the text has set underline or strikeout on.

Superscript text is small text that appears above the normal line of the text, such as 2^2; subscript text is small text that appears below the normal line of the text, such as CO_2. Again, you can turn off either of these attributes if another style applying to the text may have turned them on. If you just want to use superscript characters 1-3, you can get these by typing Alt-185, Alt-178 and Alt-179 respectively, or, even more conveniently, by holding down Alt and typing 1, 2 or 3 using the regular number/symbol keys. These characters are in the standard character set. They are available in the standard Acorn fonts, including Newhall, but may not be available in fonts from other suppliers.

The next section of the dialogue box looks like this:

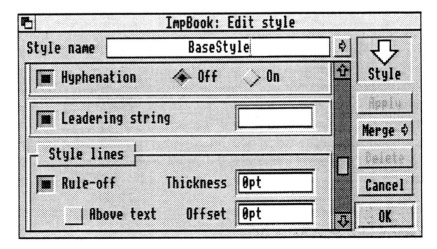

Hyphenation

You can choose whether or not Impression will automatically hyphenate long words that fall over line breaks. If you want words to be automatically hyphenated rather than carried over to the next line, turn hyphenation on. You will also have to load the hyphenation module if you want to use hyphenation. This is explained in chapter 20: *Making your own settings and customising Impression.* Words will only be hyphenated if they fall at the end of a line but do not fit on the line, have more than four characters and do not already contain a hyphen or other non-alphabetic character. Words that may be hyphenated are checked in a hyphenation exception dictionary for any special instructions about hyphenating them. If they are not in the exception dictionary, Impression applies a set of hyphenation rules to decide where to put the hyphen. Impression also takes account of a few other factors.

- If there are already hyphenated words at the end of previous lines, the word is less likely to be hyphenated and more likely to be carried over to the next line to improve the appearance of the text.

- If a large gap would be left at the end of the line by taking the word to the next line, the word is more likely to be hyphenated.

- The last word of a paragraph will not be hyphenated.

You can control the hyphenation of individual words using a soft hyphen and by editing the hyphenation exception dictionary. These alternatives are described in chapter 10: *Word-processing with Impression.*

Leadering string

A leadering string is a row of characters that will be added between tabs. In tables of figures and a table of contents, a row of dots or dashes helps to draw the eye across the page. It is common to use a sequence of three dots and then a space, like this: ... ... You could also use dots separated by spaces, like this: . . . . You can type a sequence of up to four characters to use as a leadering string.

You can use a leadering string as a way of making a bullet style, too. To do this, you will need to choose a character to use as a bullet from the font you are using for the text for bulleted items. This is likely to be the bullet character Alt-143, but you can use any other character you like. Type the character, or the Alt sequence you need to use to get the character, in the field for the leadering string and then type three spaces. For example, you would need to type:

```
Alt-143 [space] [space] [space]
```

to get this format of bulleted list

•   a bullet item.

When you make the ruler settings for the style, you will need to be careful not to leave so much space between the left margin, where the bullet character appears, and the tabbed position for the start of the text that the bullet is repeated. If the bullet repeats, you need to change the ruler setting, not the leadering string. Using this method to define a bulleted style is described in greater detail in chapter 12: *Some special effects.*

Style lines

You can add rules above and/or below text by defining rule-off lines with the Style lines part of the dialogue box.

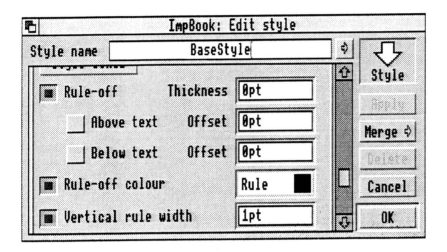

If you want to use lines, click on the button beside Rule-off to turn it on. You can then define the thickness of the lines. By default, the thickness is shown in points, but you can define it in any units that Impression recognises. If you don't change the setting, which is initially 0pt, the line will have zero thickness, so it won't be visible. Click on either or both of the buttons Above text and Below text to add a rule above the paragraph and/or below the paragraph. For the rule above the text, the offset is measured from the top of the first line of text in the style. An offset with a positive value will appear above the line of text. For rules below the text, the offset is measured upwards from the baseline of the bottom line of text. This means that a positive offset will appear above the baseline and rule through the text. This is probably not what you want. To get the rule below the line, you need to use a negative offset. Again, the offsets for rules are measured by default in points but you can use other units if you wish. If you leave the offset for both rules at zero and draw both rules, the rules will be separated by the font size. For example, if your text is 16pt, there will be 16 points between the two rules. If you use a text style with a rule above set directly beneath a paragraph with a rule below set, only the rule below will be used and the rule above from the second paragraph will be ignored.

You can add a vertical rule down the side(s) of a column of text. To do this, you need to set a vertical rule marker on the ruler. This is described later in this chapter in the section *Rulers*. You also need to turn on the button beside Vertical rule width. You can define the width of the vertical rule in the field to the right of the button. You can add more than one vertical rule; adding rules both above and below the text and to the left and right of it gives you text enclosed in a box. This is a crude but sometimes useful method of boxing text as the size of the box will alter to accommodate all the text when you edit the text. A more conventional method is to put the text into a frame with a border; this is described in chapter 8: *Frames*. A vertical rule along one side of the text can be used as a change bar if you want to show which sections of a document have been changed since you last issued it. If you want to use the rule-off function for this, you will probably want to create a text style with only one attribute, the presence of the vertical rule, and you can then use this with all your other styles. If it is a style with only this attribute set, you can remove the style from your text easily without affecting any other elements of the styling. There is an example of a changebar style in example document 6 on the disc that accompanies this book; it is described in chapter 21: *Examples.*

You can set the colour of a rule if you turn on the Rule-off colour button. The field shows a block of the colour currently being used. Click on the colour block to display the usual colour definition dialogue box and use this in the same way as you use it to set the font colour and background. If you have a suitable printer, the lines will print in the colour you choose. You can only define one colour for the rules, even if you have several rules set for a style.

Style labels

The final part of the dialogue box looks like this:

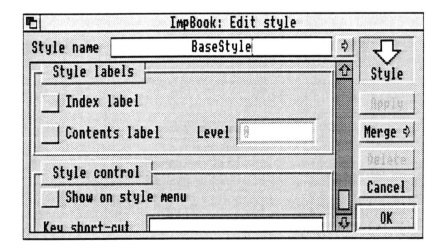

If you want to compile an index or table of contents (TOC) for your document, you can do so automatically by using a style that sets labels that will be picked up by Impression when it searches for text to include in an index or TOC.

If you want text in the style you are editing or creating to be included in an index, click on the button beside Index label. Any text using this style, whether or not there are other styles overlaying it, will be picked up and added to an index. You will probably want to create a style with only this attribute set and then use the style for all the items you want to appear in the index. For example, if you have a line of text:

There are two types of nappies: disposable nappies and terry towelling nappies

you might want to include in the index 'nappies', 'disposable nappies' and 'terry towelling nappies'. You would select each of these in turn and apply the index style to each. When you compile the index, these items will be picked up and included. Chapter 14: *Creating an index and table of contents* explains how to compile an index.

You can also compile a table of contents automatically. For this, you probably won't want to create a special style and add it to items you want to include, but will instead decide which levels of heading to include and use the Style labels facility to include all text in the appropriate styles in the TOC. For example, you might want to include all text in styles Chapter and Section in your TOC. Click on the button beside Contents label to turn this on for a style. The field to the right lets you set the level of heading the items will be given in the TOC. Typically, a table of contents shows chapter headings more prominently than section headings, for example, so these are in different styles. Set a number in the range 0-15 in the Level field. You can then create corresponding contents styles when you generate the TOC and the layout of the TOC will be partly done for you. There is more information on generating a TOC in chapter 14.

Style control

The final section of the style dialogue box allows you to control whether the style appears on the style menu and to set a keyboard short-cut to get the style without using the menu.

You might decide not to include a little-used style in the style menu in order to keep down the length of the menu. If you are using a lot of styles, the menu can get long and unwieldy. However, if a style is not included in the menu, you need to define a keyboard short-cut, otherwise you won't be able to use the style at all. A keyboard short-cut is a combination of keys you press to add a style to selected text or start that style for text you are about to type. Once you have defined a short cut, you can't then use that combination of keys for anything else.

You can define any combination of keys but obviously it isn't a good idea to use just alphabetic keys. Typically, the Control key with an alphanumeric key, or the function keys with or without Shift or Control are used for shortcuts. If you use a combination that is already defined in Impression for another function, that function will be overwritten by the style-defining function. Don't use F12 as that is used to leave the desktop.

If you use a shortcut that has already been defined for another style (and some are set up by default), it won't work for the second style you allocate it to. To remove a shortcut definition, use Edit style for the style that has the shortcut set and delete the text in the shortcut field or use Ctrl-U to remove it. You can then give a new shortcut, or leave the style without a shortcut, and use its original shortcut for something else.

Implementing changes of style

When you have finished defining a style or making changes to a style, you need to save the changes you have made.

If you began creating a style with some text selected, you can click on Apply on the Style dialogue box to save the style and apply it to the selected text in a single operation. If you just click on OK, the style will be saved but not applied to the selected text. If you have been editing a style, all text that uses the style will be changed when you click on OK or Apply.

If you change your mind about the changes you have made with the Style dialogue box, click on Cancel to remove the dialogue box without saving the changes. If you click with the Select (lefthand) mouse button on OK or Apply, the changes are applied and saved and the dialogue box removed from the screen. If you click with Adjust (the righthand mouse button), the changes are applied and saved but the dialogue box remains on screen. This is helpful if you are trying out changes in a style and want to use the dialogue box repeatedly as you make changes and look at the effect. Remember that some of the style you are changing must be visible in the window for you to be able to see the effects of the changes you make.

There are two other buttons here on the dialogue box. Delete allows you to delete a style. Merge allows you to combine the characteristics of two styles. Both are described later in this chapter.

Styles in imported text

Sometimes when you import text Impression may create some extra styles for your text. This depends on the loader module you are using and whether there was any styling in your original file. Impression will create styles to try to match some or all of the styling in your original. For example, if you import a 1st Word Plus file you may find that extra ruler styles have been created and used to try to keep the same line length as your document had in 1st Word Plus.

There is no advantage to having all your text in a style other than BaseStyle, so if this happens you should put the caret in the story, use Select text story from the Edit menu to select all the text and click on the ticked style in the Style menu to remove it from your whole story. You can delete the styles created by default if you are not going to use them. This is explained later in this chapter.

Using styles sensibly

To make your document easy to manage and easy to change, you should set just the attributes necessary for each style to achieve the effect you want. For example, if you want an indented style to use with lists, and want only the space between paragraphs and the position of the lefthand margin to differ from your BaseStyle, set only the Space above, Space below and ruler setting for the lefthand margin. Don't set the font or size; these are set by the

BaseStyle anyway, so you don't need to redefine them. If you keep your style definitions economical like this it is easy to make global changes to your document. If you had set the font for your BaseStyle and also in two related styles (say, an indented style and a bulleted style), and then decided to change the font, you would need to make the same change to three styles. If, though, you set the font only in the BaseStyle, you would need to make the change only once. Apart from saving time and trouble, this helps to prevent any untidy mistakes if you miss one of the styles you need to change.

It is also a good idea to decide on a sensible policy for naming styles and stick to it. It is important that you can tell from the list of styles in the Style menu which style you are using for different things. You can use descriptive style names, such as Heading, Bullet, Indented, Bold, and Table, or you can use style names that indicate the function of the style, such as Emphasis, Chapter, Section and so on. A common way of distinguishing between different levels of heading is to label them A-head B-head, C-head and so on, with A-head as your main heading and the other letters for progressively lower levels of heading.

Using the ruler

The Style dialogue box gives access to the ruler, which is displayed in a separate window. To display the ruler, click on Alter ruler in the Text format section of the dialogue box to display the ruler window. It looks like this:

The ruler gives you control over the placing of text. It lets you set:

- the lefthand margin (where text starts)

- the lefthand margin for the first line of text in a paragraph (where the first line starts)

- the righthand margin (where text stops)

- tab positions and types

- the position for vertical rules.

A ruler can be associated with a style or it can be stand-alone. The method for making settings is the same in each case, but the use differs. Let's look at how to make the settings first.

If you have accessed the ruler from the Style dialogue box, the OK and Cancel buttons are greyed out. These are used only for stand-alone rulers. Next to the Cancel button is a button showing the current ruler units. Click on this button to cycle through the units available: inches and tenths, picas, inches and eighths, and centimetres. To the right of this button is a series of icons:

⏋⌐⅃ ⊢⊣ ▽▽▼▽ |

These represent, in order:

- the lefthand margin position

- the righthand margin position

- the first line lefthand margin

- the starting position for a horizontal rule

- the finishing position for a horizontal rule

- a left tab

- a right tab

- a centre tab

- a decimal tab

- the position for a vertical rule.

To add one of these items to the ruler, either drag it from the row of icons or click on it in the row of icons and then click at the position on the ruler where you want it to appear. If an item is already present on the ruler, you can drag it to a new position. You can only place one copy of each of the margin icons and of the starting and finishing positions for horizontal rules, but you can place as many tabs of all kinds as you want (up to a total of 32 tabs) and as many vertical rules as you want. The different types of tabs and their functions are described in chapter 5: *Some typographical terms.* You can't set the left or first line margin to the right of the right margin, or the starting point for a horizontal rule to the right of its finishing point. If you don't define any of the margin settings (left, first and right), the frame edge will be used. The righthand margin is set relative to the righthand edge of the frame, so if you set it 1cm from the righthand end of the ruler, lines will stop and the text will wrap around at 1cm from the righthand edge of the frame. If you want to set the position of the righthand margin relative to the lefthand edge of the frame, use the Ruler set-up dialogue box, which is described below.

Dragging icons or clicking on the ruler lets you see the position at which you are setting ruler items, but it doesn't allow you to be very accurate. To give precise values for margins and tab-stops, you need to use the Ruler set-up dialogue box. Quite a good way to define a ruler is to drag the icons for the margins and tab stops to place them roughly, and then use the set-up dialogue box to give the exact values for their positions. To display the set-up dialogue box, click on the menu arrow to the right of the field for the ruler's name, or click the Menu button on the mouse when the pointer is over the ruler. The first item in the menu, Enter values, displays the set-up dialogue box. This has a button and text field for each of the items you can use only once at a time — the three text margin settings and the margins for horizontal rules — and a section for you to set tab positions.

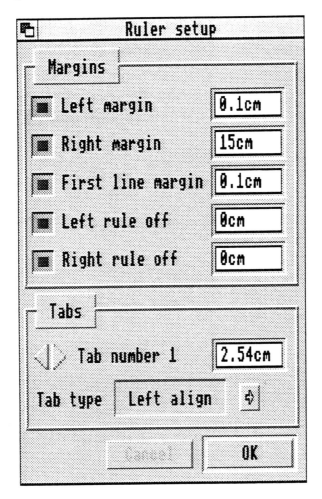

If you have already made settings for any of these items, the current settings are shown and you can change them. All the positions are measured from the lefthand edge of the current frame. To set tab positions, follow these steps:

1.   If necessary, click on one of the arrow buttons beside Tab number until the number of the tab you want to set is displayed. If there aren't any tabs set you can only set them in order, beginning with tab 1.

2.   Click on the menu button beside Tab type to display a menu showing the tab types available (left, right, centre and decimal, and vertical rule position). Click on the one you want to use and its name will appear in the field to the left of the menu button.

3.   Now delete the value shown in the field for the tab position (if there is one) and type the position you want to use for the tab. It is measured from the lefthand margin. If there are already some tabs set, you can do this before step 2 if you prefer.

4.   To set the next tab, click on the forwards arrow to the right of the label Tab number. Continue setting tabs like this. You can move backwards or forwards through the sequence of tabs you have set by clicking on the arrow buttons to the left of the tab type label.

When you have finished making ruler settings from this dialogue box, click on OK. When you have finished making ruler settings from the ruler dialogue box, you will need to click on OK or Apply from the Style dialogue box to remove the ruler display and implement the changes you have made.

Sometimes, you might want to change only the ruler settings and no other attribute of a piece of text.

You can do this by creating a style with altered ruler settings, or you can create a new ruler on its own, as a stand-alone ruler. To create a stand-alone ruler, display the Style menu and click on New Ruler. This displays the ruler defining dialogue box, but with the ruler name and OK and Cancel buttons available. The new ruler will have a default name of the form Ruler2 or Ruler3. It will use the next number in sequence that is available (not already used). It is a good idea to change the name, giving it a descriptive name that you will recognise easily when you want to reuse the ruler.

Make all the settings in the usual way, and give the ruler a new name if you want to. Click on OK when you are happy with the settings. If you click with Adjust, the ruler remains on screen for you to make further changes. Click on OK with Select to remove the ruler display. The name of the ruler will be added to the list of styles in the Style menu.

Removing ruler items

There are two ways you can remove any items from the ruler. You can drag icons from the ruler and drop them above the ruler, where they won't stick to the ruler in a new position (over the row of icons, for example), or you can display the ruler set-up dialogue box and turn the buttons off for the items you don't want and remove any tabs you don't want. To remove a tab using the dialogue box, use the arrow buttons to the right of the Tab number label until the setting for the tab you want to remove is shown, then display the Tab type menu and click on the first item, Remove tab. Any tabs after this one will be renumbered so that there are no gaps in the numbering.

Deleting a ruler

If you want to remove a ruler from a style, you can only do this by deleting all the items on the ruler, the margins, tab stops and vertical rule positions. A ruler that doesn't define anything has no effect, and any other ruler used with another style affecting the text will operate instead. However, a ruler that defines any elements at all will take precedence over any rulers attached to styles that have been overlaid (that is, styles that have been selected earlier for the same piece of text).

If you want to remove a stand-alone ruler, move the cursor to an area affected by the ruler, then choose Edit ruler from the Style menu. Display the ruler menu, by pressing the Menu button on the mouse or clicking on the menu icon button on the set-up dialogue box, and choose Remove ruler. The ruler will be deleted wherever it is used in the document.

Using existing rulers

If you create a stand-alone ruler, you can give it a name. This allows you to use the same ruler again later without having to redefine it, or to alter an existing ruler. The name of a stand-alone ruler appears in the list of styles in the Style menu.

You can apply an existing ruler to text by selecting the text and then choosing the name of the ruler from the Style menu, or you can apply a ruler to text you are about to type by choosing the ruler name and then typing. The new ruler will be applied from the cursor position if you do the second of these and will remain in force until you switch to a different ruler or apply a style that has a ruler of its own.

If you want to edit an existing ruler, select some text that uses the ruler and choose Edit ruler from the Style menu. The set-up dialogue box appears, showing the settings for the ruler in use. You can change any of these and then use OK to apply and save the changes. They will affect all text that uses the ruler.

If you have the ruler set-up dialogue box on screen, you can load a different ruler by choosing its name from the menu for the ruler display. The names of existing rulers are listed in the lower part of the menu. When you choose one, this ruler will be loaded. A warning dialogue box will appear, telling you that changes you have made to the other ruler will be lost and giving you the chance to cancel. Click on Continue if you want to carry on, or on Preserve if you want to save the changes you have already made. Any changes you make to the existing ruler will affect that ruler wherever you have used it. You can't make a new ruler that is a copy of the one you have chosen by altering its name in the name field; this just changes the name of the ruler you started with.

Clearing styles

If you want to remove all styles from a piece of text and return it to BaseStyle, select the text and choose Clear all styles from the Style menu. If you want to remove styles from a whole text story, place the cursor somewhere in the story and then choose Select text story from the Edit menu, then use Clear all styles. You can't select all the text in a document at once unless it is a single story. You will need to select each story in turn and clear it.

Deleting styles

You can't delete a style that is used anywhere in your document. This means that you can't click on the name of a style in the menu and then on Edit style and use Delete to get rid of it; since you have clicked on the name of the style, it is set on, and so is used in your document even if you haven't typed any text in it! To delete a style, first make sure there is no text in your document using the style. You can do this by selecting each text story in turn, checking to see if the style is in the ticked list of styles used in the text and, if it is, clicking on its name to remove it from the text.

When you are sure the style is not used anywhere in the document, you can delete it. Use New style to display the Style dialogue box, and display the style menu. Click on the menu button beside the field for the style name and then choose the name of the style you want to delete. A warning will appear saying that you haven't saved the changes to your new style; click on Continue. The name of the style you have chosen will appear in the field; click on Delete to remove the style completely and close the dialogue box. There is no warning or chance to confirm that you want to delete the style, so make sure you are certain you do want to remove it before you use this option. Styles aren't saved on a clipboard, so to get the style back you will have to recreate it from scratch as a new style. If you want to leave the dialogue box on screen so that you can delete several styles, click on OK with Adjust.

Merging styles

Usually, you will be able to combine styles by overlaying one style on another. However, you can merge styles so that their attributes are added together into a single style. They will then form a combined style. If you find that there are several styles that you often use in conjunction, you may want to merge the styles to save you having to apply all of them each time. When you merge styles, attributes from one or more additional styles overwrite attributes of the style you begin with, so you can't use the initial style on its own any more. If you want to combine several styles but also be able to use all the styles again separately, begin by starting a new style but not setting any attributes for it, then merging in all the styles you want to use together.

To merge styles, begin by displaying the style dialogue box either for an existing style or for a new style. Click on the Merge button to display a menu showing the styles available for merging. You can click on one or more styles to merge with the existing style; if you want to click on more than one style, use Adjust when you click so that the menu remains on screen. Any attributes that are already defined in the existing style may be overwritten by the merging style. Where there are any conflicting attributes, the setting from the most recently merged style will be used. For example, if you merge a heading with 14pt text into a style with 12pt text, the 14pt size will take precedence. If you then add another style, with 18pt text, the merged style will have 18pt set as its text size. When you have finished merging styles, you can make any other changes you want to the newly defined style, including changing its name, and then click on OK or Apply to save the changes. If you don't change the name, Impression will give the new style a name built up from the names of the merged styles.

Don't use Merge indiscriminately. It is a good idea to use it if you want to create a composite style to use where you frequently use a combination of styles, but don't use it in place of the usual mechanism of overlaying styles. If you merge, say, your BaseStyle and a bulleted style that uses many of the same text attributes, you will have an extra style to change if you decide to alter the BaseStyle. You should always define just the attributes you need for a style.

Combining styles from different documents

You may sometimes want to use the same styles in a new document as you have used in an existing document. Rather than recreating all the styles, you can load in the styles from the old document. To do this, display the style dialogue box and then drag the file icon for the old file onto the load icon (the large arrow) at the top righthand corner of the style dialogue box. The styles will be copied in and added to the style menu.

If you consistently want to use the same styles in several documents, you can alter the default new document Impression opens so that it has your styles already established. Chapter 20: *Making your own settings and customising Impression* tells you how to do this.

Refining headlines and section headings

As you become more proficient at using Impression and more critical of the appearance of your finished documents, you may want to use a couple of features that are not on the Style menu but that relate to using section and chapter headings. You may want to control the kerning of text in large point sizes, and to set page or frame breaks before headings, tables and so on.

Altering the kerning

You will probably use text in large point sizes for headings, and sooner or later you will use two letters that don't sit well together at their default kerning (letter spacing). You can alter the spacing to improve the appearance of the text. You can only set the kerning for a single pair of letters at a time. (There is a description of kerning and some examples of letters that often need special kerning in chapter 5: *Some typographical terms.*)

If you want to alter the spacing between a pair of letters, place the cursor between them and use Kern in the Misc menu to display this dialogue box:

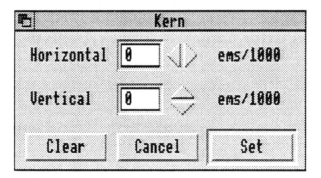

You will usually want to set the horizontal kerning. Both horizontal and vertical kerning are measured in thousandths of an em. An em is the length of an em dash (—) in the font and point size you are using. To move letters closer together horizontally, click on the arrow icon that points to the left. To move letters further apart, click on the arrow icon that points to the right. These buttons reduce or increase the kerning by increments of 10 units at a time. You can type directly in the fields if you prefer. Remember to add a minus sign (-) to make the value negative if you want to move the letters closer together.

Vertical kerning moves the letters out of alignment with each other. The arrow icon pointing upwards increases the kerning, moving the second letter up relative to the first. The arrow pointing downwards reduces the kerning, moving the second letter down relative to the first. You are only likely to use it either to create a special effect or to enhance the appearance of text that contains letters from different fonts or in different sizes. For example, you can create an effect like this:

he jumped up twice

Here the u and the space before it are given negative kerning and the p and the space following it are given positive kerning of the same number. You need to alter the kerning by quite a large value to achieve an effect like this. Start with about 300 for 24pt text.

If you mix fonts, you may want to alter the vertical kerning so that the letters look better aligned. For example, if you mix a serif and sans serif font in a headline, characters in one font may look as though they are higher up than characters in the other font. If you mix different point sizes in a headline, you may also want to adjust the vertical kerning.

Using Force to next

Sometimes you may want to force a piece of text to the start of the next page or column. This is most likely to be a heading, but it may also be the start of a table you want to keep together, or a list item. You can do this to keep the two final items in a list together so that there isn't just one item on its own at the top of a page.

To move text into the next frame, put the cursor at the start of the piece of text and choose Force to next from the Frame menu. This adds a marker into the text, and even if you subsequently edit the text so that you don't need to force it to the next frame, it will still be moved. To remove the marker, put the cursor at the start of the text again and press the Delete or Backspace key once.

Don't rely on Force to next in place of setting a Keep together value for heading styles because the method becomes inconvenient when you edit text. It is useful, though, to use it to move the start of a long table to the next frame, or any other piece of text or group of lines that you don't want split over a page break.

More about styles

Some special styles that you might want to use are described in more detail in chapter 12: *Some special effects*. This chapter explains how to create hanging indents for numbered lists and how to create outdented styles, and goes over the use of vertical and horizontal rules in more detail.

What next?

Styles are a means of setting several text attributes at once, or setting one attribute that you are going to want to set frequently. The next chapter explains when and how to use effects instead of styles. You can only set one text attribute at a time with an effect.

7   Using effects

Effects are local changes to text attributes that you set one at a time. Unlike styles, effects don't all have names that you can choose from a menu; you often pick an effect by choosing the attribute you want to set (such as text font) and then choosing the value you want from a submenu. It is often slower to use effects than to use styles as for some options you need to go through a series of submenus. This chapter explains:

- the effects you can set

- when it is better to use a style than an effect, and

- when it is better to use an effect than a style.

Text effects

The text effects you can set are:

- text font

- text size

- line spacing

- text colour

- underline

- subscript

- superscript

- justification.

All the effects are available from the Effects menu and its associated submenus. To use an effect, either select the block of text you want it to apply to and then choose the effect, or choose an effect to be used from the cursor position for text you are about to type.

To choose a font, display the submenu for **Text font** which shows the font families available, then move across to show the submenu for the family you want to use. This shows the fonts available (for example, Bold, Bold.Italic, Medium and Medium.Italic). Click on the one you want to use.

To set the size, display the submenu for **Text size**. This offers condensed and expanded text, a range of point sizes, and the option to set a point size of your own. Condensed text has the same vertical height as normal text, but is narrower, so more characters fit on the line. Expanded text has the same height but is wider. Click on the option you want to use, or move the pointer to the right over Other to set a different point size. The dialogue box for setting a point size has a button for Off as well as for On.

This allows you to remove a custom point size from text you have already applied it to. It is better to use this Off button than to set the size explicitly back to the normal size for the style (by setting it to 10pt or whatever) as otherwise the text will still be marked as having an effect set, even though the effect doesn't alter the appearance of the text. If you then change the point size for the style, the text marked with an effect will keep the size set by the effect.

To set the line spacing, display the dialogue box and give a value for line spacing. Again, there are On and Off buttons. If you want to return the line spacing to normal, you can turn the effect off from this dialogue box.

To set text colour, click on this option in the menu to display the standard colour definition dialogue box.

To set underline, subscript or superscript, just pick the option from the Effects menu.

The justification options available are the same as those available for styles. Again, just pick the one you want to use. You can apply a justification effect to just part of a paragraph, but if you apply it to less than a line it will have no visible effect. If you go on to add text within the area you have applied the effect to so that more than a line is affected, you will then see the effect. You can centre, right align, left align or justify a single line, group of lines, whole paragraph or several paragraphs.

Effect or style?

Not all of the text attributes that you can set with the style dialogue box can be set with effects and then you will obviously need to use a style. At other times, though, it may not be immediately obvious whether you should use a style or an effect. A few useful guidelines are:

- If you are going to use two or more effects together, and you are going to use the combination more than once, use a style

- If you are going to use a single effect that is easy to set (such as underline), use an effect

- If you are going to use a single effect that is not particularly easy to set because it involves using submenus (such as text font), and you are going to use it repeatedly, create a style.

- Remember that there are keyboard short-cuts for the effects you can set directly from the Effect menu without using a submenu. This makes them quick to use and means that there is no point in creating a style and giving it a keyboard short-cut.

- Try to avoid using too many styles because the style menu list will get very long and unmanageable. You can use keyboard shortcuts and remove styles from the list if it gets too difficult to manage.

- Be consistent; if you have a suitable style defined, use it all the time rather than sometimes using the style and sometimes using an effect.

You should create styles for all the levels of heading you are going to use and any other special pieces of text (such as list items, picture captions and bulleted points). If you don't create a style, you can quickly find that you have forgotten exactly the combination of effects you were using for any particular item.

Also, if anyone else has to use and edit your document, they won't know what combinations of effects you have used. It becomes very difficult to give your documents a consistent appearance if you don't use styles properly but rely on effects instead.

What next?

The next chapter explains how to use frames. You will need to use frames if you are going to create or alter master pages, add graphics, alter the position or size of text columns, or use advanced layouts.

8 Frames

Every item in an Impression document, whether it's text or graphics, must be in a frame. The frame is just a container for the text or picture. It allows you to control where text appears on the page. Unless you set a border to the frame, you won't see a frame when you print out your document.

This chapter explains how to use frames in the body text pages of a document. The next chapter explains how to use master pages, including using frames on master pages. You will need the information in this chapter before you can understand the next chapter. This chapter explains the different types of frames and shows you how to:

- create and edit frames

- add a text file or picture to a frame

- use a border with a frame

- use embedded frames.

Different types of frames

Impression recognises three types of frame that can hold text or graphics: master page frames, local frames, and repeating frames.

Master page frames can only be used on master pages, so they are described in the next chapter. If your new pages are copied from a master page that contains any master page frames, these frames will appear on your new page ready for you to use. A frame copied from a master page may be empty to hold your text and graphics or may already contain some text or a picture — perhaps a logo or header text.

Local frames are frames that you create on the page on which you want to use them. They appear only on that page and are empty; you can add text or graphics to a local frame.

A repeating frame is a frame that you add to one of the body pages of your document (not a master page) and it appears on every subsequent page in the same chapter. You can delete it from any pages you don't want it to appear on.

In addition to master page frames, local frames and repeating frames, you can create guide frames which can't hold text but help you to position and size the frames that can hold text. You are most likely to use guide frames on a master page, so they are described in the next chapter.

Creating and editing frames

The method for creating and altering a frame is similar for all types of frame. There are some settings you can't make for guide frames, but otherwise you need to learn only one method for all types of frame including master page frames.

Creating a new frame

You may want to create a new frame on a body text page to include a picture, or a table. If you are laying out a newsletter or magazine, you may not be using a master page with frames for your text and will need to create all the text and graphics frames you need on each page.

When you want to create a new frame, display the Frame menu and move the pointer over the option **New frame** to display a submenu offering three types of frame:

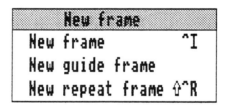

New frame gives you a normal local frame (as long as you have have accessed the menu from a body page and not a master page). **New guide frame** creates a frame that can't hold text or graphics, but that you can use to help you to position other frames. This is useful if, say, you want a lot of small frames in a column and want their left- and righthand edges to line up properly. **New repeat frame** creates a frame that will appear on the page you create it on and on every subsequent page in the same chapter.

When you have chosen one of the options the pointer changes to a pair of crosshairs. Position the centre of the cross where you want the top lefthand corner of the new frame to be, then press and hold down the Select button on the mouse. Drag the pointer until the centre of the cross is at the position for the bottom righthand corner, then release the mouse button. As you drag the second corner, the size of the frame you are defining is shown and constantly updated.

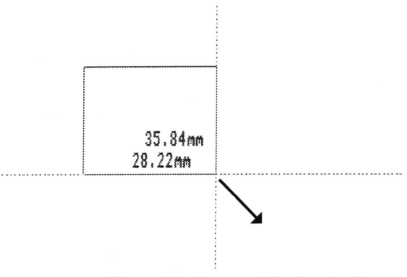

The new frame is automatically selected so that you can change its size and shape if you want to, so it has eight handles:

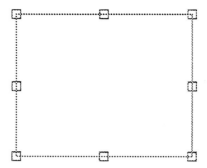

The text cursor is inside the frame, so that if you start typing the text will appear in your new frame.

If you move the pointer over one of the handles on the frame it changes to a snowflake shape. This is the shape you need to use to adjust the size and shape of a frame. You can drag a corner handle to alter the vertical and horizontal dimensions of the frame, or a side handle to change only one dimension at a time.

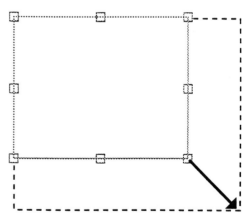

As you drag a handle, the size of the frame is reported and constantly updated.

As the new frame is selected, you can drag in a picture or text file immediately: just drag the file icon for a Paint or Draw file or a text file into the Impression document and it will be used to fill the frame you have created. There is more on importing text of various formats in chapter 18: *Working with documents,* and more on using pictures in chapter 11: *Graphics.*

Altering frames

When you have just created a new frame, you can change its size and shape by dragging its handles. You can do this with an existing local frame too if you first click in it to select it and display the handles. You can move a selected frame by putting the pointer inside it, then pressing and holding down the Select button and dragging the frame around. The pointer changes to a hand when you do this. As you drag, the vertical or horizontal position of each handle on the sides of the frame is reported. (The vertical position of the top and bottom edges and the horizontal positions of the left and right edges are shown.) However, this method allows you to move only local frames, and it is difficult to make very precise adjustments using it. You can resize or position a frame more accurately using the Alter frame dialogue box. This also allows you to make changes to a frame copied from the master page by letting you convert it to a local frame first. To display the Alter frame dialogue box, click in the frame you want to change to select it and then choose **Alter frame** from the Frame menu. (If you select a frame copied from the master page, handles are not shown but the frame's outline is shown in green when it is selected.)

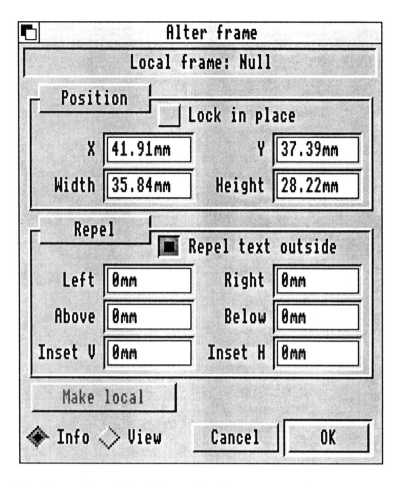

The first section of the dialogue box lets you control the position and size of the frame. This is measured from the top lefthand corner of the page. The default units are millimetres, but you can use other units if you prefer. If the frame you selected was copied from a master page, this section will report the current position and size of the frame but will be greyed out so that you can't make changes. If you want to change these, you will first need to make the frame local. This dissociates it from the master page. Any changes you make to the frame on the master page will no longer be reflected in the frame if you make it local. The frame will also no longer form part of the text flow of a story that flows across several pages. If you do want to make a frame local, click on the Make local button. This displays a warning and gives you the chance to change your mind and cancel (though the change is not actually made until you click on OK on the Alter frame dialogue box). To change the size and position settings, delete the text in a field and type the new position or dimensions you want. You don't need to specify the units if you want to use millimetres; Impression will assume the value is in millimetres unless you give another unit. Any changes you make to the local frame will have no effect on the master page frame or on other copies of it.

The next section of the dialogue box deals with repelling text. You can set this for a local frame or one copied from a master page. Text repelling means that text will not be printed right up to the edge of the frame. This is particularly useful if you are going to use a border with a frame, as text printed right up to the border may be overprinted by the border and looks messy. You can set text repelling margins for inside and outside a frame. If you want to repel text outside a frame (which you will only need to do if the frame is superimposed over another text frame), make sure the button beside Repel text outside is turned on. You can then set the space that will be kept clear of text above, below and to the right and left of the frame. Again, the default units are millimetres. Inside the frame you can set vertical and horizontal insets. The vertical inset controls the strip of space that will be kept free of text at the top and bottom of the frame; the horizontal inset controls the space that will be kept clear at the left and right edges of the frame.

There is another section to the dialogue box which allows you to control the borders and background colour of the frame. To display this, click on the button next to View in the lower left of the dialogue box. (To return to the first screen, click on Info.)

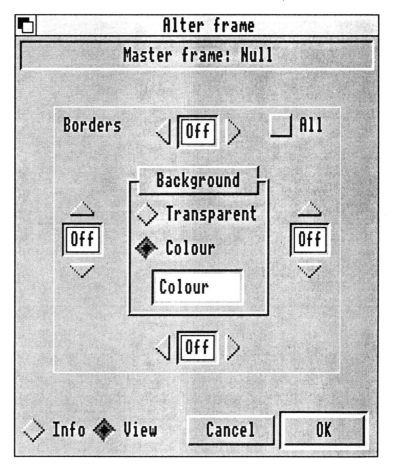

The background to a frame may be a colour or it may be transparent. If you click on the button beside Colour and then in the field below (which shows a block of the current colour, white), the standard colour definition dialogue box appears for you to set the colour. This is described in the section on the colour picker in chapter 6: *Using styles*.

You can also set a border from this dialogue box. Borders are identified by number, and can be added to one, two, three, all or no sides. You can use a different border for each side if you wish. To start with, borders are turned off for all sides. To turn on a border for a side and choose a border number, click on the forward or up arrow for that side. A number one appears in the text field. You can delete this and type another number, or use the arrow icons to move through the sequence of borders. The border is illustrated in the dialogue box. For example, if you set the top edge to have border number 10 and the bottom edge to have border number 4, the dialogue box will look like this:

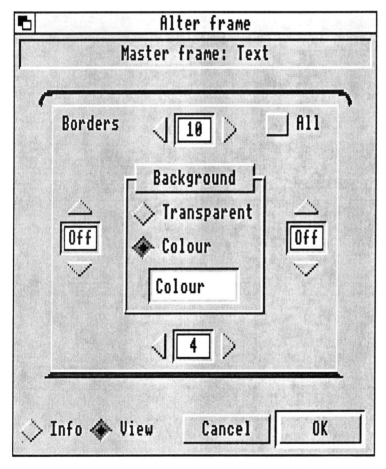

There is more on using borders in the section *Borders* later in this chapter.

Deleting, copying and pasting frames

To delete a frame, select it and then use **Cut frame** from the Edit menu or Ctrl-X. The frame is added to a clipboard and stored there until you copy or cut another frame; it is then overwritten. You can paste the frame on the clipboard back into your document using **Paste frame** in the Edit menu or Ctrl-V. When you use **Paste frame**, the pointer changes to a pair of cross-hairs for you to give the new position for the top lefthand corner of the frame.

If you delete the main text frame on a page copied from a master page and then paste it back in, the frame will have been made local and will no longer form part of the text flow through the chapter so it won't have any text in when you paste it back. You can add frames into the text flow quite easily. Click on a frame in the flow to select it, then click with Adjust on the frame you want to add; the second frame will be added to the sequence. If you have accidentally deleted a frame that is part of your text flow, you can paste it back, then click on the previous text frame in the flow and click with Adjust on the frame you deleted. You may need to use Alter frame to position it exactly so that its position matches the position of frames on other pages.

If there are no additional local frames in the chapter, you may prefer to delete the page instead as the pasted back frame is no longer linked to the master page. Impression will automatically create an extra page to hold the text in the chapter. If you are using a pair of master pages, two pages will be deleted and two automatically created. If you have frames that are not embedded and that contain graphics or other text on subsequent pages in the same chapter, don't use this method as the local frames will be attached to pages, not to places in the text, and they won't remain in the right place relative to the text. If all your graphics frames are embedded, they will move with the text so you can use this method.

To copy a frame, select it and then use **Copy frame** from the Edit menu or Ctrl-C. The frame is added to a clipboard and stored there until you copy or cut another frame. Again, you can paste it back into the document from the clipboard unless you overwrite it by cutting or copying another frame. You can paste several copies of the frame held on the clipboard; it isn't removed from the clipboard until you overwrite it with another.

Adding text and pictures to frames

When you create a new frame it is empty; an empty frame is called a *null frame*. You can add text or graphics to a frame, and then it will become a *text frame* or a *graphics frame*.

You can add text either by typing in a frame or by importing a text story you have already created. If you want to import a text story, select the frame and then drag into it the icon of the text file you want to use. You can drag in a plain text file (Edit file) or, if you have a suitable loader module loaded, a file created with a word-processor. Chapter 18: *Working with documents* explains when and how to use loader modules.

If you drag the icon of a text file into a frame copied from the master page and there is too much text to fit in the frame, Impression will automatically create additional pages and fill their frames with the story until it has all been fitted into the document. This is the default setting. You can, if you prefer, instruct Impression to copy the previous page rather than the current master page. It will then copy all the local and repeating frames as well as any frames copied from the master page. When you begin a new chapter you can instruct Impression to copy the previous page rather than the master page when creating pages automatically, but once a chapter exists you can't change this setting. (Impression Junior files always copy the previous page because they don't have master pages. This option in Impression allows documents to be fully compatible with Impression Junior.)

If you import a text story into a frame that is not copied from a master page, and there is too much text to fit in the frame, Impression won't know where to put the rest of the text. A red arrow at the bottom righthand corner of the frame indicates that there is more text that doesn't fit. You can link frames together so that they can hold a text story flowing between them. To do this, click Select in a frame holding part of the text, and then click Adjust in any other null frames you want to link to it. Click in them in the order you want the frames to be used to hold the story. Once they are linked, the text story will flow between them as you edit the text or resize or delete the frames. You can link frames before or after importing the text story, but you can't link any frames that already contain other text or graphics, and you can't include repeating frames in the sequence.

Text will always flow through frames on a page in the order in which you linked them, but will fill linked frames on one page before going to the next.

This means that if you create three frames on page 1 and add a text story to them, then add a linked frame on page 2 to the flow and then add a fourth frame on page 1 which you link to the others, the text will flow through all four frames on page 1 before flowing into the frame on page 2. If you want to look at the order of flow, use the option **Show flow** from the Impression icon bar menu. This indicates the order in which frames are linked by drawing an arrow from the bottom right of one frame to the top left of the next, like this:

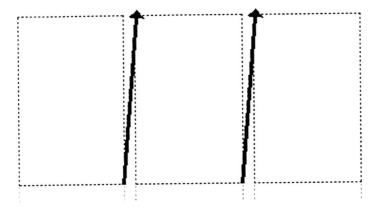

To remove the arrows, click anywhere in the document.

If you want to add graphics to a frame, select the frame and drag in the icon of a Draw or Paint file. The picture will be scaled to fit the frame, but retaining its aspect ratio so that it isn't distorted. There are some adjustments you can make to a picture once you have imported it, but you can't make changes to the picture itself. Chapter 11: *Graphics* explains how to move, rotate or resize a picture and how to change its aspect ratio.

Using borders

Using a border is a good way of making your text stand out. It is useful if you are presenting a single sheet that is going to stand alone, such as a menu, perhaps, or an OHP slide, or a form. Your border can be as plain or fancy as you like. Try to choose a border to match the image you want to create with your document. A simple, smart border looks elegant, but fun or fancy borders may be more engaging in some types of document.

You can add a border to any combination of the sides of a frame, or to all the sides using the Alter frame dialogue box. Borders are identified by number. You can have up to 255 borders. By default, there are ten borders defined, but more borders are supplied on Impression disc 3. You can also buy extra borders. The first three default borders are simple black lines with thicknesses of 0.25pt, 1pt and 4pt.

You can look at the borders allocated to each number and add new borders to your set up using the **Borders setup** option from the Frame menu. It displays this dialogue box:

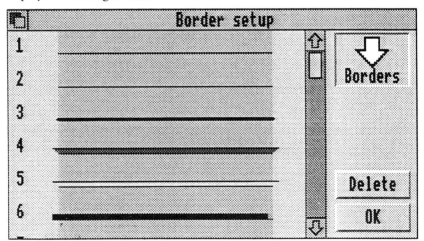

Use the scroll bar to move through the sequence and see the borders allocated to each number. You can delete a border by clicking to select it and then clicking on Delete. (Borders aren't stored on a clipboard; if you delete a border and then change your mind you will have to reinstate it by copying it back from the original disc.) You can't delete borders 1-10. If you delete a border that is used somewhere in the document, the border number is still stored by the frame(s) that used it and if you create a new border for that number it will be used by the frame(s) that used the old border.

You can add new borders that you have bought or created yourself. A border must be a Draw file. To add a new border, drag the Draw file to the load icon (the arrow) at the top right of the dialogue box. It will be loaded as a border allocated to the next free number. You can now use the border.

Borders that you add take up space in your document even if they are not used anywhere in it. A complex border uses a lot of space. These considerations should encourage you to use borders sparingly, but even if you have a lot of spare disc space remember that over-using borders will make your document look fussy, crowded and unprofessional.

When you want to use a border, use the View part of the Alter frame dialogue box. If you want to use the same border on all sides, click on the All button and then choose the border for one side: it will be used for all sides. If you don't remember which borders are allocated to each number, move the pointer so that it is over or just outside the white rectangle that shows the borders so that it changes to a menu shape, and display the menu to see the borders and their numbers.

Multiple selecting and grouping frames

Sometimes you may want to group several frames together so that you can edit and move them as a group. You may want to do this if you have a set of illustrations that you want to keep together, for example, or if you have several columns of text and want to adjust the size of all the columns equally. You can group frames temporarily by multiple selecting them, or permanently by using the **Group** option in the Frame menu.

To multiple select frames, click in one and then hold down Shift and click in each of the others in turn. All the frames will be selected. If you want to perform just one operation with them as a group (such as moving or resizing them) you can do this by dragging one of the frames or dragging the handles on the frame that shows handles. Any change in size will be matched in the other frames, and the frames will move as a group. However, when you click in a frame that isn't selected, all the others will be deselected and they will no longer be a group.

If you want to keep frames together in a group, select them all and then use **Group** from the Frame menu. A bounding box around the whole group is shown instead of the outlines of individual frames. Handles appear on this bounding box, and the individual frames are resized in proportion as you alter the size of the group's bounding box. You can move the group around by putting the pointer inside the bounding box and pressing and holding down the Select button until the hand shape appears and then dragging the bounding box. A group of frames remains grouped together when you save the file and later reopen it.

You can ungroup frames that you have grouped together by selecting the group and then using the **Ungroup** option from the Frame menu.

Embedding frames

Sometimes you may want to keep a frame in its position relative to text in another frame. For example, if you have a frame containing an illustration to your main text, you will want to keep the illustration near the text it refers to, even if you alter the text. You may have seen user manuals for other RISC OS applications that have many small pictures scattered throughout the text, often appearing in the middle of a sentence; these are embedded frames in Impression files.

To import a picture into an automatically created embedded frame, position the cursor where you want the picture to appear and then drag the Draw or sprite file icon into the Impression document window. An embedded frame will be created to hold the picture.

You can also embed a frame stored on the clipboard. To embed a picture that already exists in your document, cut or copy its frame so that it is on the clipboard and then you can embed it in the text. To embed a frame from the clipboard, place the cursor where you want the frame to appear and use **Embed frame** from the Frame menu. You can edit an embedded frame in the same way as a local frame, changing the background colour, border, size and so on. You can't embed guide frames or repeating frames. You can't flow a text story through an embedded frame and other frames, though you can import a text story just into an embedded frame.

Locking frames in place

You may occasionally want to lock a frame in position so that you or anyone else can't accidentally or deliberately delete or move it. You can't lock a frame copied from a master page, as you would need to make it local before moving or deleting it anyway. Don't lock an embedded frame, either (it won't have any effect if you do — the frame moves with the text it is attached to).

If you want to lock a frame in position, select the frame and then use **Alter frame**. At the top of the Info part of the dialogue box is a button labelled Lock in place. It is greyed out if you have selected a frame copied from a master page. Turn this on to lock a frame. A locked frame can't be moved, resized or deleted, and handles aren't shown when it is selected. If you try to move a locked frame, the pointer shape turns to a key to show you that the frame is locked. You can unlock the frame by turning off the Lock in place button if you do want to move, resize or delete the frame.

Ordering frames

Sometimes you may want to overlay one or more frames on another. At the simplest level, this may involve just adding a frame containing an illustration on top of the frame containing your main text. If you just add one frame on top of another like this, you shouldn't have any difficulty with the order of frames. However, if you have several frames overlaying or overlapping each other it is important to get frames in the right order. Frames higher up the stack (nearer the top) will obscure frames lower in the stack. If you have several opaque frames containing pictures and text, you may want to overlap them to create a special effect. Remember that if you turn text repelling off for a frame, text in any frame it overlaps may be hidden behind the overlapping frame. If you want text to come right up to the frame border but not continue behind the frame, set text repelling on but with margins of zero all round.

To control the stacking order of frames you need to use two options in the Frame menu, **Put to back** and **Bring to front**. Each of these works on the selected frame. It is easy to select a frame that is in front and send it to the back of the stack, but to see frames that are obscured by others you may need first to move some of the frames that are in front of it, or send them to the back of the stack, so that you can see the frame you want and then select it and bring it to the front of the stack. When you create a new frame it is always on top of any frames it overlays or overlaps. This means that by default frames are stacked in the order in which you created them. There is a little more about stacking frames in chapter 12: *Some special effects.*

Repeating frames

A repeating frame is one that will be copied from the page on which you create it to all the subsequent pages in the chapter (or in the whole document, if it has only one chapter). To create a repeating frame, use the option **New repeat frame** from the New frame submenu. Create the frame in the usual way using the cross-hairs to give positions for its top left and bottom right corners. You can adjust the size and position of the frame in the same way as an ordinary frame, either by eye or using the Alter frame dialogue box. However, a repeating frame will be copied onto the following pages of the chapter. If you create a repeating frame on page 7 of a twelve page document, it will appear on pages 7-12. Any text or graphics you add to it will also be copied. If you make any changes to the size, position or contents of any of the copies of the frame, the same change will appear in all the other copies. However, you can delete the repeating frame from individual pages without removing it from other pages. Because repeating frames aren't continued from one chapter to another, they are a useful way of adding a running header that you want to appear on each page of chapter. If you want some text or graphics to appear on every page of a whole document, though, it is better to add it to the master page(s).

What next?

There is quite a lot of overlap between frames and master pages. The next chapter explains how to use master pages, and covers the types of frames that you are most likely to use on a master page. This chapter has concentrated on local frames, but for many types of document you are likely to keep most of your text in frames copied from a master page.

9 Master pages

Master pages are one of the most powerful features of Impression. They can save you time and effort, and help you to give your documents a consistent appearance. A master page is a template used when creating new pages. It holds information such as the size and shape of the page, and usually has at least one null fame that will be copied onto new pages to hold your main body text. It can also have frames containing text or graphics that you want to appear on all the body pages. It is worth spending a little effort to learn to use master pages properly as they can make a big difference to how well and efficiently you can use Impression.

There are always some default master pages in any new document you create. You can use or modify these, or build your own master pages from scratch. You can choose when each master page is used as a template for new pages, and can make local changes to pages copied from master pages, although if you change frames copied from a master page the page won't later then be updated if you change the frames on the master page. The greatest advantage of Impression's way of operating master pages is that any changes you make to a master page are applied to all the pages that already exist and were copied from that master page, as well as any pages you create in the future. This chapter explains how to look at, modify and create master pages, and how to use them to best effect in your documents.

Looking at master pages

Master pages are always displayed in a separate window; you can look at a master page at the same time as looking at an ordinary body page. To display the master pages, use the option **View master pages** in the Edit menu. A new window appears:

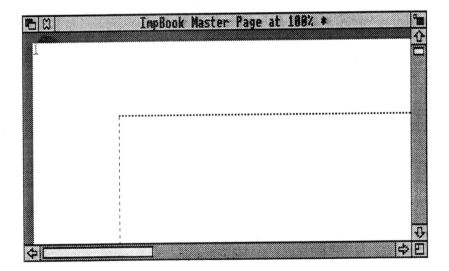

It has a figure one in the top lefthand corner showing that you are looking at the first master page. The title bar shows that you are viewing the page at its full size — 100%. You can scroll through the master pages using the scroll bar and scroll arrows, but it is easier to do this if you first adjust the view size so that you can see one or more full pages in the window. To do this, move the pointer into the master page window and choose **Scale view** from the Document menu. This displays a dialogue box for you to choose a size. You can pick one of the options for a scaled view (33% of the current size, for example), or type a scale in the field, or scale the view to fit in the window or fill the screen using the buttons Scale to window and Scale to screen. A good size for looking through the master pages is 33%. You will probably need to adjust the window size with the adjust size icon to show the whole page at this scale.

You can now easily look through the master pages that are created automatically for a new document. Some are arranged in pairs; these are used to create different left- and righthand pages. It is a useful feature if you are going to print on both sides of the paper and then bind the pages as you will probably want different margins on the inside and outside edges of the page to allow space for binding or punching holes. The first three master pages use a single column; the next three use two columns. Pages 2 and 3 and 5 and 6 are double pages, allowing different lefthand and righthand pages. Pages 7 to 9 have guide frames rather than null frames. You can't put any text or graphics in a guide frame, but you can use it to help you to align null frames that you create. These three pages are useful masters if you want to create a newsletter layout with different size columns for different stories and pictures. The guide frames will appear on the pages copied from these master pages and you can be sure that if you use them to help you position the null frames you create, your columns will be equally spaced and positioned on each page. Page 10 is an A4 landscape page: an A4 page on its side. Pages 11 to 16 are A5 pages (half of A4) with one or two columns, and page 17 is an A5 landscape page. You are not limited to these pages or page sizes; you can create your own master pages at any size you like.

Modifying master pages

Often, you will be able to modify one of the existing master pages rather than creating your own completely new page. You will need to create a new page if you want to use a size other than A4, though. Creating new master pages is described later in this chapter. We will concentrate for now on modifying the default pages.

To alter a frame on a master page, follow the same procedure as to alter a local or repeating frame on any other page. Click in the frame to select it. You can then drag the handles or move the frame, or use the **Alter frame** option from the Frame menu. A master page frame can have a border and a background colour, but you can't make it local.

To create a frame on a master page, use the menu option **New frame** from the Frame menu. You can add an ordinary frame, which will become a master page frame because it is on a master page, or a guide frame. A guide frame has an orange outline (in appropriate screen modes on colour monitors) to distinguish it from ordinary frames, which have green outlines. You can't add text or graphics to a guide frame. If you create an ordinary frame with no text or graphics in, it will appear as a null frame on each page that is copied from the master page. You can also create a frame and add some text or a picture. The frame, with the text or picture, will then appear on all pages copied from the master page. For example, you might want to add a logo at the bottom of each page, or a frame with the page number. To add a page number to a frame, you need to use the **Current page number** option from the Insert submenu from the Misc menu. This has a submenu of its own offering different formats for the page number. The page number can be numeric (1, 2, 3, etc), upper-case Roman (I, II, III, etc) or lower-case Roman (i, ii, iii, etc).

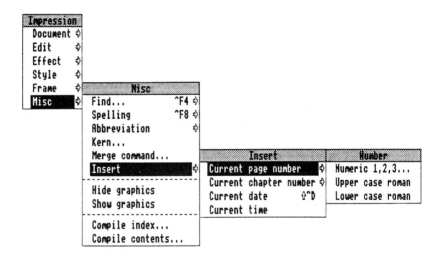

You can type any other text you want in the frame, too, and use the Insert option at the point at which you want the page number to appear. On the master page, the page number is represented by <pn>, but on each page of the document it will be replaced by the current page number. For example, on the master page it may look like this:

Seasonal report, July 1993   *<pn>*

On each page, the current page number will be substituted for the <pn>. You can use styles and effects for the text (including the page number) in the same way as on ordinary body pages. You can control the page number that the counter starts from, and you can reset the counter at the start of a chapter if you like. The first option is useful if your document will eventually be part of a longer document. The second option is useful if you want to have chapter or section numbers shown as an element of the page number. For example, you could number pages through appendices A, B and C in the form A-1, A-2, A3..., B-1, B-2, B-3..., C-1, C-2, C3... If you want to include the current chapter number, use the Insert option **Current chapter number**. Again, you can choose whether it will have numeric, upper-case Roman or lower-case Roman form. You can control the number at which the chapter counter starts, too. There is information on setting and using the page and chapter counters in chapter 13: *Multi-chapter documents.*

If you want to add a logo or other graphic, create a frame and drag in a Draw file or sprite file in the usual way.

Remember that if you add text or graphics to a frame, you can't then use that frame to hold a text story that is flowing through other frames. This means that you need to create separate frames on the master page to hold any text or graphics you want to repeat on the body pages, you can't put them in the main text column frames.

Creating master pages

If you want to use an A4 or A5 page, you can just
edit one of the master pages supplied. However, if
you want to use a completely different page size you
will need to create your own master page. It may
also be easier to create a new master page than
modify an existing one if you want to use a different
number of columns, different margins and any
frames for header or footer text, particularly if you
are going to use a pair of master pages and would
need to alter both. To create a new page, display the
master pages and choose **New master page** from
the Edit menu. This dialogue box appears for you to
make settings for the new page:

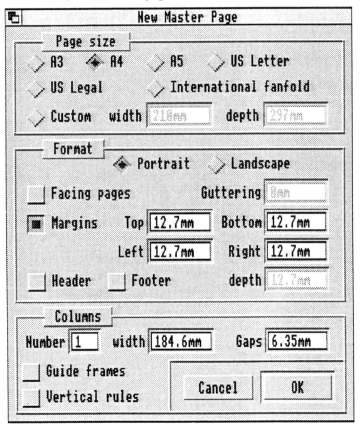

The first part of the dialogue box lets you choose a page size. You can choose one of the standard sizes, or define your own size. The standard sizes are:

- A3: 297mm x 420mm

- A4: 210mm x 297mm

- A5: 148.5mm x 210mm

- US letter: 8.5" x 11"

- US legal: 8.5" x 14"

- International fanfold: 8.25" x 12"

To define your own size, click on the button beside Custom and then type the values you want for the width and height (depth) of the page. The default values are the dimensions of the last page size selected. When you start up Impression, this is an A4 page, but if you have clicked beside any of the other options the dimensions of that page size will appear in the fields instead. Delete the figures you don't want to use with the Delete or Backspace key or by pressing Ctrl-U, and then type the dimensions you want. If you don't specify a unit, Impression will assume you want to use the units originally shown in the field. You can use any of the units Impression recognises:

- millimetres: mm

- centimetres: cm

- inches: in

- points: pt

- picas: pi

- feet: ft

- yards: yd

- metres: m.

The next section of the dialogue box allows you to set the format of the page. This can be portrait (a page that is taller than it is wide) or landscape (a wide, short page). If you want to use different layouts on the left and right pages so that you can print or photocopy your work double-sided and bind it, click on facing pages. If you do this, two master pages will be created, one for lefthand pages (even numbers) and one for righthand pages (odd numbers). Pages will always be created and deleted in pairs. They will be displayed on the screen side by side, which means that at view sizes near 100% you won't ever see the righthand page of the pair unless you move across with the scroll bar at the foot of the window. If you are using facing pages, you might want to change the view size to 50%, or some value that lets you see both pages (this value will depend on your monitor and the screen mode you are using as well as the page size).

If you click on Facing pages, the Guttering option becomes available. Guttering is the space between the inside columns on the facing pages; it will be added to the left and right margins you specify. For example, if you set left and right margins of 10mm, and guttering of 40mm, Impression will calculate where to put the frames like this:

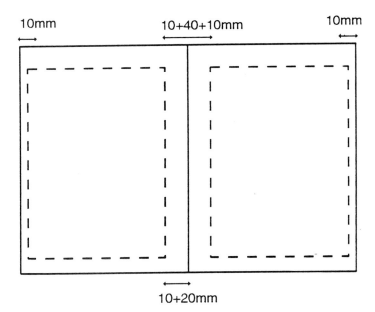

10mm   10+40+10mm   10mm

10+20mm

Guttering can also be used to refer to the space between columns on a single page, but Impression uses the word only for the space between text on two facing pages. The space between columns on the same page is controlled by the Gaps setting in the next section of the dialogue box.

You need to set margins for the top, bottom, left and right of the page. If you are using a single page, the margins alone will determine the position of the default frames on each page. If you are using facing pages, half of the guttering will be added to the inside margin on each page (that is, the left margin on odd-number pages and the right margin on even-number pages). The margins will be used for an automatically created frame on the master page (or frames, if you choose to use more than one column). They don't limit where you can put frames either on the master page or on any page copied from it.

You can add a frame to hold a header and/or a frame to hold a footer if you like. A header is a piece of text that will appear at the top of every page; a footer will appear at the foot of every page. If you choose one or both of these, you can also set the depth of the frame that will be created. The header frame will begin at the top margin position and will have the depth you specify. It will extend between the left and right margins you have set, or between the outer margin and the inner margin plus half the guttering if you are using facing pages. The gap between the header and the main text frame(s) is controlled by the Gaps setting in the next section of the dialogue box. Remember that these settings (top margin and gaps) control the positioning of the frames only; the position of the text within the frames will be determined by the style you use for the text. You can add a frame to hold header or footer text later rather than with this dialogue box if you prefer. The advantage of setting it at this point is that Impression will automatically use the margins you have set for the main text and so you can be sure that the frame is in exactly the right place. You can move or delete the frame created if you later change your mind about the position or whether you want it at all. You will have to move or alter the header or footer frame if you don't want to leave the same space between it and the text as you are leaving between the columns on the page, or if you want frames of different sizes for the header and footer, as you can't set these separately.

The final part of the dialogue box lets you control the columns. In the first field, give the number of columns you want. You can then set the width of the columns or the gap you want to leave between them; Impression will calculate the value for the one you don't set. For example, if you have a page 210mm wide and leave a left and right margin of 15mm, you will have a total text width of 210-30 = 180mm. If you decide to have three columns each 55mm wide, Impression will calculate that you need gaps of $(180 - 165) \div 2 = 7.5$mm. On the other hand, if you chose to have a gap of 5mm, Impression would calculate the width of the columns: $(180 - 10) \div 3 = 56.67$mm. If you only have one column, the Gaps setting will still control the spacing between the header and footer frames and the main frame.

If you change the left or right margin setting or the number of columns, Impression will recalculate the width of the columns, using the same gap.

If you want vertical rules to be inserted between columns, down the centre of the gap, turn on the button beside Vertical rules. If you want to create only guide frames and not master page frames that will be copied to give null frames on the page, turn on the button beside Guide frames. If you choose to use guide frames, you can still add frames to the master page too with the **New frame** option from the Frame menu.

When you have finished making settings, click on OK. Impression will report the number of the new master page you have created. You can't use this dialogue box to alter the settings for a page after you have created it, but you can edit the frames that have been created and you can add new frames.

Using several master pages in a document

If you have a document with several chapters, you may want to use more than one master page. Even if you use the same master page (or pair of master pages) for all the main text, you might want to use a different master page for an index, for example, or pages of references. When you want to begin a new chapter in your document, use the option **New chapter** from the Edit menu, which displays this dialogue box:

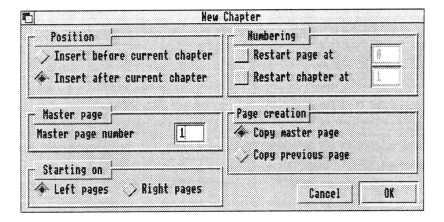

There is a field for you to give the number of the master page you want to copy to create pages in the chapter. Give the number of the master page you want to use; if you want to use a pair of facing pages, give the number of the lefthand page. If you don't know the number of the page you want to use, click on Cancel and then look at the master pages. There is more on using this dialogue box and creating new chapters in chapter 13: *Multi-chapter documents.*

What next?

The next chapter explains how to use Impression as a word-processor. Whether you type your text directly into an Impression document or import it from a file that already exists, you may want to edit your text. Impression is a fully-featured word-processor as well as a desktop publishing program, so you can type your text in and edit it easily.

10 Word-processing with Impression

Because Impression has full word-processing facilities, you will probably want to type your text directly into an Impression document rather than prepare it in another system first.

We have already looked at how to type text in Impression in chapter 3: *Starting work*. Once you have typed your text and read through it, you are likely to want to make some changes, and then you will need to use the editing facilities. As well as the standard features of cutting, copying and pasting text and finding and replacing letters, words or phrases, Impression has a spell checker to help you ensure that there are no spelling or typing errors in your document and an abbreviations facility so that you don't have to type in full each time a long word or phrase you use frequently. Finally, it allows you to insert a few items of special, current information in the text. You can add the current date, time, page number or chapter number at any point in the text using the **Insert** menu option. This chapter explains how to use Impression as a word-processor and describes:

• moving around the document

• text editing features such as cutting, copying and pasting text

• search and replace routines

• using the spelling checker

• using abbreviations

• inserting special information.

Moving around the document

Unless your document is very short and all fits on the screen at once, you will need to move around it when you want to edit it or add styles. You can move around a short document using the scroll bars and scroll arrows in the same way as you would use them with any other window. However, to move around a longer document it may take you a long time to find the area you want just using the scroll bars. You can instead move to a particular page or chapter, or search for a piece of text. Both of these use the **Find** option in the Misc menu. To move to a particular page or chapter, display the Find submenu from **Find** in the Misc menu:

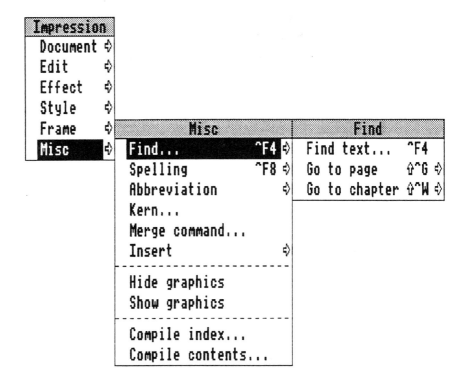

The two options **Go to page** and **Go to chapter** both display a dialogue box for the number of the page or chapter you want to move to. Type the number in the field and click on OK or press Return. The cursor will move to the top of the page or start of the chapter and the window display will change to show this area of text. This may not always be the page or chapter you expect. This is because the Find option works on the real page and chapter count, which may not be the same as the page or chapter number shown by use of **Insert Current Page number** or **Insert Current Chapter number**. These two Insert options use a number taken from the page or chapter counter, which you can reset at the start of any chapter, while the real page and chapter counts always start at one and increment sequentially each time a new page or chapter is added. For example, you might number your contents and other preliminary pages i-x, and then start your main text, resetting the page counter to 1. The page that has number 1 is actually the eleventh page in your document. If you use Go to page 2, page ii will be displayed; to display page 2, you will need to use Go to page 12. There is more on page and chapter counters in chapter 13: *Multi-chapter documents.*

You may want to move to a particular word or phrase, or subheading. You can do this using the **Find** option in the Misc menu. This is described later in this chapter, in the section *Finding and replacing text.*

You can move to the end of the current chapter using Control and the down arrow key, or to the top of the current chapter using Control and the up arrow key. You can move up or down a screen at a time using Shift with the up and down arrow keys.

Editing text

Once you have found the area of text you want to work on, you will probably need to use the cut, copy and paste options to modify your text. Unless the changes you want to make are very small, these options are quicker than using the Delete or Backspace key to remove text and typing in again any bits that you want to copy.

Deleting text

When you want to delete more than a few characters, select the text by dragging across it with the Select button on the mouse and then choose **Cut text** from the Edit menu or use the key combination Ctrl-X. The text is stored on a clipboard. You can paste it back into your document or into another document. The text is stored on the clipboard until you copy or delete another piece of text, when it is overwritten. Only one piece of text can be stored on the clipboard no matter how many documents you have open. This means that if you cut or copy some text from one document, it will overwrite any text already on the clipboard from the same or any other document. This allows you to move text between documents.

You can also use Delete Text or Ctrl-K to remove text and not store it on the clipboard. You can't then paste it back in.

Copying text

You can copy a piece of text to re-use in the same document or another document. To do this, select the text you want to copy and choose **Copy text** from the Edit menu or press Ctrl-C. The text is copied onto the clipboard, but the original remains in your document. Again, it is kept on the clipboard until you overwrite it by cutting or copying another piece of text. When you copy a piece of text, the original is not altered if you make any changes to the copy after pasting it.

Pasting text

To paste text, put the cursor where you want the text to be inserted and use **Paste text** from the Edit menu or press Ctrl-V. A copy of the text on the clipboard is inserted into the document. You can paste in multiple copies of the text on the clipboard as it isn't removed from the clipboard when you paste it. To paste a piece of text into another existing document, open the document by double-clicking on its icon in the directory display or using New view from the Impression icon bar menu (if it is already loaded), put the cursor where you want the text to appear and use Paste. To open a new document to paste the text into, click on the Impression icon on the icon bar and then click in the new document to make it active before using Paste. You can move text between documents by cutting or copying it from one document and pasting it into another document.

Finding and replacing text

You may sometimes want to find a piece of text somewhere in your document, perhaps because you want to look at or edit text near it. You will probably want to replace all or some instances of a piece of text at some point, too. For example, you might have written a report saying that your project will be finished in October and then find that your schedule is slipping. You could find all instances of the word October and change them to November using Impression's search and replace facility.

Finding text

To find a word or phrase, again use the Find submenu but this time choose **Find text** to display the Find dialogue box:

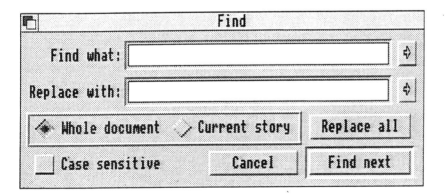

Type the text you want to find in the first field. You can use upper and lower case as you want to find it and then use the Case sensitive button to make sure Impression only finds instances of the text that match the case you have used in the Find what field. You can also use wildcards in the Find what field. A wildcard is a character that stands for one or more unknown or variable characters. There are three wildcards you can use when searching for text:

- # to stand for any single character

- * to stand for any group of characters within a word, and

- @ to stand for any group of characters whether or not they are within the same word.

Here are some examples:

- 'sin#' would find 'sine', 'sing' and 'sins'

- 'sing##' would find 'singer', 'single' and 'singed'

- 'si*' would find 'sin', 'sing', 'sight', 'sides', & 'sip'

- 'si@on' would find 'sign on', 'sit on', 'sit with your mother on' and 'situation'.

If you want to restrict the search to text in a particular style, click on the menu arrow to the right of the text field to display a list of styles. Click on the style you want to limit the search to before you type the text. This feature is of limited usefulness because of the way Impression works. Impression searches for text in a style by looking for the style marker and the text in combination. If the text you want to search for is not at the start of that particular use of the style, it won't have the style marker directly before it and so Impression won't be able to find the combination. Also, if you have applied two or more styles to the text, the order in which the invisible style markers appear in the text will affect the search. If you save an Impression text story with its styles and look at it in Edit you will see that the style markers appear in this form:

{"bullet text" on}weasels

stoats{"bullet text" off}

If you search for stoats in bullet text style, Impression won't be able to find this as the marker that turns on bullet text does not come directly before the text 'stoats'. Despite these limitations, the ability to search for text in a style can be useful if you are looking for a particular subheading or other piece of text where you know you can type the start of the string.

You can search through the whole document or just the current story. The search will begin from the cursor position and go forwards if you search the current story, but starts at the beginning of the document if search the whole document. When you click on OK to begin the search, Impression will look for the next occurrence of the string, using the style and case you have specified, if you have chosen to use these options. If it finds the string, the Text found dialogue box will appear:

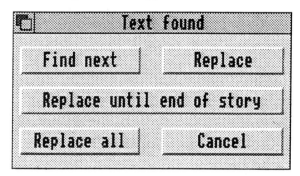

You can click on Find next if it isn't the instance you wanted, or on Cancel if it is. Cancel stops the search.

Don't use any of the replace options as you will overwrite the found text with whatever the contents of the Replace with field were in the Find dialogue box — probably nothing, so you will just lose the found text.

Replacing text

You will probably more often want to find one piece of text so that you can replace it with another, rather than just find it and move on. To find and replace text, you again need to use **Find text** from the Misc menu. This time, type the text you want to find in the first field and the text you want to replace it with in the second field. You can set a style for the text you are looking for, but the same limitations apply as if you are just finding the text. You can also set a style for the text you are replacing it with. This means that you can use the find and replace facility to change the style of text as well as or instead of changing the words. For example, if you wanted to change all references to The Times to italic, you would need to create a style that just sets the font to Trinity italic (or whatever font you want to use) and then use the dialogue box to tell Impression to search for The Times and change it to The Times, but using the italic style. Choose the style before you type the text for the Replace with field.

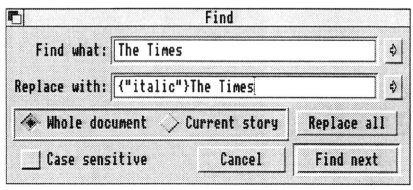

As with Find, you can choose whether to limit the search to the case you have used in the dialogue box (making it case sensitive) or whether to ignore case and change all instances of the text. If the example above were case sensitive, the search would only find instances of 'The Times'; it wouldn't find 'the times' or 'the Times' or 'THE TIMES', for example. Again, you can search the whole document or just the current chapter. The search goes forward from the cursor position if you search the current story, or starts at the beginning of the document if you search the whole document.

If you are sure that you want to replace all instances of the text, click on Replace all when you have made the other settings. Impression will then automatically change every instance of the Find what string with the Replace with string, without prompting you to accept the replacements. If you are going to use this option, make sure that only text that you want to change will be affected. For instance, if you decide to make your document less sexist by changing 'man' to 'person', you will find that you also change 'management' to 'personagement' and 'demand' to 'depersond'. You can avoid this by putting spaces either side of a single word you want to change (' man '), but remember that then plurals, other verb forms or the word followed by a punctuation point won't be changed. If you want to change 'wish' to 'want' and you type ' wish ´ in the first field, 'wished' won't change.

If you are at all unsure, click on Replace and then Find next instead. This allows you to step through all the instances of the text that Impression finds and accept or reject the change for each one. When Impression finds the text, it displays this dialogue box:

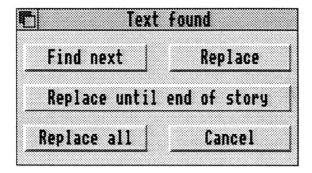

You can:

- replace the single instance found (Replace)

- replace all instances in the story (Replace until end of story)

- replace all instances in the document (Replace all)

- stop the search (Cancel)

- find the next instance (Find next).

You can replace the single instance and then go on to find the next one, as the dialogue box remains on screen if you choose Replace. Alternatively, you can use Find next on its own to leave the current instance unchanged and move on. At any point you can change all the remaining instances in the story (Replace until end of story) or the document (Replace all) or stop the search (Cancel).

Using the spelling checker

Impression has a spelling checker to help you avoid typing mistakes and spelling errors. You can use this to flag possible misspellings as you type, or to check your document when you have finished.

Spell checking facilities are available from the Spelling submenu, from the Spelling option in the Misc menu. If you choose one of these menu options when there is no dictionary loaded, a dialogue box will appear giving you the chance to load the default dictionary.

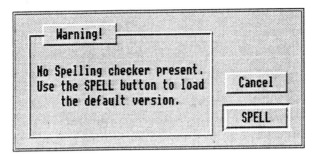

The dictionary will be loaded from disc, unless you have bought and installed the SpellMaster dictionary on ROM and instructed Impression to load and use it. This is described in chapter 19: *Getting the most from Impression.*

To check your spellings as you type, choose **Check as you type**. A beep will sound whenever you type a word that Impression's dictionary doesn't recognise. It takes a space, full stop, tab or Return as indicating the end of a word. It won't check a word if you move the cursor away from it with the cursor keys or the mouse, or use another punctuation point, such as a comma, at the end of the word. If you hear the beep, it means that the word is not in Impression's dictionary. It may be correctly spelled if it is a name or an obscure or foreign word that isn't in the dictionary, but if you have any doubt you can check in the dictionary. To do this, choose **Dictionary** from the Spelling submenu to display this dialogue box:

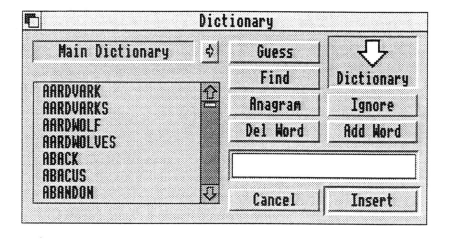

Type the word in the text field as you think it should be spelled. The dictionary window will scroll through the dictionary following your typing so that it moves closer to the word you want. For example, if you thought communicate should be spelt 'comunicate', Impression would follow your typing of this, moving to the first word beginning with 'c' as you type the 'c', then to words beginning 'co' as you type the 'o', then to words beginning 'com' as you type the 'm', and so on. You may well be able to see the word you want as you do this. If you can see the word you want, click to put it in the editable field and then click on Replace. If you can't see the word you want, click on Guess. The dictionary will show its best guess at the word you wanted. It will assume that you have made a single error, such as missing out one letter, adding an extra letter or transposing two letters. If this still isn't right, you can use Guess again, which performs a different type of guess: it looks for any words that sound like the word you have typed. If you find the word you want, click on Replace to replace the spelling in the document with the correct spelling.

You can also check the document from the current cursor position to the end, or check the whole document. In both cases, Impression checks until it finds a word that isn't in its dictionary, then highlights the word, moving the text through the window to show it if it is off screen, and displays the Dictionary dialogue box. The dialogue box has the suspect word in the editable field and the dictionary's guess displayed.

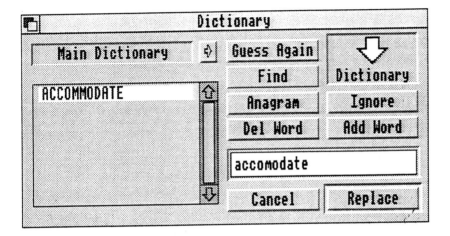

If the guess is wrong, you can use Guess again. If it still isn't right, or if Impression doesn't give a guess, you can use Find to display the dictionary entries near the word you have typed. If you can see the word you want, click to put it in the editable field and then click on Replace.

So far we have only considered words that you have typed incorrectly. You may have typed a word correctly but the dictionary doesn't contain it and so flags it as an error. You can do three things about this:

• you can take no notice, and type on
• you can add the word to a user dictionary
• you can tell Impression to ignore the word in this document.

The first is the easiest, but if the word is going to come up a lot it will be irritating if the spelling check stops at it each time or the beep sounds each time you type it. In this case, you will do better to add it to a dictionary or tell Impression to ignore it.

You can add the word to a user dictionary by clicking on the Add word button in the Dictionary dialogue box. The word is automatically added to a special user dictionary (not the main dictionary) which is built up from words you decide to accept. (User dictionaries are described below.). If you haven't loaded a user dictionary, a new one will be created. If you are likely to want the word in your documents in future, it is worth adding it to a user dictionary. However, if you are only going to use it in the current document you may choose to instruct Impression to ignore it for the present. For example, if you were writing a reference for Mr Mangwendeza, you wouldn't want Impression to flag his name as an error each time you typed it. Whether you added his name to a user dictionary or told Impression to ignore it would depend on whether you expected to use his name in other documents. You can save your user dictionary when you have finished, and can reload it later.

If you tell Impression to ignore it, the word will only be flagged as an error if you spell it incorrectly (so that it doesn't match the word being ignored). Any words that you tell Impression to ignore are added to an ignore dictionary. You can save this and load it again at another session if you like. This may be useful if you think you may use the same names or special words again, but don't want to add them to a user dictionary. This might be because, although they are valid in some of your documents, they are the same as a common misspelling and so you don't want Impression to ignore them in most of your documents. The procedure for saving and loading an ignore dictionary is the same as that for handling user dictionaries described below.

User dictionaries

A user dictionary can hold up to around 1500 words and you can have up to eight user dictionaries loaded at any time. If you create a user dictionary using Add word, it will have a default name. You can also create a user dictionary explicitly using the menu option **Create** from the menu in the Dictionary dialogue box. (Press the Menu button on the mouse or the menu arrow to the right of the dictionary name on the dialogue box to display this menu.) To save a user dictionary, move across to the submenu from its name in the Dictionary menu. All the user dictionaries in use are listed at the bottom of the menu. You can save it as a dictionary file, in which case you will be able to reload it another time, or as a text file. You can save the ignore dictionary using the submenu from **Ignore** in the menu.

You will need to save the dictionary if you want to use it again in the future. Impression will warn you if you try to quit without saving the dictionary. If you save a user dictionary as a user file, you can reload it in another session by dragging its icon to the load icon (the large arrow) at the top right of the Dictionary dialogue box. You may want to use only one user dictionary for all your extra words, but if you have two or three areas of work each with their own specialised vocabulary you might like to keep a separate dictionary for each. As a dictionary can hold about 1500 words, you are not particularly likely to run out of space even if you use only one. You can save as many user dictionaries as you like, but can only have eight loaded at once.

You can delete words from a user dictionary by typing the word in the editable field and clicking on

Del word. You can't delete words from the main dictionary like this.

Anagrams

If you like to do crosswords or play Scrabble, you might like to use the Anagram button on the Dictionary dialogue box. This searches through the dictionary to find any words in the dictionary that can be made with the letters typed in the editable field. You can also use the Find button to help with crosswords. If you have some of the letters of a word, you can use the wildcard # in place of the letters you don't know and click on Find to look for possible words. You can do this even if you don't know the first letter. For example, if you type '##ec#p#t#te', Impression will come up with 'precipitate'.

Limitations

The dictionary has its limitations, of course. If you are making a fundamental error, such as spelling 'physics' with an initial 'f', the dictionary won't get near the word you want, but the same would be true if you were trying to look it up in a conventional dictionary. The dictionary can't tell you if you are using words inappropriately (such as 'there' for 'their') or if you have actually misspelled a word but by coincidence it is a correct spelling of something else ('my cat as black feet', for example). The dictionary will beep when you type a proper name or foreign word, even though it may be correctly spelled, because it isn't listed in the dictionary. You can, though, add words to a user dictionary or store and accept them temporarily as explained above. Another limitation is that the dictionary will not pick up spelling errors of a couple of letters, such as 'tp' for 'to' as it doesn't check two-letter words. Since 'tp', and 'ti' (for or 'it' 'to') are common typing errors, you still need to check your text carefully.

Hyphenation exception dictionary

The hyphenation exception dictionary is a special dictionary that helps Impression to hyphenate words sensibly. Hyphenation is set on or off for each style using the Style dialogue box. If you want to use hyphenation, you also need to set hyphenation on using **Preferences** from the Impression icon bar menu; this is described in chapter 20: *Making your own settings and customising Impression*. The rules Impression follows when hyphenating words are the same for all styles. The rules give sensible hyphenations for most words, but some words are hyphenated unusually and sometimes two words that are spelt the same but pronounced differently need to be hyphenated in different ways. If just by applying rules Impression could come up with two apparently appropriate hyphenations, it may not use the one you would prefer. For example, hyphenation tends to break words into syllables but sometimes it may not be clear just from the spelling which one of two possible syllables a word is using. The word anteater could have a first syllable 'ant' (which it does) or 'ante', which is also a common first syllable. If the word is hyphenated 'ante-ater', it is difficult to recognise. To deal with difficult cases like this, Impression has a hyphenation exception dictionary which stores a list of exceptions to the standard rules. You can add to this dictionary, and specify the points at which you want a word to be hyphenated.

You can only add hyphenation preferences to the dictionary when there is a hyphenation module loaded. Choose **Exception** from the Dictionary dialogue box menu; if there is no hyphenation module loaded, a dialogue box appears giving you the chance to load the default hyphenation module. The hyphenation exception dictionary is then shown in the dictionary window.

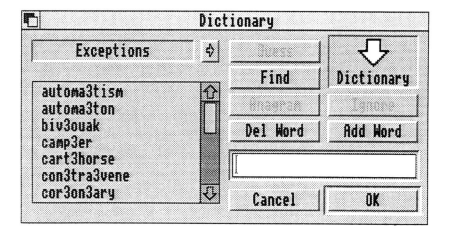

To add a hyphenation preference to the hyphenation exception dictionary, type the word in the editable field of the Dictionary dialogue box but use the figures 1, 3 and 5 to indicate points at which you would accept a hyphen. Use 5 for your preferred hyphenation point, 1 for the worst point you would accept and 3 for a point in between. You don't need to use all the numbers. For example, you would probably specify that anteater could only be hyphenated ant-eater. It wouldn't matter which number you used to mark the hyphenation point, but it is conventional to use 3 for a single hyphenation point. You would need to type ant3eater in the editable field. When you have typed the word, with its hyphenation points marked, click on Add word to add it to the exception dictionary.

You can also change the hyphenation of any words in the dictionary, or delete any words that you want to hyphenate following the standard rules. To change the hyphenation of a word, click on it so that it appears in the editable field. You can then edit the text and click on Add word to add your new hyphenation. The original version won't be deleted automatically, so click on it to show it in the editable field and then click on Del word to remove it from the dictionary.

When Impression has to hyphenate a word, it will look first of all in the hyphenation exception dictionary to see if there is a preferred hyphenation. If the word isn't in the exception dictionary, Impression will apply the standard rules to decide the hyphenation.

You can save or delete a hyphenation dictionary using the options in the Exception submenu from the Dictionary dialogue box menu. You can reload a hyphenation exception dictionary by dragging its icon to the load icon (the arrow) at the top right of the dialogue box.

Using abbreviations

Impression has an abbreviation expansion facility to help you type long words or phrases that you use frequently without having to type them in full each time. For example, if you were writing about the British Broadcasting Corporation, and wanted the name to appear in full each time, you could use the abbreviation bbc and tell Impression to expand this to the full name.

Before you can use abbreviations you need to set them up in an abbreviation dictionary. To start with there are no abbreviations stored in the abbreviation dictionary. To create a new, empty dictionary display the Abbreviations submenu from the Misc menu and choose **Dictionary**. If there isn't an abbreviations dictionary loaded, one is loaded or a new one is created when you do this. To add abbreviations to the dictionary type the abbreviation, then a space and then the full form in the editable field. Abbreviations are case sensitive, so you will always need to use upper or lower case as you have typed it in the editable field. For example, to register bbc as the abbreviation for British Broadcasting Corporation, type 'bbc British Broadcasting Corporation', in the field:

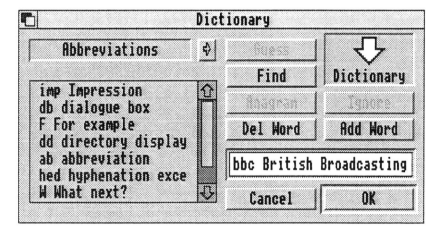

It doesn't matter that British Broadcasting Corporation is too long to fit in the field; it will scroll across as you type, and although it won't all be displayed in the dictionary window it will expand properly when you type bbc. Remember that each time you type the abbreviation it will be expanded, so don't use as an abbreviation a word or contraction that you may want to use in its own right — don't use 'man' as an abbreviation for 'Manpower Services', for example.

Impression will expand the abbreviations as you type if you choose **Expand as you type** from the Abbreviations submenu. An abbreviation will be recognised if it is followed by a space, full stop, slash (/), hyphen (-) , Return or tab but not a comma or other punctuation point.

You can save your abbreviation dictionary either with the default name, in which case it will be loaded next time you load abbreviations, or with another name. You can drag any abbreviation dictionary icons to the load icon at the top right of the Dictionary dialogue box to load them.

To delete an abbreviation from the dictionary, click on it in the dictionary window and then on Del word.

Click on OK when you have finished setting up or modifying abbreviations. Clicking on Cancel does not cancel any completed operations (setting up or deleting abbreviations) but does abandon an abbreviation you haven't completed if you have not typed a space yet.

You can also edit the abbreviations dictionary from the Dictionary dialogue box brought up with the **Dictionary** option from the Spelling submenu.

What next?

The next chapter explains how to use graphics with an Impression document. You can't draw any graphics in Impression, but you can import Draw files and sprites to illustrate your work. You can modify the size, aspect ratio and rotation of graphics once you have imported them.

11 Graphics

You can include pictures in your Impression documents by importing Draw files or sprite files into frames. Impression doesn't have any drawing tools of its own, so all graphics must be prepared in Draw, Paint or a program that produces files compatible with either of these. Once you have imported a graphics file, you can use it several times in a document without needing to import it again. You can also change the size, rotation and aspect ratio of one or more copies, but you can't do any graphic editing. This chapter explains how to:

- import graphics

- change the size, position or rotation of graphics

- use the same graphic in several frames

- fix the position of a picture by embedding the frame

- hide or show graphics

- use greyscale dithering to enhance a monochrome image on screen.

Importing graphics

You can import a Draw or sprite file into any null frame. This may be a frame you have created specially to hold graphics, a frame copied from the master page or a repeating frame that doesn't already hold some text. You can only import a picture into a frame that holds text if you place the cursor where you want the picture to appear, allowing Impression to create an embedded, empty frame to hold the graphics. To insert a picture into your text, you can either create a new frame to hold the picture or place the cursor where you want to embed a new frame. This is described later in the chapter in the section *Fixing the position of a position of a picture*. You can embed the frame to keep it in the right place; this is described later in the chapter.

To create a new frame to hold graphics, follow the instructions in the section *Creating and editing frames* in chapter 8: *Frames*. You can only import a picture into a selected frame; click in a frame to select it. If it is not a master page frame, its handles will appear to show that it is selected. Now drag the file icon of the picture you want from the directory display. The picture will be loaded so that it fits in the frame, using the same aspect ratio (X:Y proportions) that it had in the original file.

Adjusting a picture

Although you can't make any changes to the graphics, you can move, rotate or resize a whole picture, and change its aspect ratio.

Moving a picture

You can move the picture around within the frame by dragging it. Move the pointer onto the picture and then press and hold down Select. The pointer will change to a hand, showing that you can drag the picture.

If you accidentally drag the picture so that you can't see it in the frame any more, you can retrieve it using the **Alter graphic** option from the Frame menu. This also lets you make some other settings, including adjusting the position of the picture more precisely.

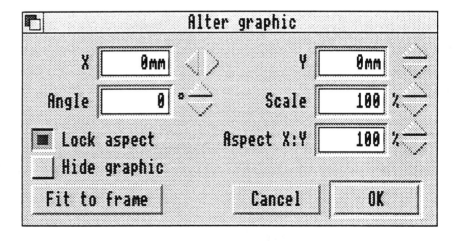

You can change the position of the graphic within the frame using the arrow icons or by deleting the text in the X and Y position fields and typing the position you want. By default, the position is measured in millimetres from the bottom lefthand corner of the frame. If you import a Draw file, an invisible bounding box around the objects will define the area imported. The bottom lefthand corner of the bounding box will be positioned at the bottom lefthand corner of the frame, which may mean that the graphic objects actually appear a little up and to the right of the corner if they don't fill the bounding box.

Besides changing the position of a picture with in a frame, you can move the frame around in the usual way. The position of the picture in the frame will not be affected by this.

Resizing a picture and changing its aspect ratio

You can set the scale of the picture using the Scale field, in which case both the height and width (Y and X directions) will be scaled by the same amount, or by setting the X:Y aspect. The second option allows you to rescale one dimension relative to the other. For example, if you set this to 50%, the picture will shrink in width by 50% but stay the same height. (The size of the frame isn't affected.) If you set it to 200%, the picture will become twice as wide but the height will stay the same.

Whether or not you have changed the aspect ratio, you can lock it with the Lock aspect button so that the picture won't be distorted if you change the size and shape of the frame. If you want the picture to fill the frame, click on Fit to frame. This is useful if you change the size of the frame and want to adjust the size of the picture to fit it again. With aspect ratio locked on, Fit to frame makes the picture as large as possible so that it all fits in the frame without being distorted. With aspect ratio unlocked, the picture will fill the frame, even if it means that it has to be distorted. If you change the size of the frame, the size of the picture won't alter until you use Fit to frame.

Rotating a picture

You can rotate a picture, either by dragging it with Adjust or using the Angle option in the dialogue box. You can rotate imported Draw files, but can only rotate sprites with RISC OS 2 if the Enhanced graphics option is set. To set this, choose **Preferences** from the Impression icon bar menu and click to turn on the button beside Enhanced graphics. There is more information on Enhanced graphics in chapter 19: *Getting the most from Impression*. With RISC OS 3, you can rotate sprites without using Enhanced graphics.

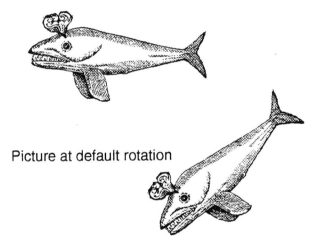

Picture at default rotation

Picture rotated through 45 degrees.

Fixing the position of a picture

If your picture refers to a particular piece of text and you want to keep it with the text you can fix it in place so that if you edit the text the picture will move with it. To do this, you need to embed the frame. Put the cursor in the text where you want the picture to appear and drag the Draw or sprite file into the Impression document window. An embedded frame of an appropriate size will be created to hold your picture. If the picture is too big, it will be cropped and you will need to use Alter graphic to change its scale and then move it all into view.

You can also embed a frame that is held on the clipboard, so you can copy or delete an existing graphics frame and then paste it back in as an embedded frame. Copy or cut the frame so that it is on the clipboard. Next, place the cursor where you want the frame to appear and use **Embed frame** from the Frame menu. The frame will be inserted at the cursor position and will remain in that position relative to the text however the text moves.

Repeating a picture

If you want to use the same picture in more than one frame, you can save memory by linking the frames so that the picture is copied from one to another. To do this, click with Select on a frame containing the picture, then click with Adjust on a null frame. The picture will be copied from one to the other. You can alter the aspect ratio, size or rotation of any copy of a picture without affecting the other copies, and you can delete some frames that contain the picture; the other linked frame(s) will still contain the picture.

Turning on and off the display of graphics

You can turn the display of a picture off so that it won't be shown on screen, and will not be printed if

you print out the document. This can be useful if
you have a lot of pictures or are using complex
pictures as redrawing them can slow down screen
redraws and storing them uses computer memory.
To turn off or on the display of a picture, click on
the button beside Hide graphic. You can turn off
the display of all graphics using **Hide graphics** in
the Misc menu. Use Show graphics in the same
menu to turn the display back on again.

Greyscale dithering

Greyscale dithering is a means of getting a better
monochrome image on screen by rendering more
greyscales. It can give pictures a better appearance
on screen, but won't affect the printed picture if you
print out your work. Greyscale dithering becomes
available when you turn on Enhanced graphics from
the Preferences dialogue box. To display this
dialogue box, click on **Preferences** in the
Impression icon bar menu. Turn on the button
beside Enhanced graphics, and then the Greyscale
dithering button beneath it. To do greyscale
dithering, Impression will change the palette so that
it has 16 grey scales which can be used for rendering
monochrome graphics. The whole desktop and all
graphics will be shown in monochrome, with grey
scales.

On some monitors and with RISC OS 3, the
mapping of grey scales can make the menus
unreadable (white text on a white background) and
the document unusable. It is then not possible to
see the dialogue box to turn greyscale dithering off
again, and you will have to reset the computer
before you can use it. For this reason, save your
work before trying out greyscale dithering. If you

don't remember to do this, press Ctrl-F3 to save your Impression document with the same name when you can't see to use the menus.

What next?

The next chapter explains how to achieve some special effects using Impression. This includes detailed instructions on using rules, and explains how to create dropped capitals and bulleted styles and how to overlay frames.

12 Some special effects

Impression is very versatile and with a little patience and imagination you can achieve some very striking effects. This chapter explains how to achieve some of the standard effects you may have seen elsewhere. It tells you how to:

- Use !FontDraw to add special text effects, including dropped capitals at the start of a paragraph, and rotated text

- overlay text and graphics

- flow text around pictures or into shapes

- create effects with frames

- add horizontal rules

- create bulleted and indented styles

• create styles with boxes and lines to make up tables.

Using !FontDraw

!Fontdraw offers a means of creating text as a draw object that you can manipulate, enhance or distort before including it in your document as a graphic. It is a useful way of getting some special effects — such as text with different fill and outline colours — that you can't achieve just with Impression.

!FontDraw is in the directory Utils on Impression disc 2. Double-click on its icon to open this window:

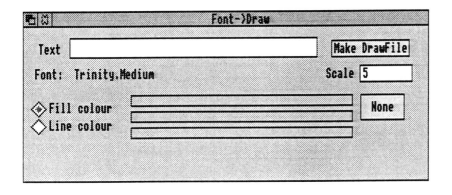

Click in the editable text field and type the text you want to use. It could be a single letter, if you wanted to add a large capital at the start of a paragraph, or a whole word or phrase in mixed up and lower case.

Press the Menu button on the mouse to display a menu listing the fonts available in !Fonts and choose the font you want to use. If you are using RISC OS 3, !FontDraw won't work with any of the fonts held in ROM (Corpus, Homerton and Trinity) because it takes the font outline information from !Fonts. (It is worth remembering that the default font is Trinity medium, which you can't use with !FontDraw in RISC OS 3). You can, however, use Trinity with !FontDraw in RISC OS 3 if you keep copies of the original Corpus, Homerton and Trinity outline fonts in your disc-based !Fonts directory. You can't use a bitmap font with either RISC OS 2 or RISC OS 3; !FontDraw works only with outline fonts. The name of the font you choose from the menu is shown below the text field and the text in the field changes to the font you have selected.

You can set the scale for the conversion in the editable field on the right of the dialogue box. The default scale is 5, which produces large characters. You can resize the resulting Draw file when you have dragged it into your Impression document, but using a large size to start with will make sure that the curves are smooth and even. Don't set the scale to zero or a negative number. If you intend to manipulate the text in Draw first, you can use a scale of 2 instead.

You can set the colour used for the outline of the letters and the colour used to fill them by adjusting the proportions of red, green and blue used to make up each colour. There is no block of colour to look at which shows you the colour you are defining, but you can change the line and fill colours in Draw anyway. Click on None if you want the fill or line colour to be transparent. When there are no colours shown in the red, green and blue bars, the fill or line colour will be black. If you fill all the bars with colour, it will be white. Click on the button beside Fill colour to define the colour used to fill the strokes that make up the letters, and then on the button beside Line colour to define the colour for the outline of the letters. Here is an example of a letter with a black line and white fill colour:

When you are ready to make the Draw file, open a directory display to drag the Draw file icon to when it is complete, then click on Make Drawfile. A Draw Save as icon will appear for you to give a name for the file and save it in a directory.

Once you have created the Draw file, you can edit it in Draw or use it immediately in Impression. In Draw, you can distort or rotate it. If there is more than one character, you can ungroup the characters and manipulate each one separately. Here are a few examples, using Newhall.

Here one character has been lifted up.

Here the characters have been rotated and moved. The letters of 'and' were rotated as a group, the others were rotated and moved separately.

Here the letters have been ungrouped and regrouped in whole words. The groups have been changed; 'wide' has been stretched widthways, and 'tall' has been stretched vertically, and has had its fill colour changed to white. The fill and line colour of '&' have been changed to grey.

To add your Draw file text to Impression, put the cursor where you want the text to appear and drag the file icon into the document. Impression will automatically create an embedded frame to hold the picture. Alternatively in an empty frame and drag the title icon onto it.

Once you have added the graphic, you can alter its scale, move it around in the frame and change the size of the frame in the usual way. These procedures are described in chapter 8: *Frames* and chapter 11: *Graphics*.

If you are using RISC OS 3, you won't be able to use the fonts from ROM with !FontDraw, but you will be able to convert text to graphics in Draw (which you couldn't do in RISC OS 2). This means that you can achieve all the effects that you can with !FontDraw just by using Draw, including specifying different fill and line colours. Alternatively you could copy Corpus, Homerton and Trinity from !Fonts on Impression disc 4 into your own !Fonts, which would cause the computer to ignore the ROM-based versions. (Chapter 19: *Getting the most from Impression* explains how to copy fonts into your !Fonts directory.) If you want to use both disc and ROM-based versions, you must rename the disc-based versions. To do this properly you will need the !FontEd application. Simply renaming the font directory will confuse the computer. For example, you might copy Trinity into !Fonts and rename it TrinNew. Don't use these copies of the fonts for anything else besides !FontDraw — use the fonts loaded from ROM instead. Click on !Fonts after you have copied the fonts. When you next use !FontDraw, choose one of the new names you have used from the font menu and you will be able to create text in Corpus, Homerton or Trinity. This is not an approved procedure; it's a work-round that will only work if you change all the names of the fonts consistently through the directory structures.

Dropped and raised initial capitals

A dropped capital is a large capital, usually put at the start of a paragraph, like the A at the beginning of this paragraph. It is used to add emphasis to the beginning of a section or chapter. There are two ways you can create a dropped capital; you can create a frame to hold the letter, then position the frame and size the text as you want it, or you can use !FontDraw. If you are using RISC OS 3, remember that !FontDraw won't work with the fonts held in ROM (Corpus, Homerton and Trinity) unless you follow the workround described above.

To make a frame to hold your large initial capital, use **New frame** from the frame menu in the usual way. Click in the new frame to place the cursor in it and type the capital you want to use. You can use a style or effect to set the font, size, colour and line spacing you want to use. Alter the size of the frame and the text repelling if you want to until it gives the effect you want. Remember that a letter will not come right to the edges of a frame as a graphic would and so is more difficult to resize precisely. This is one advantage of using !FontDraw to prepare an initial capital.

To use !FontDraw to create a large initial capital, click on FontDraw to display its window, choose the font you want to use and type the capital in the text field. Open a directory display to hold the saved file, and click on Make Drawfile. Give the Draw file a name and drag the file icon to the directory display. Now create a new frame in your document where you want the initial capital to be and then drag in the Draw file containing the letter. You can alter the size of the graphic and the size of the frame if you want to. An easy way to adjust the size precisely is to make the frame the right height and then use the Alter graphic option Fit to frame (with the aspect ratio locked). If the letter doesn't use the full height of your frame it is because the frame is too narrow. Make it wider and then try again.

Remember that, whichever method you use, the letter is not in an embedded frame, so any edits to the text may cause the rest of the paragraph to move away from its initial capital. Check that the large capitals are in the right places before printing your document. (If you edit your text substantially, or add or delete any pages before the page with the dropped capital, you may find that the capital is no longer on the same page as the text it belongs to.)

If you want a raised capital at the start of the paragraph, like the I at the start of this line, you can just type the letter in the main text and then use styles or effects to adjust its size, colour and font.

Overlaid text and graphics

You may sometimes want to layer text and graphics like this:

DANGER

It is dangerous to lean out of the vehicle while it is moving.

This example shows text overlaid on a !FontDraw image, but you could overlay one text frame over another, or text over a Draw or sprite file. To achieve this effect, create a frame to hold the graphic (or background text) and add the picture or text you want to use. Next, create the frame you want to superimpose on it. You will need to use **Alter frame** to set Repel text outside off and to give the frame a transparent background (this is in the View part of the dialogue box). There is a full explanation of how to make these settings in chapter 8: *Frames*. If you need to make any changes to the background frame, you may need to move the superimposed frame or send it to the back of the stack of frames before you can select and alter the background frame. You must put the frames back into the right order when you have finished.

If you use more than two frames in a layered arrangement, you might find difficulties with the text repelling mechanism. Sometimes text isn't repelled when it should be if you have three frames that overlap or are superimposed. You may have to experiment to find an order or method of overlaying frames that gives the effect you want.

Giving text a shape

Frames are always rectangular, but if you want to give your text an unusual shape you can do this by linking rectangular frames into a more intricate shape. To make a single line of text follow a shape, use !FontDraw or prepare it with an application that allows you to 'flow' text around a shape and then import it as a picture. To make your text story follow a shape, build up the shape from an arrangement of frames. Here are some examples:

The Grand Old
Duke of York
He had ten
thousand men;
First he marched
them up to the top
of the hill, then he
marched them down again.

The Grand Old
Duke of York
He had ten
thousand men;
First he marched
them up to the top
of the hill, then he marched them
down again.
The Grand Old
Duke of York
He had ten
thousand men;
First he marched
them up to the top of the hill, then he
marched them
down again.

The first example was created by typing text into frames arranged like this and grouped so that text flows between them:

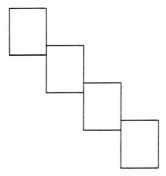

To group frames in an arrangement like this so that text will flow from one to the other, select the first frame and then click with the Adjust button in the other frames in sequence. You can drag in a text story or type in the first frame and text will overflow into the following frames as necessary.

In the second example, the text is all in one frame, but an arrangement of frames to the left repels the text from the lefthand margin of the main frame. The frames are arranged like this:

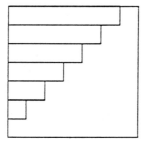

The frame holding the text has a black background and the text is white. Each of the frames forming the 'steps' is 26pt high, the height of two lines of text (the text has 13pt leading). You can change the units of measurement for frames to points using **Preferences** in the Impression icon bar menu. This is described further in chapter 20: *Making your own settings and customising Impression.*

Other effects with frames

Chapter 8: *Frames* explains how to add a border to a frame. By using frames imaginatively, you can create some special effects. For example, you don't need to use the same border (or indeed any border) on all sides of a frame. You can also layer frames so that there is more than one border on one or more sides by hiding a larger frame behind your text frame and giving this a different border. You will need to send the larger frame to the back of the frame stack after you have created it.

Jack and Jill went up the hill to fetch a pail of water. Jack fell down and broke his crown and Jill came tumbling after. Jack and Jill went up the hill to fetch a pail of water. Jack fell down and broke his crown and Jill came tumbling after. Jack and Jill went up the hill to fetch a pail of water. Jack fell down and broke his crown and Jill came tumbling after.

You need to be careful when using more than one border on a frame, or superimposing frames with borders. Too enthusiastic an application of borders can make your work look messy and unprofessional. Even so, it's worth experimenting if you think you have a good idea.

Don't forget that you can use tinted frames to create some effects, too. The following heading is introduced by a tinted frame to the left of it:

 # This is a heading

In the example, the frame is embedded. To embed a frame that doesn't contain graphics you need to create the frame, delete or copy it so that a copy is stored on the clipboard, position the cursor where you want the frame to appear and then use **Embed frame** from the Frame menu. (To embed a graphics frame, just put the cursor where you want the picture to appear and drag the picture file into the Impression window.)

The default position for the frame is aligned with the baseline for the text. We have also used **Alter frame** to set the text repelling value for outside the frame to leave a little space between the frame and the text. An embedded frame may not appear in quite the right place. If you wanted the frame to appear in a different place in relation to the heading, you would need to add the frames by hand and move them when you edit the document rather than embed them.

You can also add a coloured frame along the edge of each page, either putting it on a master page or using a repeating frame. This can be a useful way of marking different sections of a long document, like this:

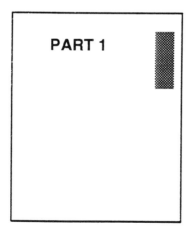
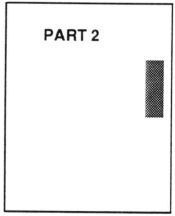

You can to try to use frames in more imaginative ways, but once you have several frames layered and are using text repelling to achieve special effects, you might run into problems. It's worth trying, especially as Impression is constantly being updated and in the version you have layered frames may work well.

Rhubarb rhubarb, rhubarb rhubarb. rhubarb rhubarb. Rhubarb rhubarb, rhubarb rhubarb. rhubarb rhubarb. Rhubarb rhubarb, rhubarb rhubarb. rhubarb rhubarb. rhubarb rhubarb. Rhubarb rhubarb, rhubarb rhubarb.

❝ Rhubarb is the best thing since sliced bread ❞

rhubarb rhubarb. rhubarb rhubarb. Rhubarb rhubarb, rhubarb rhubarb. rhubarb rhubarb. Rhubarb rhubarb, rhubarb rhubarb. rhubarb rhubarb. Rhubarb rhubarb, rhubarb rhubarb. rhubarb rhubarb. rhubarb rhubarb.

Rhubarb rhubarb, rhubarb rhubarb. rhubarb rhubarb. Rhubarb rhubarb, rhubarb rhubarb. rhubarb rhubarb. Rhubarb rhubarb, rhubarb rhubarb. rhubarb rhubarb. Rhubarb rhubarb, rhubarb rhubarb. rhubarb rhubarb. Rhubarb rhubarb, rhubarb rhubarb. rhubarb rhubarb. Rhubarb rhubarb, rhubarb rhubarb. rhubarb rhubarb. Rhubarb rhubarb, rhubarb rhubarb. rhubarb rhubarb. Rhubarb rhubarb, rhubarb rhubarb. rhubarb rhubarb. Rhubarb rhubarb,

The example shown has frames arranged like this:

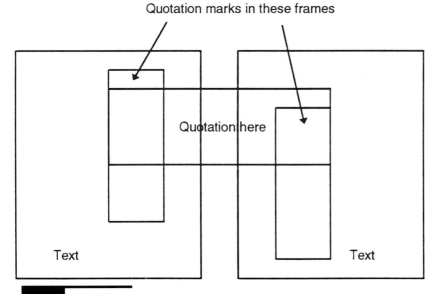

Quotation marks in these frames

Quotation here

Text

Text

The text is in two linked columns; the inset quotation is in the wide frame across the middle, which has text repelling set on. The quotation marks are each in a separate frame with text repelling set off. The size of the frames holding the quotation marks is determined by the amount of space needed to draw the character; although the quotation marks don't take up the whole height of the frame, that size frame is needed for them. You could achieve the same effect using a smaller frame if you prepared the quotation marks with !FontDraw.

Vertical rules

It is sometimes useful to add a vertical bar down the side of text that you have changed since the last issue of your document. This is called a change bar. It is easy to add change bars in Impression. The best way is to create a style or ruler which has only the vertical rule attribute set and then apply this style to any text that has changed.

To create a change bar style, use **New style** or **New ruler** from the Style menu. If you are creating a style, click on the Alter ruler button to display the ruler. Add a vertical line tab to the position on the ruler where you want the rule to appear. This will probably be at the left or right margin. You might want to move the right margin for the text in slightly to make room for the rule. You can add a horizontal rule at each side of the text if you like. Any text that you apply the new style or new ruler to will have the vertical rule(s) added. If you didn't have any other tabs or ruler items on the text you apply it to, the new ruler or style won't change the layout of existing text. However, whenever you apply a ruler to text, it takes precedence over any ruler already in use. This means that if some of your text was tabbed or indented, you will lose these effects when you apply the change bar ruler. You can make several change bar rules incorporating the other ruler characteristics if you need to. When you want to issue your document without the change bars, simply remove each style from all the text you have applied it to.

Bulleted and indented styles

Because Impression allows you to set the lefthand margin of the first line and the lefthand margin for the rest of the paragraph separately for each style, it is easy to create bulleted styles, hanging indents and outdented styles.

Bulleted styles

A bulleted style is used to mark unnumbered points. For example, you might use a bulleted style like this to:

- list a group of alternatives

- itemise the stages of a process, or

- list the items you are going to cover in the next part of your document.

To create a bulleted style which will use the same font settings as your BaseStyle (or another style applied to the text) you need to set the left margin, a tab stop and a leading string.

You need to set the first two of these from the ruler dialogue box. Use **New style** from the Style menu to bring up the New style dialogue box. Give the style a name and click on Alter ruler to display the ruler. Now display the ruler menu and choose **Enter values** to display this dialogue box:

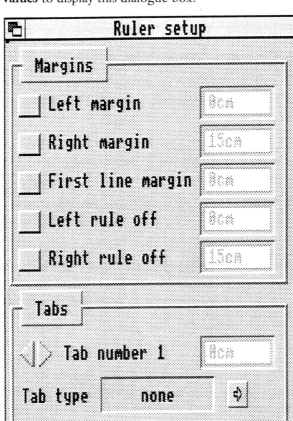

To set up a ruler for a bulleted style that has the bullet flush with the lefthand margin and the text indented about 5mm from the bullet point, set the left margin and first tab at 0.55cm. This assumes that you are going to leave the first line left margin at the default position for BaseStyle set up by Impression, which is 0.0635cm. You can indent the bullet as well. If you want to do this, set the first line left margin to the bullet position and then set the left margin and tab position 5mm further across.

When you have made the ruler settings, click on OK. Move through the style dialogue box until you get to the field for a Leadering string. Put the cursor in the field and press the Alt key and hold it down while you type 143 using the numeric keypad. The bullet character • will appear. Type three spaces after it in the field. If you miss out the spaces, the bullet character will repeat between the margin and the text. Save your new style.

If you are using 10, 11 or 12 point Trinity or 10 or 11 point Homerton, this definition will produce a style with a single bullet before the text. If you want to use 12pt Homerton, you will need to add only two spaces to the leadering string after the bullet character. If you want to use other sizes of text, experiment until you find the right tab and margin setting and the right combination for the leadering string.

When you want to use your bullet style, click on it in the style menu and begin the first line of the bulleted item with a tab. When you press Tab, the bullet will appear and the cursor will move to the tab position. Type the text. As the text wraps round to the next line, it will line up under the tabbed text because the left margin and tab are set at the same position. When you want to add the next bulleted item, press Return and begin the next line with a tab.

Hanging indents

A hanging indent is useful if you want to create a numbered list. It is similar to a bulleted style, except that no leadering string is set. This allows you to type a number or other character before the tab. The following all use the same hanging indent style:

This is a hanging indent style, but there is no tab in the first line, so the text is not lined up with the subsequent lines.

1   This line shows how to use a hanging indent in a numbered list. The text in subsequent lines is lined up under the start of the text in the first line.

xiii This line shows a hanging indent used with a roman numeral. Again, the text in subsequent lines is lined up under the text in the first line.

a   You can use a hanging indent for lists that use letters, too.

Because you are not restricted by the length of the leadering string, you can have more space between the first line margin (where you will put the number or letter) and the left margin (where the text will begin). Again, set the tab position and the left margin position to the same values with the ruler dialogue box.

When you want to use the style, click on it in the style menu and then type the number or other character you want to begin the first item and press Tab. If the text wraps round to a second line it will automatically align under the tab as the left margin is set to the same position. Don't add a space after the tab, and if you are changing text that you have already typed, delete any spaces after the letter or number and before the start of the text. If you don't, the following lines won't line up properly under the first one.

Outdented styles

An outdented style is the opposite of an indented one. It has its first line margin and/or its left margin set further to the left than the start of the body text. You can only use a style like this if your BaseStyle is indented so that it doesn't begin at the lefthand edge of the frame. You may like to use an outdented style to set subheadings to the left of your text. There is an example on the disc that accompanies this book that uses outdented headings. If you want to use outdented headings, you will need to make sure that the BaseStyle and any other styles that set a ruler have both the left margin and the first line margin set in by at least an inch or so (2.5cm). This will give an outdented style enough space to be conspicuous. Remember that each time you set a ruler it overrides the rulers set by other styles applying to the text, so you will need to set the margins for all your rulers.

Boxes and tables

You can combine horizontal and vertical rules to build up tables, add boxes and create other effects with lines. Use the rule-off setting in the style dialogue box to add horizontal lines, and Line tabs to add vertical lines. Remember that you will need to turn on and set the thickness for both types of rule in the style dialogue box. To add vertical lines, use the Line tab option in the Enter values dialogue box opened from the ruler menu. You also need to set the left and right end positions from the ruler to control the length and position of the horizontal rules. These are called Left rule off (the starting position for the line) and Right rule off (the end of the line). For example, if you wanted to draw a box using just rules, you would need to set rule-off above and below the text, and set a line tab at the same positions as the left and right rule off points. If you want to create a table, remember that you will also need a tab position for the text; you will need to use tabs in the sequence line — left (or however you want the text positioned) — line for the first cell of the table, and left — line for each subsequent cell.

One of the default styles in a new Impression document is called Table and sets up a table using rules. Use Edit style to have a look at this style and its ruler settings to see how to construct a table. There is an example document on the disc that accompanies this book that uses rules to make up boxes.

What next?

The next chapter explains how to use multiple chapters in an Impression document. It tells you how to build up a multi-chapter document, how to use different master pages of chapters, and which operations you can use with a whole multi-chapter document and which only within a chapter.

13 Multi-chapter documents

If you are creating a short document such as a letter or brochure you will probably use only one chapter. However, a long document like a book or a long report may benefit from being broken up into several chapters. The main advantage of having different chapters is that you can use a different master page for each, if you wish. You can also perform some operations on just a chapter. A chapter is like a mini-document within your document.

This chapter explains how to use chapters, how to begin a new chapter, alter some details of an existing chapter and delete a chapter.

If you are building up a long document from several chapters, you may want to use Impression's facility to generate a table of contents and index automatically. These are described in the next chapter.

Features of a chapter

A chapter is a self-contained unit within a document; it is not just a separate text story. A chapter may contain several text stories, as the single chapter generally used to create a newsletter may. A chapter always begins on a new page. If you like, each chapter can have its pages copied from a different master page or pair of master pages. When you edit the text of a chapter, the chapter will gain or lose pages as necessary to accommodate changes in the text. The text won't flow backwards or forwards into the previous or next chapter, though the page numbers of the next chapter will be changed if necessary. In this way, a chapter is similar to a document; it can grow and shrink as you edit it, without affecting neighbouring chapters. You can also change the master page used for one chapter without necessarily changing any of the other chapters (as long as other chapters use different master pages).

You can use repeating frames within a chapter to hold text or graphics that you want to add to several or all pages. This can be useful if you want to include the title of the chapter in a header, for example. If several chapters use the same master page you can't put this information on the master page, but as repeating frames are not continued from one chapter to the next you can use them to hold a header instead.

The document information dialogue box displayed by **Info** from the Document menu or by pressing

Ctrl-F1 shows information about the current chapter as well as the whole document.

Deciding whether to use chapters

When you begin a new document, it is worth giving some thought to whether you are going to divide it into chapters. Probably an important reason for using chapters will be to allow you to use different master pages for different parts of the document or different text in repeating frames. Although all your body text chapters may use the same master page, you might want a different master page for appendices, for example, or for the index, table of contents and preface or abstract. It is also useful to break a large document into chapters so that it's easier to move around it. You can use **Find** to go to a specified chapter, and use the cursor keys to move to the beginning or end of the current chapter. Pressing Control with the up - arrow key will move the cursor to the start of the current chapter; Control with down - arrow moves the cursor to the end of the chapter.

Another important factor that you should bear in mind is that splitting your document into chapters enables you to make more efficient use of the computer's memory. You can tell Impression to hold only the current chapter in memory and leave the rest of the document stored on disc. This reduces the amount of memory Impression needs to use and is particularly useful if you are using a 1Mb machine and want to create long documents. To do this, display the Impression icon bar menu and click on **Minimise memory**. This option is described further in chapter 19: *Getting the most from Impression.*

The first chapter

When you first open a new Impression document a new chapter is begun automatically, copying its pages from the first master page. You can edit this master page or, if you want a completely different page layout, you can instruct Impression to use a different master page for the chapter. To do this, use **Alter chapter** in the Edit menu. It displays this dialogue box:

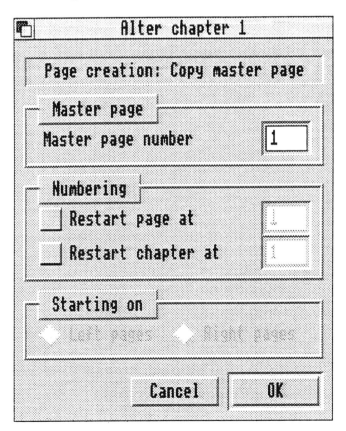

The first field lets you set the number of the master page you want to use. Delete the number in the field and type the number of the master page you want to use. If you don't know which you want to use, look at the master pages first using **View master** pages in the Edit menu. If you want to use a pair of master pages so that you can have different left and right pages, give the number of the first of the pair. For example, master pages 2 and 3 are a pair, and you would need to type 2 to use this pair. Remember that the first master page of a pair is usually the second to be used as it is the lefthand (even-numbered) page.

If you use a pair of master pages, the Starting on options are available. You can choose to start the chapter on a lefthand page or a righthand page. You can make this setting separately for each chapter. It is quite common to start chapters in books on a righthand page, even if this means having a blank page facing the start of the chapter because the previous chapter finishes on a righthand page. It is relatively unusual to begin a document on a lefthand page, but you may want to do this if you have other pages for the document stored elsewhere. If you start a document on a righthand page, the first page will be copied from the second master page in the pair. The 'space' before it will be shown as a dark grey area when you scroll through the document.

You can set the page numbering within a chapter, either to restart at 1 or to start from some other number. You can also set the counter for chapter numbers to restart. You might want to restart page numbers from 1 if you are using a page number format that shows the chapter number and page number together: 4-1 for page 1 of chapter 4, for example. To set a page number like this, you would need to set the text holding the page number with this sequence: **Insert Current chapter number** (from the Misc menu); hyphen; **Insert Current page number** (from the Misc menu). The correct chapter number and page number will automatically be added to each page that has this text. You may want to restart the page numbers at the start of a document to a number other than one if the chapter comes part way through a document (perhaps because you are creating a very long document and some is stored in another file) or if there will be some preliminary pages that take up the first few page numbers and that are not part of your Impression document. You may want to reset the chapter counter to a number other than one if other chapters are held in another document. There s more information on the page and chapter counters later in this chapter.

When you have made the settings you want, click on OK. If you have chosen a different master page for your first chapter, the page will be redrawn using the new master page.

Creating a new chapter

When you want to create a new chapter, which is not the first chapter, you can make similar settings. There are a few other options, too. Use **New chapter** from the Edit menu to display this dialogue box:

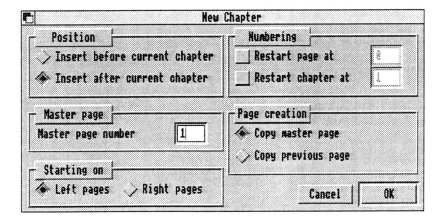

You can add a new chapter after the current chapter or before it. In either case, a new page will be created to hold it and it won't affect the existing pages in other chapters in any way other than renumbering them. As you add text to the chapter, extra pages will be added to hold it. In this way, a new chapter can be squeezed in between existing chapters and all the following chapters will move forwards to make room for it. You can only add a new chapter before or after a chapter, not in the middle of an existing chapter.

Again, you can reset the page or chapter numbering to 1 or another number, you can begin the chapter on a left- or righthand page and you can give the number of the master page you want to use. If you start a new chapter on a righthand page and the previous chapter finished on a righthand page, the intervening, blank lefthand page will be shown as a dark grey area when you scroll through the document. Nothing will be printed on it when you print out the document. This happens so that left and right pages don't get out of sequence, with an even-numbered page appearing on a copy of a righthand master page, for example.

There is one other option when you are creating a new chapter that you aren't offered when altering an existing chapter and this is to copy the layout of the previous page (the last page of the preceding chapter) rather than a master page. You are not especially likely to want to do this, but it is supplied so that documents from Impression Junior (the cut-down version of Impression) can be used; Impression Junior doesn't have a master page facility.

When you click on OK, the new chapter will be created on a new page. You can type in the frames created or drag in text or graphics in the usual way. If you have copied a master page that has guide frames only, you will need to create some local frames before you can add text or graphics. This is described in chapter 8: *Frames.*

Adding and deleting pages

When the cursor is in a frame, you can add a new page or delete the page the cursor is on using the options **Insert new page** and **Delete page** from the Edit menu.

Insert new page adds a new page after the page the cursor is on. It is copied from the appropriate master page, but text is not automatically flowed through the frames on the new page. If you want to add the frames on the new page to the text flow, click on the last frame in the text flow before the new page, then click with Adjust on each frame on the new page in turn. The frames on the new page will be added to the text flow and text will move back from later pages to fill them. You must click on the frames in the order in which you want them to be used (usually from left to right across the page).

You are not likely to need to add new pages if your text flows through your document from page to page as enough pages are created to hold all the text automatically. You are more likely to add new pages if you are creating a newsletter or other document which has no single main story.

To delete a page, put the cursor on the page you want to delete and use **Delete page** from the Edit menu. A warning dialogue box appears for you to confirm that you want to lose all the local frames, text and graphics on the page.

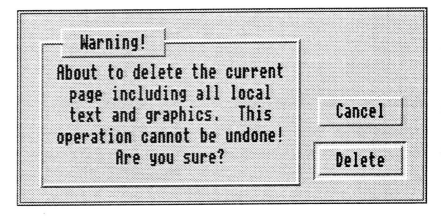

If you delete a page, only local text and graphics are lost. If your text is all in frames copied from the master page and is part of a story that flows from or to other pages, deleting the page will not cause you to lose the text because it will just flow through the chapter and appear later. Extra pages will be created to hold it if necessary. Similarly, you won't loose pictures in embedded frames. However, if you have added any extra frames and put text or pictures into them, these will be lost. They are not stored on the clipboard, so you won't be able to retrieve them after you have deleted the page. If you have any extra frames for graphics on subsequent pages, and they are not embedded, the text and pictures will become out of sequence. This is because the graphics frames are local frames attached to a page rather than to the text; as the text moves forward through the document away from the deleted page, it will move away from its associated pictures.

Deleting a chapter

If you are sure that there is a chapter you no longer need, you can delete it. Don't do this unless you are absolutely certain you won't want it again, as the text and graphics will be lost and are not stored on a clipboard, so you can't paste them back in if you change your mind. To delete a chapter, use **Delete chapter** in the Edit menu. The cursor must be in a chapter or you won't be able to choose this option. Impression issues a warning and gives you the chance to cancel before it deletes the chapter. If you click on Delete on the warning dialogue box, your chapter will be lost. Any later chapters in the document will move back to fill the gap.

You can't delete a chapter just by deleting all the pages or text and graphics in it. One page or pair of pages of a chapter will always be left, even if it hasn't got and text or graphics on it. If you try to use **Delete page** to remove this page, you will be told by Impression that you can't delete it because it is the only page in the chapter. You will have to use **Delete chapter** to get rid of this final page.

Information about chapters

You can display some information about the current chapter and the document as a whole using **info** from the document menu Ctrl-F1. It displays this dialogue box:

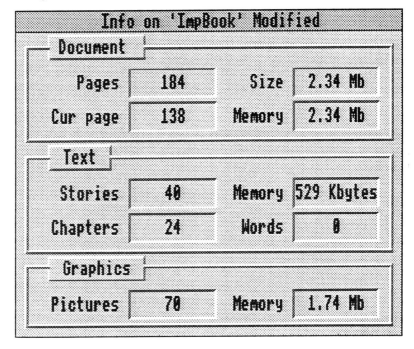

The word count shows the words in the current chapter. To remove the dialogue box, click anywhere in the Impression window.

Automatic chapter and page numbering

Impression keeps a chapter counter which it updates each time you add a new chapter to a document, and a page counter which is incremented each time a page is added. If you want to display the chapter or page number anywhere — such as in a header or footer, or in the title of the chapter — use the Insert submenu from the Misc menu and choose the option **Current chapter number** or **Current page number**. You can choose the format in which it will appear from a submenu. It can be in upper-case Roman numerals (eg XI for eleven), lower-case Roman numerals (xi for eleven) or arabic (11 for eleven). You can use the automatic chapter and page numbering to help you move around the document, too. Use Find from the Misc menu, with the option **Go to chapter** or **Go to page**. There are several limitations and special features you need to bear in mind with both the page and chapter counters.

The page number counters are rather easier to understand than the chapter number counters as there are fewer possible complications. There are two counters, one you can reset and an internal counter which counts from the first page as page 1 sequentially through the document. For example, you might number the table of contents and other preliminary pages i-xii and your text pages 1-100, then the index ci-ciii. To do this, you would need to:

- add the page number to a frame on the master page for the preliminary pages using **Insert, Current page number, Lower case roman**

- use **Insert, Current page number, Numeric** for the main text by adding this to a frame on a different master page

- reset the page counter to 1 at the start of the first chapter of the main text either with the New chapter dialogue box or the Alter chapter dialogue box

- use **Insert, Current page number, Lower case roman** for the index pages by adding this to a frame on the master page (it could be the same master page as you used for the preliminary pages, or a different one). You don't need to reset the page counter this time: the numbers will continue in sequence from the main body of the text, but will use the different format you have specified.

The **Insert** option will use the page number stored in the counter you can reset so the correct numbers will appear on all the pages. However, Impression's internal counter will be used by the Find option **Go to page** so this will count sequentially from the beginning of the document. If you have four pages of contents or preliminary matter and then begin the body of the text with the page counter reset to 1, using Go to page 5 will display the first page of the body text as this is the fifth page of the document. If you want to know the number of the current page on the internal counter, use **Info** from the Document menu (or Ctrl-F1) to display information about the document including the number of the current page.

Chapter counting is more complex, but you may not need to use it. Again there are two chapter counters: one that you can reset, which controls the chapter number inserted if you use **Insert Current chapter number**, and an internal chapter counter that counts all the Impression chapters in your document. It can become complicated, because you may choose to use more than one Impression chapter in a single 'real' chapter of your document. (You may want to begin a new Impression chapter for a new subsection of a chapter in your document, for example.) Both counters will count each new

Impression chapter whether or not it corresponds to the beginning of a new 'real' chapter in your document.

You can reset the chapter counter at the start of a new Impression chapter; this counter will be used for **Insert** if you want to include the current chapter number anywhere in the document. However, if you use the Find option **Go to chapter**, the internal chapter counter is used. The table below shows how resetting the chapter counter at the start of a chapter affects only one of the counters. The first counter is used for **Insert**; the second is used for **Go to chapter.**

Book chapter	Impression chapter	Counter	Internal counter
TOC	1	1	1
Introduction	2	2	2
Chapter 1, counter reset to 1	3	1	3
Chapter 2	4	2	4

If you use more than one Impression chapter in a 'real' chapter, it gets more complicated. For instance, if each chapter of your book has two different Impression chapters within it, the chapter counters will be increased by two, not by one, for each chapter. If you wanted to use **Insert Current chapter number**, you would then have to reset the chapter counter at the start of each Impression chapter within a document chapter:

Book chapter	Impression chapter	Counter	Internal counter
TOC	1	1	1
Introduction	2	2	2
Chapter 1, section 1			
counter reset to 1	3	1	3
section 2,			
counter reset to 1	4	1	4
Chapter 2, section 1	5	2	5
section 2,			
counter reset to 2	6	2	6

Go to chapter always uses the internal counter, so if you used Go to chapter 2 in the document described in the table, the cursor would appear at the start of the introduction; to move to the start of chapter 2, you would need to use Go to chapter 5.

If you have only one Impression chapter for each chapter of your document and no extra Impression chapters (for a table of contents, for example), the real chapter number will match the number held in the counter.

The automatic chapter numbers will be updated wherever they appear in the text if you alter the document by adding or deleting chapters.

What next?

The next chapter explains how to generate a table of contents and an index automatically. This is particularly useful with a long document. These operations are particularly useful with a long document

14 Creating an index and table of contents

One of the more laborious and time-consuming chores of creating a long document when you are not using Impression is compiling an index. Even a table of contents takes some time, especially if you want to include several levels of heading. Impression saves you lots of time and makes sure your index and table of contents are perfectly accurate by offering automatic generation of both. Both the index generation and the table of contents (TOC) generation work by picking up markers attached to styles. This chapter explains how to generate a TOC and how to generate an index.

Generating a table of contents

A TOC lists the page numbers of different chapters or sections of your document. To build up a TOC in Impression, you need to decide which levels of heading you want to include and use **Edit style** to give their styles TOC labels.

Near the bottom of the style dialogue box is a section called Style labels. This allows you to mark a style to be picked up by the indexing or TOC generation procedure. When you generate a table of contents, Impression will include in the table all text in styles which have the TOC label set on. Typically, you will want to include all chapter headings or main headings, and some levels of subheadings. Use **Edit style** to turn on the contents label setting for each style of heading you want to include.

Levels of heading and styles

You can also set a level, in the range 0 to 15, for the entries in the TOC. This controls the style that will be given to the text when it appears in the table of contents, enabling you to distinguish easily between headings of different levels. If you set levels, Impression will automatically put the different levels of heading into styles called Contents0, Contents1 and so on. You need to create any Contents styles you want to use before compiling the TOC, so if you have set levels 0, 1 and 2, you will need to create styles Contents0, Contents1 and Contents2 using **New style**. You don't need to define any attributes for these styles yet, but you do need to create the styles with their names. For example, you might decide to include three styles in your TOC, called Chapter, Main heading and Sub-heading. You would need to use Edit style to turn on the contents label for each of these, and to set the level of Chapter to 0, Main heading to 1 and Sub-heading to 2. When the TOC is generated, all text taken from Chapter style will be given the style Contents0, all text taken from Main heading will have style Contents1 and all text taken from Sub-heading will have the style Contents2.

Any text that uses any of the styles with the contents label set on will be picked up by the contents compiler and included in the TOC. It doesn't matter whether the style has been overlaid with another style; it will still be included. If your table of contents is to be accurate, it is obviously very important that you use styles properly, using your heading styles for all your headings appropriately, and not substituting effects for styles occasionally.

Compiling the TOC

You will probably want to compile the TOC when your document is finished or you are ready to issue a draft. If you edit the document so that the chapters and sections fall on different pages your TOC won't be correct any more, so you will need to regenerate the TOC after changing the document.

When you are ready to compile the TOC, use **Compile contents** from the Misc menu. It displays this dialogue box:

```
Compile contents
Chapter style  [                    ]  ⇨
Title style    [Main Heading        ]  ⇨
Category style [Sub-heading         ]  ⇨
■ Capitalise entries        □ Chapter numbers
   Master page: [    1    ]   Cancel    OK
```

The editable fields are for you to set the styles that will be used for the whole chapter (the TOC forms a new chapter) and the title of the chapter (which will be Contents). The last field, Category, is only used for generating an index and you can't set this for a TOC. You can type the name of a style you want to use in each field, or choose from the menu, either by clicking on the menu arrow to the right of the field or using the Menu mouse button. By default, Basestyle will be used for the whole text of the chapter, and Main Heading will be used (if it exists) for the title. You can choose another style for either. If you have defined any Contents styles these will be applied over the style you choose for the whole chapter.

If you want all entries to have an initial capital Letter whether or not they do when they appear in the main text, turn on Capitalise entries. It is fairly unlikely that you will have chapter headings and subheadings that don't start with capitals unless you specifically wanted lower case. This button is more useful for index generation.

If you want chapter numbers to be inserted before the page numbers, turn on the button beside Chapter numbers. Again, this is more likely to be useful for an index.

The chapter numbers are taken from the counter you can reset (the one used by **Insert**); there is a description of the behaviour and limitations of this counter in chapter 13: *Multi-chapter documents.*

Finally, choose a master page that will be copied to create the pages for the chapter. You will probably want to use a master page that is different from the pages in your main text. Even if you don't want a particularly different layout for the TOC, you are likely to want to separate the page numbering for the TOC from the page numbering for the rest of the document. This is usually done by giving the pages a separate scheme of numbers in lower-case roman numerals (pages i, ii, iii, iv and so on). You need to set this on the master page you have used for the TOC. To insert the page number in a frame, with or without other text, use **Insert** from the Misc menu, using the **Current page number** option and choosing **Lower case roman** from the submenu. If you change the format of the page number on a master page you have used elsewhere in the document, the page number format will be updated on the other pages that use that master page too, so you need a separate master page for the TOC pages.

When you have made the settings you want, click on OK to compile the TOC. The generated TOC will be added at the start of the document, forming a new chapter of its own. This has some disadvantages. The first is that the new chapter immediately becomes chapter 1, so the first real chapter of the document becomes chapter 2. This is awkward if you are using automatic chapter numbering to insert the chapter number either in chapter titles or in page numbers. Go to the first chapter and choose **Alter chapter** from the Edit menu, then turn on Restart chapter at, delete 2 from the field and type 1. You now have two chapters which are numbered 1; Impression's internal counter will still think of the new chapter 1 as chapter 2, and you will find that if you use the Find option **Go to chapter** that it counts from the TOC as chapter 1. Another problem is that the TOC has page numbers, yet your main text starts at page 1 (and is shown as doing so in the contents list). Use the Restart page at option from the Alter chapter dialogue box to restart the pages of the chapter after the TOC at 1.

You can edit the TOC and set or alter attributes for the Contents styles used. If you didn't choose to use Contents styles for different levels of heading, you can still apply different styles to the different levels at this stage. It is often useful to reduce the space above and below the paragraph to avoid excessive space between the lines. You will probably want to set a tab stop over to the right of the page, too, for the page numbers. The page numbers are all preceded by a tab character so they will move over as soon as you set a tab. If you have not already set up a tab in one or more of the Contents styles but there are tabs in the Basestyle, the page numbers will already be at tab positions, though they may not line up if there is more than one tab set in the style. When you set a suitable tab position for the Contents style, this will override the tab stops for Basestyle and the numbers will line up. There is an example of a document with a table of contents on the disc that accompanies this book.

You can regenerate the TOC if you need to (because you have edited the document and it is no longer correct) and the different levels of headings will look as you want them to immediately because the attributes of the Contents styles are now set up.(If you do regenerate the TOC, a new chapter will be created to hold it — it won't overwrite the existing TOC chapter. You will need to use **Delete Chapter** to remove the old TOC).

Generating an index

The process for compiling an index is similar to that for compiling a TOC and uses the same dialogue box (though with a different title). Again you need to begin with styles, though this time you need to create a style specifically for attaching index markers to text. You can create a style, perhaps called Indexmark, which sets only one attribute: turning on the Index label in the Style labels section of the dialogue box. Next you need to go through the whole document applying this style to all the words and phrases you want to include in the index. It can overlay other styles, but it doesn't matter if you later apply another style, overlaying this one — the index compiler will still pick it up.

Marking text for the index

Text will appear in the index exactly as it appears in the text (except that any styles and effects will be ignored). This means that you will need to edit the index to make it consistent. For example, you might end up with separate index entries for 'saving files' and 'save a file'. You can minimise the work you have to do by bearing this is mind as you mark text for including in the index. Decide how you want the entry to appear — saving files, for example — and mark this phrase wherever possible instead of a phrase that means the same. If you want items to appear in the singular in the index ('file type', for example, rather than 'file types'), you can still mark plurals for the index, just miss out the final 's' or 'es' when applying the index marker style (so apply the style to 'file type' only).

If you are developing an application of your own that you want to sell, you may need to apply to Acorn for filetypes for the files your application generates.

Impression will record in the index only the text you mark and the number of the page it appears on. If you have a topic that is described over several pages, it will therefore only list the first page in the index unless you mark an entry on each page separately. If you are likely to edit your text, it is worth marking the indexed topic in each paragraph so that if the page breaks change when you edit the text you are less likely to miss any pages in the indexing. Alternatively, if a topic continues over a large page range, you might want to add the range by hand when the index has been generated and just mark the text at the first occurrence.

Compiling the index

When you have marked all the text you want to include, use **Compile index** from the Misc menu. It displays the same dialogue box as **Compile contents**. Again, set the style that you want to use for the whole chapter and for the title, which will be

Index. This time, you can also set a style for the item Categories; this will be used for the subheadings for the different letters (A, B, C, etc). If you want all entries to begin with an initial capital, turn on Capitalise entries. You can add chapter numbers before the page numbers by turning on Chapter numbers. Choose a master page for the index to be copied from and click OK when you are ready. Although this time you don't need to use a separate master page so that you can set the page number in a different format, you will probably want to set the index in two columns to save space and improve its appearance. For a long document with a lot of index entries marked, it may take a long time to generate the index, so do it when you aren't going to need to use the computer for something else immediately.

Editing the index

However careful you have been, there are likely to be a few changes you want to make to the text of the index after it has been generated. If you have not used Capitalise entries, for example, you may want to remove initial capitals from the entries that start with capitals because the text you marked had a capital. You may want to change a list of page numbers to a range of pages by deleting the pages listed between the first and last and adding a hyphen or, better, an en-dash (Alt-151) between the two numbers. (For example, you would change 34, 35, 36, 37 to 34 — 37). The usual convention in indexing is to show a range only if the same discussion of a topic continues over all the pages, but to list pages separately if there is a separate mention of the topic on each page. This means that if you describe installing a printer driver on pages 9, 10 and 11, you could mark this in the index as 9—11, but if you mention the need for a printer driver on page 7 and then, after discussing some other topic, say where printer drivers are stored on page 8, you would make the index entry 7, 8. This is very laborious, and you need to know the text very well to do it. It is much easier to change all lists to ranges.

If you change your document at all, the index is likely to become wrong as items are shuffled from one page to another but the page numbers shown in the index aren't updated. You will have to re-do all your edits to the index if you regenerate it. For this reason, don't generate the index until you are certain you have finished the document and aren't going to make any more changes.

What next?

The next chapter explains the saving options that you can use to save your document and to extract text stories from your document. It also describes Impression's auto-save facility, which will save your document periodically without you needing to do it explicitly.

15 Saving your work

At some point, you will want to save your document. This should be sooner rather than later, as it is always advisable to save your work frequently in case there is a computer or power failure, or you accidentally delete a lot of your work. (If you delete a chapter, for example, you can't reinstate it as it isn't stored on a clipboard.) You can save your document as an Impression document, but you can also save a text story from it, with or without Impression's styles marked in it. As well as saving your document yourself, you can instruct Impression to save your document periodically. This is useful if you think you might forget to do it yourself, but it has some disadvantages. This chapter explains:

- how to save your work

- how to save a text story from your document

- how to use Impression's auto-save option.

Saving a document

When you want to save your work, open a directory display for the directory you want to save your document into. You may need to put a new, formatted disc in the disc drive if you are using a computer with only a floppy disc drive. Use **Save document** from the Document menu to display this Save as icon:

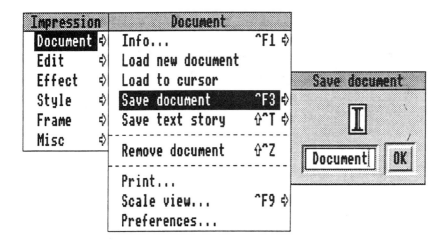

If it is a new document, the default name will be Document. Delete this using the Delete or Backspace key or Ctrl-U, and type the name you want to use. Impression will add a ! character in front of the name if you don't do so yourself; the name must not be more than nine characters long if you don't add a !, and only ten characters long if you do include the !. The ! shows the computer that the icon represents an application directory.

Impression does not save a document as a single file, but as a directory which splits it into chapters and stores text, graphics and instructions about layout separately. You can type a full pathname and then click on OK or press Return, or drag the icon into the directory display for the directory you want to store it in.

If you are changing a document that already existed, the full pathname of the document will be shown in the editable field. Click on OK to use the same name, overwriting the original copy, or delete this name and give another name. You can type a full pathname, or just a file name and then drag the icon to a directory display. Saving a document does not close it down.

It is a good idea to save your work periodically, even if you haven't finished, to limit the amount of work you can lose if there is a power failure or if you make a serious mistake such as deleting a chapter or using **Delete text** instead of **Cut text**.

Saving a text story

Sometimes, you may want to save just a text story from your document. This might be because you want to give it to someone else to work on, who is not going to use Impression. Maybe you have to give your book to a publisher as ASCII text for the publisher to lay out to a different style on another system, for example. To do this, open a directory display to hold the text and use **Save text story** from the Document menu. This displays a dialogue box offering several options:

You can save any combination of linefeeds, return characters and style descriptions with your text. Whether you want linefeeds or Returns will depend on what you are going to do with the text. If you save linefeed characters, a linefeed will occur at the end of each line, and return characters will be replaced by linefeeds. If you look at the document in Edit, you will see that the text begins a new line in the same places as it did in the Impression document, though it may wrap around first if the line is too long for Edit. If you save Returns, a Return character will be inserted at the end of each line and at each Return. In Edit, these are shown by the hexadecimal character code [0d]. If you change your mind about whether you wanted linefeeds or Returns, you can open the file in Edit and use the Edit menu option CR<=>LF to switch Returns for linefeeds or vice versa.

If you save styles, the style information for the document will be added to the text file. This doesn't mean that the document will be displayed on screen in any other program using the styles you have set, but that the style information will appear as text. Here is an example taken from the start of this chapter:

```
╔══════════════════════════════════════════════════╗
║ 🗐 ⊠     ADFS::Disc_87.$.TextStory          🗎 ║
╠══════════════════════════════════════════════════╣
║ define style "BaseStyle";                     ⇧ ║
║  font Homerton.Medium;                           ║
║  fontsize 11pt;                                  ║
║  spaceabove 6pt;                                 ║
║  spacebelow 6pt;                                 ║
║  leftmargin 1.8pt;                               ║
║  rightmargin 0pt;                                ║
║  returnmargin 1.8pt;                             ║
║  condframethrow 0pt;                             ║
║  rulewidth 0pt;                                  ║
║  ruleoffset 0pt;                                 ║
║  fontaspect 100%;                                ║
║  fontcolour rgb=(0,0,0);                         ║
║  linecolour rgb=(0,0,0);                         ║
║  rulecolour rgb=(0,0,0);                         ║
║  justify left;                                ⇩ ║
╚══════════════════════════════════════════════════╝
```

The file begins with a list of styles and style definitions. The styles applied to a piece of text are shown in the form {"chapter" on} and {"chapter" off}.

You may want to save the style information if you are going to drag the text into another Impression document at some point, or if you are going to use the text in some other desktop publishing program. For example, you could make the text suitable for use in Ventura Publisher by making replacements such as changing{"style" on} to @style =. You could make it suitable for Acorn Desktop Publisher by replacing {"style" on} with <style>.

To save a text story, give a name for it and drag the file icon to a directory display. The story is saved as plain ASCII text, and you can look at it and change it in Edit.

Auto-saving

If you find it difficult to remember to save your work regularly, you might like to use Impression's auto-saving option. This instructs Impression to save your document regularly at an interval you specify whenever the document is open. You can ask Impression to prompt you before saving, or just to save without a prompt. Auto-saving saves the document with the same name, so it overwrites your existing copy of the document on disc.

To set this option, choose **Preferences** from the Document menu to display this dialogue box:

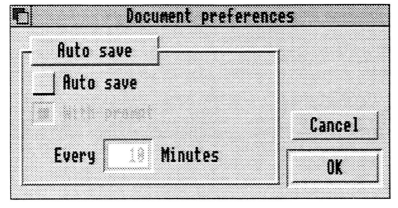

If you turn on auto-save, you can then specify the interval in minutes that you want between saves. You can also choose whether or not to be prompted before the save. When Impression is ready to auto-save your document, and if you have set prompting on, a dialogue box appears telling you that Impression will save the document and giving you the chance to postpone the save, go ahead or cancel it. It is often useful to have the prompt, because the save might happen when you have just a large chunk of text but not yet pasted it in. You won't want the save operation to overwrite the saved file that contains the text with a version that doesn't have the text in at all, so it's useful to be able to cancel or postpone a save occasionally. It is also useful to have the prompt in case you make a mistake, such as deleting a chapter that you wanted to keep, and the save occurs almost immediately afterwards and overwrites the existing copy that had your complete document. If you choose to postpone the save, you can say by how many minutes you want to postpone it. If you cancel it, Impression will wait until the next auto-save is due and issue the dialogue box again. However, you might find the prompt tiresome. As long as you keep regular back-up copies in a different directory, you may decide it's safe to turn off the prompt. Even if you set prompts off, the prompt will appear the first time the document is due to be saved in a session.

Squashing Impression documents

If your computer uses RISC OS 3, you may want to use **Squash** to compress your Impression documents and save disc space. If you do this, you *must* remember to turn on **Squash apps** from the Squash icon bar menu, as each Impression document is held as an application directory. If you don't turn on **Squash apps** and squash an Impression document as though it was a file, the squashed version would be incomplete — all the text and graphics are lost. If you save the squashed document with the same name as the original (the default name for it) you will lose your document completely.

What next?

The next chapter explains how to print Impression documents. You will need to connect a printer and install a printer driver before you can print anything. The chapter explains how to choose and install a printer driver and describes the print options available from impression.

16 Printing Impression documents

Before you can print any documents, you need to load a suitable printer driver and make sure a printer is connected to your computer. You can then set print options and send documents to print. Usually, this is very straightforward. Impression uses the standard RISC OS printer drivers, which are described fully in the *User Guide* supplied with your computer. There is also a draft print option available for some printers which allows you to print text only more quickly than using the standard, high-quality mode. This chapter explains how to:

- choose and install a suitable printer driver

- use the **Print** option to send a document to the printer

- print a pamphlet

- prepare files for typesetting.

Installing a printer driver

You need to install a suitable printer driver before you can print any Impression documents — even if you only want to print them to a file to send to a printer later.

What is a printer driver?

A printer driver is a piece of software that tells the printer how to interpret the codes it is sent from the computer. When you send an Impression document to the printer, the printer may receive the information in one of two ways:

- it may receive a *bit-map image* of the screen. This is an image of the text and graphics on screen in the form of a 'snapshot'. It gives the printer instructions to print one dot black, leave the next white, and so on.

- it may receive instructions that tell it when to begin text, which fonts to use, where to draw a line, and so on.

The first method is characteristic of dot-matrix printers and LaserJet-type laser printers. The second method is used by PostScript laser printers. Whichever method your printer needs to use, the printer driver translates the text, the codes that describe the special formatting and styling options you have used, and the graphics in an Impression document into a form your printer can understand.

Printing from a network

If you are using one computer on its own you will be able to see whether there is a printer attached. It will be plugged into one of the data ports on the back of the computer, the serial or parallel port. However, if your computer is connected to a network (in a school, for example), there may be no printer attached to your own computer. This doesn't mean you won't be able to print anything — there is probably a printer somewhere on the network and you should be able to use this. Ask the network manager whether there is a printer, how to use it and how to set up your printer driver.

Choosing a printer driver

Impression uses the standard RISC OS printer drivers. Versions of the RISC OS 2 printer drivers are supplied on the Impression discs. If your computer runs RISC OS 3.0 or later, don't use the printer drivers supplied with Impression, but use the RISC OS 3 printer drivers supplied with your computer. If your computer runs RISC OS 2, check to see whether the versions of the printer drivers supplied with Impression are more up-to-date than the copies you have already. Always use the most recent version you have. Chapter 2: *Getting ready to use Impression* explains how to check the version number of a printer driver.

Which printer driver you need to use will depend on what type of printer you have and whether your computer runs RISC OS 2 or RISC OS 3.

For a RISC OS 2 computer, use:

• PrinterPS for a PostScript laser printer

• Printer LJ for a LaserJet laser printer

• PrinterDM for a monochrome dot matrix printer

• PrinterIX for an Integrex colour ink jet printer.

To load a RISC OS 2 printer driver, open a directory display for the directory holding it and then double-click on its icon to install it on the icon bar. You can then make some adjustments to the printer driver, setting the paper margins and resolution, for example, and set the connection as parallel, serial or network. The *User Guide* supplied with your computer explains fully how to do this.

For a RISC OS 3 computer, there are many more printer drivers and should be one specifically for the printer you want to use. To load a printer driver in RISC OS 3, first load !Printers in App1 by double-clicking on its icon in the directory display. If you have already used a printer driver and saved your settings in !Printers, a printer driver may be loaded, with its name and icon already on the icon bar at this point. Otherwise you will see the Printers icon, like this:

Printers

Display the icon bar menu for this icon and choose
Printer control. If there are no printers loaded, the
window will be empty:

If you have any printers loaded, but inactive, they
will be listed in the window, like this:

If there is a printer driver that you want to use and it
is inactive, click on it to highlight it, then display the
menu and choose **Active**. The printer driver status
will change to Active and the icon on the icon bar
will change to show the printer driver now in use.
For example, if you make the Epson FX-80 driver
active, the icon on the icon bar will look like this:

FX-80

If there are no printer drivers listed, or if the one
you want to use isn't listed, you will need to load
one. Open the directory Printers in App2 and find
the directory that is likely to hold printer drivers for
your printer. For example, if you have an Epson FX-
80, open the Epson directory. Now display the icon
bar menu for the !Printers application and choose
Printer control. When the printer control window
appears, drag the icon for the printer driver for your

printer to the window. The name of the printer appears in the window, and it automatically activated. Its icon appears on the icon bar. If there is another printer driver also active, the second icon may be grey. Inactivate the other printer driver (the one you don't want to use) by clicking on its name in the printer control window and choosing Inactive from the menu. Once you have loaded a printer driver, you can make some settings to control how it is connected and how it will behave. The *User Guide* supplied with your computer explains how to do this.

Printing a document

When you have installed a printer driver, make sure your printer is connected to the computer, turned on and on-line and has some paper in it. You can then print a document. To print a document, use **Print** from the Document menu. It displays this dialogue box:

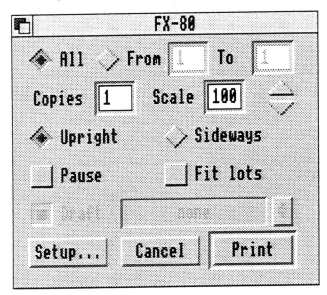

The title bar shows the printer driver you have loaded (and have active, in RISC OS 3). You can make these settings from this dialogue box:

* print all the pages or choose a range of pages to print

* print one or more copies

* print the document at its normal scale or specify another scale

* print the document upright or sideways on the paper

* pause between sheets (if you need to insert one sheet at a time, for instance)

* fit lots of pages onto a single sheet of paper (if you are using a smaller page size than your paper size or are using a small scale)

* use draft mode

* change the set up.

Let's look at each of these in turn.

Page range

If you want to print all the pages, make sure the button beside All is turned on. To print a range of pages, turn on the button beside From and then type the number of the first page you want to print in the first editable field and the number of the last page you want to print in the editable field beside To. The numbers refer to the actual numbers of the pages, with 1 always being the first page, not to any numbers shown on the page (which may be different). (There is more on the page number counter in chapter 13: *Multi-chapter documents*.) If you don't know the number of a page (perhaps because you aren't showing page numbers in your document or the page numbers shown don't correspond to the real page numbers), click in a frame on the page and then use **Info** from the Document menu or press Ctrl-F1 to display a dialogue box that shows you information about the document, including the number of the current page.

Number of copies

You can print one or more copies of your document. If you print more than one copy, you can choose whether to have all copies of each page printed together, (all copies of page 1, then all copies of page 2, and so on) or print the whole document several times (one copy of the document, then the next, and so on). This is controlled using the Set up dialogue box described below. For many printers, it is quicker to print all copies of a page together and sort them out yourself than to print the whole document several times.

Scale

By default, the pages will be printed at full scale, so an A4 page will fill an A4 sheet of paper. If you want to, you can adjust the scale, perhaps reducing your A4 page so that you can print two side by side. This is described below.

Upright or sideways orientation

You can print upright or sideways on the page. Upright is the usual way, with the text going across the width of the page using portrait orientation. Sideways prints landscape. You will need to choose this if you want to print two A5 pages side by side on an A4 sheet of paper. Not all printers may be capable of printing sideways, so if you try this and it doesn't work it is probably because your printer isn't capable of it. However, it is worth looking in the printer manual to see if there are any settings you can make to get it to print sideways. Depending on the type of printer, you may have to put the paper in sideways or make some dip switch settings.

Pausing between pages

You may need to pause between pages if you have to feed each page separately. The printer will pause after printing each page and display a dialogue box allowing you to continue printing when you have inserted the next sheet (Continue), or cancel the print run (Stop).

Fitting lots of pages on a single sheet

If you are using a small page size in Impression, or are reducing the scale of your pages, you can use Fit lots to fit as many pages as possible onto a single sheet of paper. This saves paper, particularly if you are printing drafts rather than final copies. If you are printing A5 pages, you can use this option with sideways printing to print two A5 pages side by side on an A4 sheet. If you want to reduce A4 pages to A5 and print two side by side, set the scale to 66%.

Draft printing

Some types of printer can use Impression's draft printing mode. This is a quick way of printing text only and is often useful for drafts that you want to check rather than final copies that you want to issue. Draft mode uses only the resident fonts in your printer, so if these don't look like the fonts you have used in the document, your printout won't resemble the document in appearance, though the content of the text will be the same. Draft mode doesn't print graphics at all. The advantage of draft printing is that for some printers it is much quicker than the standard high-quality mode. There is no point in using draft mode with a PostScript laser printer as it can print using RISC OS fonts as quickly as with the printer's resident fonts and simple graphics print nearly as quickly as text anyway. You can achieve better speed with complex graphics by turning off printing of illustrations. This is described below as an option from the Set up dialogue box.

Before you can use draft mode, you need to have installed a draft printing module. These are supplied on the Impression discs. Installing them is described in chapter 2: *Getting ready to use Impression*. Click on the button beside Draft to see which draft module is loaded; its name is shown in the field beside the button. You can display a menu by clicking the Menu button on the mouse or clicking on the menu arrow to the right of the text field to see a list of the modules that are installed and available. Click on the one you want to use. If you have a printer that offers NLQ (near letter quality) mode, you can use this with draft printing to make the text look better. NLQ gives a higher density print-out, with more ink used to print each letter, making it blacker and more solid. If your printer doesn't have NLQ mode, make sure this option is turned off or it may confuse the printer. (NLQ mode is turned on if it is ticked; click on it to turn it off.)

Draft printing uses only the fonts your printer has in its own hardware or software; it doesn't take any fonts from the computer. As long as you make sure that you use fonts and point sizes that your computer can match, you will get quite a good result from draft printing. If you use inappropriate sizes or fonts, you may find that lines are truncated or run on to the next line, and that text appears in a different font. You can correct the first problem by adjusting the text size you use in your document. The second problem is likely to be significant only if you have used symbols in mathematical formulae, for example, or non-English characters that don't match the character set of your printer.

Set up

Click on Set up to display a dialogue box that allows you to make some settings for your print-out.

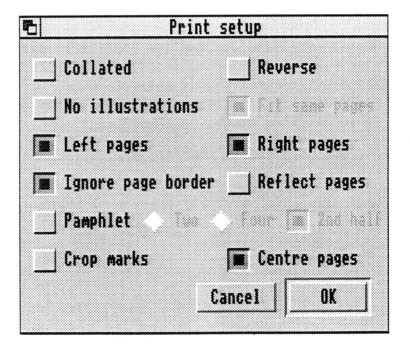

This allows you to:

- *collate pages*: print several whole copies of the document rather than all copies of page 1, then all copies of page 2 and so on. This only has an effect if you are printing more than one copy of a document. Dot matrix printers typically take as long to print each copy of a page as to print the first copy, so you might as well save yourself the effort of sorting the pages afterwards and use Collated. Laser printers, though, store an image of the page in their memory and can print multiple copies of a page in little more time than it takes to print one copy. It is then quicker to collate the pages (sort them into order) yourself after they have been printed. The difference is more significant with LaserJet-type printers than PostScript laser printers.

- print pages in *reverse order*: begin with the last page of the document and print pages in reverse order. This is useful if your printer ejects pages the right way up, so that you need to reverse their order after printing when you print forwards. Some printers stack pages upside down so that when you turn the stack over page 1 is on top. If your printer does this, don't use the reverse order option.

- print *no illustrations*: miss out any graphics to speed up printing. Any areas occupied by pictures show a cross to indicate the position and size of the picture.

- *fit* several copies of the same page on a sheet of paper: fit as many copies as possible of the same page on a sheet of paper. This is only available if you are using Fit lots to print more than one page on a sheet. If it is turned off, copies of different pages will be printed on the same sheet, but if it is turned on, several copies of the same page will be printed on each sheet. As many copies of the page will be printed as fit, regardless of the number of copies you have requested. For example, if you specify one copy, but choose a scale at which two pages will fit on a sheet, two copies of the same page will appear on each sheet.

- print only *left* or *right* pages: with either of these turned on, Impression will print only lefthand pages (usually even numbers) or righthand pages (odd numbers). Turn both buttons on to print all pages. You can't turn both buttons off. You might want to use these buttons if you want to print on both sides of the paper. You would then print all the righthand pages first, then turn over the paper and print all the lefthand pages. With some laser printers, the paper may wrinkle and jam if you feed it straight back in after printing one side, so you may want to leave it to cool down and flatten before printing the second side.

- *ignore page border*: ignore the non-printing page border set by the printer. Printers do not generally print right to the very edge of the paper and have default margins of their own which they use. Impression takes account of these and centres a page between the margins. If your printer has a larger border on one side than on the other, the text won't be centred between the edges of the paper. Turn on Ignore page border to disregard the printer's own margins and centre the text column(s) on the paper. Sometimes, this allows larger scale printing than is otherwise possible when you are using Fit lots. Fit lots takes account of the page borders for each page even though several pages are appearing on the same sheet. This means that space is wasted accounting for page borders unnecessarily and the text has to be printed slightly smaller than necessary to fit on the page.

- *reflect pages:* print mirror images of pages. This is useful if you want to produce typeset film for printing plates. It gives you the option of producing a positive or negative image.

- print *pamphlet* layouts: This is described below.

- print *crop marks:* print marks to indicate where to cut the paper to get the edges of the page in the right place. Crop marks are printed in the area of the page that will be cut off and discarded and are used by printers to line up the guillotine before cutting. They look like this:

⌟   ⌞

⌐   ⌐

You can use crop marks if you are printing a small page on larger paper, or if you are using Fit lots. You will need extra space around the page to hold the crop marks and so using Fit lots will have to use a smaller scale to fit them in. Use a scale of 62% to fit two A4 pages sideways on an A4 sheet with cropmarks.

- *centre* the pages on the sheet: centre the page on the sheet of paper rather than setting it relative to the top lefthand corner of the sheet. This makes a noticeable difference if, for instance, you print an A5 page on an A4 sheet of paper.

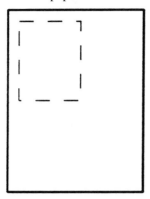 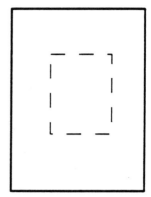

Default position

Centred position

When you have made any settings you want, click on OK to return to the main dialogue box. If you now click on Print, the document will be sent to the printer immediately, and printed using the settings you have made. If you want to store the settings and save them with the file, but not print the document immediately, click on Print with the Adjust mouse button. The settings will become current, and will be displayed in the dialogue box next time you open it. If you save the file, the settings will be saved with it. When you print a document, too, the current settings are stored and saved with the file when you have done it. This means that you don't need to keep changing from the default settings to the settings you want each time you print your document.

Printing pamphlets

One of the options on the Set up dialogue box allows you to specify pamphlet printing and select a layout. Many people use programs like Impression for printing small pamphlets and brochures. If you have used other desktop publishing programs for this you are probably used to having to print each A5 sheet and then cut and paste the sheets to get the right arrangement for photocopying. Impression allows you to do this automatically, though you do have to turn the page over to print the reverse (unless you have a printer that can print on both sides of the page). Normally, to photocopy a pamphlet onto two sides of a sheet of an A4 page to make an A5 pamphlet when folded, you need to print page 1 on the right of the page and page 4 on the left for the outside, and page 2 on the left and page 3 on the right for the inside. You can lay out two A5 pages in an A4 document like this (though you won't be able to use automatic page numbering if you do it this way), but Impression allows you to set this option at the printing stage and create your pages in order as A4 pages.

When you click on Pamphlet, another three buttons become available, labelled Two and Four. Two allows you to set up a pamphlet which will be folded in two (an A4 page folded to give an A5 pamphlet, for example) and Four lets you set up a pamphlet which will be folded in four (an A4 page folded twice to give an A6 pamphlet, for example).

To print an A5 pamphlet, create your pages in order (1, 2, 3, 4) on A4 pages. When you are ready to print the pamphlet, display the Print dialogue box as usual. You will need to turn on Fit lots and set the Sideways option to print two pages side by side.

You will need to scale your pages, too. Use 66% to fit two A4 pages on a single A4 sheet, or 70% if you also turn on Ignore page border. If you are going to print four pages on a sheet, you will probably want to use Upright and scale them at 49% for A4 with Ignore page border set. Again, use Fit lots. There are examples of A5 and A6 pamphlets on the examples disc that accompanies this book.

When you click on Print, Impression will print pages 1 and 4 of a four-page pamphlet or pages 1, 4, 5 and 8 of an eight-page pamphlet on a single page, and then prompt you to turn over the paper. Always wait until the printer has finished printing before you turn over the paper — this may be a few seconds or even a few minutes after the Impression message is displayed. If you don't want to feed the paper back in, just click on Continue to use the next sheet of paper. You can then photocopy one set of pages onto the back of the other. If you do feed the paper back in, make sure you put it the right way up. You may find that feeding paper back into your printer causes a paper jam. This is often a problem with laser printers as the paper gets quite hot and wrinkles slightly when it is printed the first time and then cannot feed through the printer easily the second time. If this happens, either resign yourself to photocopying on the back of the sheet, or try a different weight paper, or leave the page under something heavy for a while to flatten out before refeeding it. If you need to do the last of these, you can use the 2nd half option on the Set up dialogue box to print just the reverse side of your pamphlet. Print the first half, then click on Stop to halt printing, smooth out your paper under some heavy books and then later use 2nd half and put the paper back in when it is smooth and cool and less likely to jam.

If you print a pamphlet to a file (described below) or only print the first page, Impression will still prompt you to turn the paper over, even though it is not appropriate. Click on Continue; the pamphlet will still be printed to a file if that is what you are doing, and subsequent pages won't be printed if you have only specified page 1 in the page range. (You don't need to turn the paper over before clicking on Continue if you are only printing page 1.)

Downloading fonts to a PostScript printer

If you are using RISC OS 3 and have a PostScript laser printer, you can download extra fonts from your computer to your printer. When you print a file from a RISC OS application, the printer driver adds some information to the data sent to the printer that tells the printer how the Acorn font names correspond to names for fonts that the PostScript printer recognises. If you have bought and used any extra fonts that your printer may not have, you can download these so that they can be used in your documents. However, downloading fonts takes quite a lot of printer memory. You may need to buy extra memory for your printer (not your computer) if you want to download many fonts. You can't download fonts if you are running RISC OS 2, or if you have any other type of printer. (You won't need to download fonts with any other type of printer as other printers use a different method to print text.)

To download a font, you need to use the application FontPrint. Make sure the appropriate PostScript

printer driver is loaded and active before you begin,
as FontPrint needs to save the settings you make
into the printer driver application. Open directory
App1 and click on !FontPrint to load FontPrint
onto the icon bar:

Click on the icon to display this window:

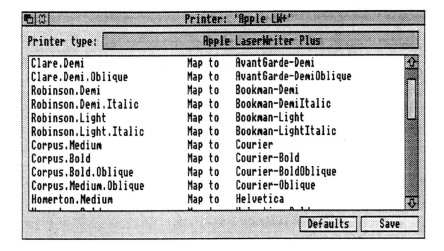

Move the pointer over the FontPrint window and
display the menu. Move the pointer over the option
Add font to display a list of fonts available on your
system and click on the font you want to download.
It will be added at the bottom of the list with
'Download' in place of 'Map to'. Click on **Save** to
save the set-up; a window will appear asking for the
password to download to your printer. The default
password is zero, which is in the field already. Click
on Return to use this. If you know the password is

not zero, type the password in its place and press Return. You may need to give the password when you start up the printer driver in future. Once the font has been downloaded, you can use it when you print from any application that is capable of handling the font. (If you are printing over a network and the password is rejected, ask the system manager what the printer password is.)

Preparing files for image

If you want to prepare a document for professional printing, you will need to produce a PostScript file that you can take to an imagesetter. An imagesetter will probably use a Linotype machine which can output text and graphics using higher resolutions than an ordinary laser printer. A standard laser printer uses a resolution of 300dpi (dots per inch), though some laser printers can go up to 600dpi. A Linotronic 200 typesetter uses 1270dpi as a standard resolution and can go up to 2500 dpi. The image will be printed on a special high-gloss material which produces a much sharper image than paper, so even at lower resolutions a Linotype bromide is better than a laser-printed image on paper.

There are one or two imagesetting bureaux around the country that will take files on Archimedes discs for typesetting. If you are using such a bureau, you may be able to supply them with just your Impression document on disc. If not, you will need to output your document as a PostScript file and then put it onto a PC-format disc. You can do this if you have the PC emulator, MultiFS (from Arxe Systems), PC Access (from Minerva) or PCDir (from Norwich Computer Services), or if you have

RISC OS 3, or if there is a PC connected to a network shared by your computer.

If you have Impression Business Supplement, this provides extra support for typesetting; read chapter 22: *Impression Business Supplement* and follow the instructions there rather than using the procedures described below.

You can produce files for a typesetter without Impression Business Supplement; you only need the Supplement if you want to produce full-colour separations or specify whether you want positive or negative film produced.

When you print to a file, there is no paper output to show that you have got everything right. It is best to print out your work and check it very carefully before printing to a file and taking it to a typesetter. If you make any corrections, print the document and check it again before printing it to a file. You can't make corrections in the PostScript file.

Producing PostScript files with RISC OS 2

When you are ready to generate a file for typesetting, load PrinterPS. Display its icon bar menu, move the pointer over the option **File** and off to the right to display an editable field and type a full pathname for the file you want to create. For example, to send output to a file called PS1 on a floppy disc in drive 0, type :0.$.PS1 and press Return. The label beneath the printer icon shows that output is directed to a file. Now print the document from within Impression in the usual way. A PostScript file is large, and you might find that you need to print a long document in batches of a few pages at a time and spread it over several discs. A warning message will appear if the disc gets full. Remember if you are printing to a file on your hard disc that you will have to copy the file to a floppy to take it to the imagesetter, so the size of files you can use is still limited. You can fit 800K on an Archimedes E-format disc, but if you are going to put the file(s) on a PC disc you will only be able to fit 720K on the disc (unless your computer can read and write 1.44MB discs. The PC emulator uses 720K; RISC OS 3 can format, read and write to 720K or 1.44MB PC discs.)

Any fonts that the Linotype machine doesn't recognise or can't identify from the font mapping in the PostScript file will probably be printed as Courier (Corpus). PrinterPS maps the following fonts:

- Clare: Avant Garde

- Corpus: Courier

- Dingbats: Zapf Dingbats

- Greek: Symbol

- Homerton: Helvetica

- NewHall: New Century Schoolbook

- Pembroke: Palatino

- Robinson: Bookman

- Selwyn: Zapf Dingbats

- Trinity: Times.

Producing PostScript files with RISC OS 3

When you are ready, load the printer driver application !Printers from App1 by double-clicking on its icon. You then need to load and make active a suitable PostScript printer driver. Two linotype drivers are supplied, for Linotronic 100 and 200 machines. You may need to ask your imagesetter which s/he uses. However, these two produce files that have font mappings only for the standard Acorn fonts Corpus, Homerton and Trinity. If you are using any other fonts, you should use an Apple Laser Writer printer driver. Any fonts that the Linotype machine doesn't recognise or can't identify from the font mapping in the PostScript file will probably be printed as Courier (Corpus). Don't use FontPrint to download extra fonts to the Linotype printer driver as the file will contain the whole font mapping and will be very large. There is an explanation in chapter 22: *Impression Business Supplement* of how to use FontPrint to map new fonts to their PostScript equivalents; you don't need Impression Business Supplement to do this if you have RISC OS 3.

To load a Linotype printer driver, open the directory Printers and then the directory Linotype. Now display the icon bar menu for the printer driver application and choose the option **Printer control**. Drag the file icon for the Linotype printer driver you want to use into this window. You may need to make it active and make any other printer driver you have loaded inactive. The icon on the icon bar will show that you have a Linotype printer driver active.

Linotype

If you want to use other fonts, use an Apple LaserWriter printer driver, such as the LW+ in the Apple directory of Printers. This has more font mappings than the Linotype drivers. (The mapping is the same as that for the RISC OS 2 printer driver PrinterPS described above.) It is a good idea to check with your imagesetting bureau that they can handle the fonts you want to use and a PostScript file compatible with an Apple LaserWriter.

What next?

The next chapter explains how to close windows and documents and leave Impression. It is a good idea always to save your work before you close an impression window in case you turn off your computer without remembering to save your work first.

17 Leaving Impression

Impression is unusual in distinguishing between closing a window and closing a document. In most RISC OS applications, if you close the window you close the file and if you have any unsaved work you are reminded that you will lose it by closing the window. However, Impression lets you hold several documents in memory at the same time and open and close windows onto them without actually closing the documents and removing them from memory. This chapter explains:

- the difference between closing a window and closing a document

- how to close down Impression.

Closing a window and closing a document

If you click on the close icon of an Impression document, the window closes. Even if you have unsaved work in the window, the window closes without a warning dialogue box. This is because closing a window doesn't close a document; your document and any changes you have made since saving it are still stored in Impression's memory.

If you have finished working on a document, save it if you want to keep your changes and then use **Remove document** from the Impression icon bar menu or from the Document menu. This doesn't delete your document from the disc, but it removes it from Impression's memory, closing it down. If your document has any unsaved changes when you choose this option, Impression issues a warning dialogue box to let you cancel the operation, or save your document before closing it down, or close down without saving. You might want to do the last of these if you have made a mistake, perhaps deleting a chapter you want to keep, and want to revert to the previously saved version of the document.

If you have closed a document window and later want to look at the document again, use **New view** from the Impression icon bar menu. This has a submenu showing you the documents currently loaded; choose the one you want to look at. You can use **New view** while you already have a window onto a document open. This is useful if you want to look at two documents or at different areas of the same document at the same time, and enables you to copy or cut and paste text between different areas of a document without the need to move backwards and forwards through the document all the time. If you have more than one window open, click in the one you want to use to activate it. Closing one window doesn't close the other.

Closing Impression

When you have finished using Impression, close it down using **Quit** from the Impression icon bar menu. Do this even if you are going to turn the computer off immediately. It gives Impression a chance to check that you don't have any unsaved work — including dictionaries — which you might have forgotten about. If it finds any unsaved work, it gives you the chance to save it before closing down. (If you have RISC OS 3 and use the **Shutdown** option when you turn off your computer, this will also check whether you have any unsaved work, including Impression documents, and give you the chance to save it first.)

If you don't get into the habit of always using **Quit**, you may find that you have lost work that was in closed windows. Because Impression doesn't prompt you to save your work before closing a window — as the document remains open even when the window is closed — it is easy to forget that you have unsaved work in documents that aren't on screen. It is a good idea to save your documents before closing their windows. This helps to protect you against losing work if you forget and turn the computer off without quitting Impression first, or if there is a power cut or computer failure.

What next?

The next chapter gives you some advice about working with documents. It covers loading text that is in alien file formats using the special loader modules supplied with Impression, and copying styles from one document to another to keep a consistent appearance to your full set of documents.

18 Working with documents

If you use Impression a lot, you will probably develop several styles that you want to use for many of your documents. You can create template documents if you want to use elements of the text and layout repeatedly, or you can copy styles between documents if you only want to use the same styles. These techniques will help you to keep a consistent appearance to all your documents. If you ever work with text created in other systems, perhaps by someone else, you can load this into Impression using one of the loader modules supplied. This chapter explains how to:

- use template documents

- copy styles between documents

- load text in alien file formats.

Using templates

Impression doesn't have any special facility for saving and re-using master page layouts from one document to another, but you can create your own document templates that you can re-use. For example, you could create a letterhead document which you load each time you want to create a letter. You can put all your address details and any logo or other graphics you want to use on the master page so that it automatically appears on the first page of each letter you start. Save each letter you type with a different name so that you don't overwrite your template document. This is an easy way to make all your letters look the same. You can use the same technique for any type of document you use repeatedly, such as invoices, simple newsletters or memos. There are some examples of templates of this type on the examples disc that accompanies this book.

Remember that you can save a document that doesn't contain any text at all, just saving the styles and the layout of the master pages. This can save you a lot of time recreating your layout every time, and avoids the possibility of being inconsistent.

Sooner or later, you are likely to overwrite one of your templates by saving the document with the same name. It is easy to recover it. Open the document, put the cursor in the text and use **Select text story** from the Edit menu, then **Cut text**, or **Delete text** also from the Edit menu. This selects all the text in the story and deletes it. You can then resave your template as an empty document. If you have added several text stories or chapters, you will need to select and delete each in turn. Make sure you have finished with the document or saved it with another name first.

If you like, you can save all your master page templates in a single document and then make this the default document that Impression loads when you open a new document. The procedure for changing the default document is described in chapter 20: *Making your own settings and customising Impression.* There is an example on the disc that accompanies this book of a document set that has master pages for different types of business document.

Copying styles between documents

If you frequently produce reports, pamphlets, newsletters or other documents in which you want to use the same styles but not the same layout or elements of the same text, you can copy styles between documents to make sure they always look consistent.

To copy the styles from an existing document into the document you have open, display the Style dialogue box by using **New style** or **Edit style** and then drag the Impression file icon of the other document onto the load icon (the large arrow) at the top right of the dialogue box. All the styles will be copied from the other document into the open document. If there are any name clashes, the newly-loaded styles will have a number added to their name (Sub-heading2, for example). You can delete any styles that you don't want, whether they came from the original document or the document you have dragged in. Chapter 6: *Using styles describes* how to delete styles that you don't want.

Loading text in other file formats

Most of the time, you will probably type your text in Impression as it has full word-processing facilities. However, you may sometimes want to use text you have already prepared in another application, or text from someone else who did not use Impression. You can load text produced by any of the following programs using the standard loader modules supplied with Impression:

- Edit (or other ASCII text)

- 1st Word Plus

- Acorn Desktop Publisher

- Inter-Word

- View

- any program that produces CSV (comma-separated value) files.

You can also load BASIC programs.

There are several extra loader modules supplied with Impression Business Supplement.

Text saved in Edit or otherwise as ASCII text can be loaded at any time, as can Impression documents. Impression automatically loads a module to read both these. To load the other types of file correctly, you first need to install and load a suitable loader module. These are supplied on the Impression discs. If you didn't install them when you installed Impression, you can install them later or just load them when you need them. You don't need to re-run the install program to do this, though you can re-install it if you like. Re-installing will overwrite your previous copy of Impression (unless you install the new copy somewhere else) and so any changes you have made to the way Impression runs, either using the **Preferences** option from the icon bar menu or using the techniques described in chapter 20: *Making your own settings and customising Impression*, will be lost.

If you want loader modules to be started up automatically when you load Impression, you can copy them directly into the Impression application directory. If you just want to use a loader module occasionally, you can save memory by double-clicking on it when you want it rather than copying it into the Impression application directory.

To copy loader modules into Impression, hold down the Shift key and then double-click on the !Impress icon in the directory display to open the application directory. If you have already installed any loader modules you will see their icons.

The loader modules are:

- LoadFWP for loading 1st Word Plus files
- LoadDTP for loading Acorn Desktop Publisher files
- LoadIWord for loading Inter-Word files
- LoadView for loading View filesLoadCSV for loading CSV filesLoadBasic for loading BASIC files.

The loader modules are stored on Impression disc 1 in the directory Extensions. Open a directory display for this directory and drag into the !Impress directory any of the loader modules you want to be able to use.

If you already have Impression loaded, save any unsaved work, quit from Impression, copy the loader modules into !Impress and then reset your computer. When you re-load Impression you will be able to use the loader module(s) you have just copied in.

To load a module that is not installed, open a directory display for the directory Extensions on Impression disc 1 and double-click on the loader module you want to use. It will be loaded and you will be able to use it immediately.

When you are ready to import a file of any format, click in a null frame or text frame in the Impression document to select it and then drag the icon for the file to the Impression window. If you try to drag in a file of a type for which you don't have a loader module installed, Impression may display a dialogue box saying that it is going to use another loader module. You can click on OK to go ahead, or on Cancel if you don't want to use that loader module. If you click on Cancel, Impression may offer you the chance to use a different loader module or may load the file as though it were plain ASCII text (like an Edit file).

Some of the loader modules can read some formatting commands from the files they import. For example, if you import a 1st Word Plus file using LoadFWP, features such as bold, italic and underline will be retained and interpreted as effects in Impression. However, the loader modules can only handle text; no graphics will be imported from files that contain graphics.

If you want to import text from a spreadsheet program such as Schema or Pipedream, you will first need to save the file in CSV (commas-separated value) format. When you want to load it into Impression, use the CSV loader. You must have opened a directory display for !System or !Scrap before using a CSV loader.

Problems with 1st Word Plus and Inter-Word files

You may have a problem trying to import 1st Word Plus files from very early versions of 1st Word Plus, or Inter-Word files from the BBC version of the program. This is because neither of these sets the filetype, which RISC OS needs in order to interpret the file. To solve this so that you can load the files, you need to set the filetype yourself. The procedure for doing this varies depending on whether you are using RISC OS 2 or RISC OS 3.

If you are using RISC OS 2, press F12 to leave the desktop and go to the command line at the very bottom of the screen. To change a file to 1st Word Plus format, type

```
SETTYPE pathname  AF8
```

and press Return. For example, to change the filetype of a file called Letter1 in a directory Letters on a disc in floppy drive 0, type:

```
SETTYPE :0.Letters.Letter1 AF8
```

and press Return. Press Return again to go back to the desktop. If you want to change an Inter-Word file, set the filetype to D80, e.g.:

```
SETTYPE :0.Letters.Letter1 D80
```

It is rather easier to change the filetype with RISC OS 3 as you don't need to use the command line. Open a directory display for the directory holding the file you want to use, select the file and then display the **File ' '**, submenu. Move the pointer across the option **Set type** to display an editable field. In the field, type AF8 or 1WPDoc to change the file type to a 1st Word Plus document, or D80 to change it to an Inter-Word file.

Additional loader modules

If you want to import text from PC programs, you may be able to use one of the extra loader modules supplied with the Impression Business Supplement. This is an additional add-on program that supplements the facilities of Impression by providing some extras that are generally useful for people who use Impression professionally. The Business Supplement is described in chapter 22.

Other text formats

If you have text in a format for which there is no loader module, you can probably still load it although you will lose all the styling and formatting information. Begin by dragging the text file into Edit so that you can see the special control codes and characters that are used to format and style the text. Here is an example of some text from a Ventura Publisher document:

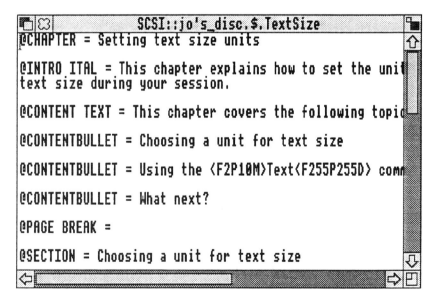

```
SCSI::jo's_disc.$.TextSize
@CHAPTER = Setting text size units

@INTRO ITAL = This chapter explains how to set the unit
text size during your session.

@CONTENT TEXT = This chapter covers the following topic

@CONTENTBULLET = Choosing a unit for text size

@CONTENTBULLET = Using the <F2P10M>Text<F255P255D> comm

@CONTENTBULLET = What next?

@PAGE BREAK =

@SECTION = Choosing a unit for text size
```

Use the Find option in the Edit menu to find all the control codes and characters and replace them with nothing. You may need to use the magic characters facility. This is described fully in the RISC OS *User Guide* or *User and Applications Guide* supplied with your computer. If there are a lot of styling commands used in the document and you want to try to keep some of them rather than re-doing all the styling, you may be able to use **Find to** replace the codes with Impression's own version of the codes.

Here are some codes you may find useful:

{"style" on}   turn on style (type the name of the style you want to use in place of style).

{"style" off}   turn off style

{font NewHall.bold}   change the font, as an effect, to NewHall.bold (type another font name you want to use in place of NewHall.bold, but you need to use the form of the font name used in the **Effect Font** submenu — so type Homerton.medium.oblique, not Homerton.italic, for example)

{font}   revert to the default font set by the style

{underline 1}   turn underlining on

{underline}   turn underlining off

{script super}   turn on superscript

{script sub}   turn on subscript

{script}   turn off superscript or subscript

{justify centre}   centre text as an effect

{justify right}   right-justify text as an effect

{justify full}   turn on full justification as an effect

{justify}   return to   left justification or turn on left justification as an effect

{tab}   move to the next tab stop

{\ n}   where n is a number between 128 and 255: insert the alternate character obtained by typing Alt-n.

{next frame}   force the following text to the start of the next frame.

To change the chunk of Ventura text shown above, you would need to use **Find** to make these replacements:

- Find \x0d and replace with nothing (magic characters on)

- Find @CHAPTER = and replace with {"Chapter" on}

- Find @INTRO ITAL = and replace with {"Intro ital" on}

- Find @CONTENTTEXT = and replace with {"ContentText" on}

- Find @CONTENTBULLET = and replace with {"ContentBullet" on}

- Find @PAGEBREAK = and replace with {next frame}

- Find @SECTION = and replace with {"Section" on}

- Find <F2P10M> and replace with {font Homerton.Medium.Oblique} (if you want to set the text in Homerton Oblique)

- Find <F255P255D> and replace with {font}

At the end of each style section you would have to set styles off with, for example, {"Chapter" off}.

If you don't feel happy making these changes to the file, remove all the control codes and characters and import the file just as plain text. If you do decide to try to convert the styles, make a back-up copy of your file first in case anything goes wrong.

Remember that some word-processing and desktop publishing programs have an option that allows you to save the text as plain ASCII text. If yours has such an option, using it may save you a lot of time and trouble. If it doesn't, there may be an option to remove all styling and formatting; this will help you to convert the file by reducing the number of codes you need to find and delete.

PC and Apple Macintosh discs

If you are using text prepared on a different type of computer, you may need a special program to read the discs. RISC OS 3 can read PC DOS discs anyway and shows their contents in an ordinary directory display, but to read PC discs with RISC OS 2 you will need either the PC emulator or a program for reading PC discs, such as PCDir from Norwich Computer Services, PC Access from Minerva or MultiFS from Arxe Systems. If you use PCDir, rename any files that have one of these suffixes: .TXT, .DXF, .C, .H, .SCR, .DOC, .ME, .PAS. These suffixes can cause problems if you are using WordStar or WordPerfect files. You can rename the file from DOS using the Rename command.

If you have a Macintosh file, you will first need to move it to a PC DOS disc before you can read it with your RISC OS computer. If your Macintosh has a Superdrive, save the file directly onto a DOS disc. If not, you will need a DOS mounter program. If you don't have either of these, take your disc to a bureau for conversion.

What next?

The next chapter explains how to set up Impression to give optimum performance on your computer and how to set some preferences about the way you want Impression to run.

19 Getting the most from Impression

There are some settings you can make and some extra items you can install to optimise the performance of Impression and tailor it to your own requirements. This chapter explains how to:

- choose the best screen mode for your computer

- make the most efficient use of your computer's memory

- add new fonts to your system.

Screen mode

Besides all the standard screen modes that your computer can use, some extra screen modes are supplied on the Impression discs. You might like to experiment with these and decide which is the best for your computer and your requirements. The most important factors to bear in mind are:

• the resolution of the screen display; this is how many dots (pixels) are used to render each inch of screen area

• the number of colours available; this may be 2, 4, 16 or 256

• the amount of memory required by the mode

• the frequency.

Generally, the higher the resolution and the more colours offered, the more memory the screen mode will need. High resolution modes and those that use many colours take more time to redraw the screen, too. You need to balance the quality of the screen display with the speed of redrawing the screen and the amount of memory your computer has. If you use a mode that has an inappropriate frequency for your monitor, the screen will probably flicker a lot. It is unpleasant and may be dangerous to use a flickering screen, so switch to another mode.

The appearance of the desktop with each mode and whether it is an improvement on the modes generally available will also depend on whether you have an ordinary monitor or a multisync monitor and whether you are using RISC OS 2 or RISC OS 3. Some of the new modes can only be used with multisync monitors. Chapter 2: *Getting ready to use Impression* describes how to load and try out the new modes supplied on Impression disc 2. Save any work you have open before trying out screen modes in case you set the machine to a mode that is so poor on your system that you need to reset the machine to restore a usable mode. Here are some guidelines on choosing a mode:

- 66 and 67 give a larger desktop on ordinary and multisync monitors. Because 67 has more colours than 66 it gives a better appearance — but it uses 240K rather than 120K. This is a large overhead, particularly on a 1Mb machine.

- 72 to 87 are for multisync monitors only. 72, 76, 80, 84 are poor quality monochrome modes that are not really good enough for text processing at a view scale of 100% unless you are using very large text. 73, 77, 81, 85 are better quality monochrome modes that are usable at 100% scale for normal sized text

- 88 to 91 give a larger logical desktop and can be used with ordinary and multisync monitors. On some monitors, they give an unusably small display.

- 92 to 95 are for multisync monitors only. Again, they give a very small display that isn't really usable for text of a normal size at 100% scale view.

The following table shows the memory requirements, number of colours and frequencies of different screen modes and indicates whether each is suitable for an ordinary monitor.

Mode	Colours	Memory	Frequency		Description
86	16	140K	63Hz	no	Acceptable colour display
87	256	280K	63Hz	no	Slow redraw; uses a lot of memory
88	2	20K	50Hz	yes	Poor quality monochrome; small display
89	4	40K	50Hz	yes	Better quality monochrome; small display
90	16	80K	50Hz	yes	Small display
91	256	160K	50Hz	yes	Small display; uses a lot of memory
92	2	40K	50Hz	no	Poor quality monochrome; small display
93	4	80K	50Hz	no	Better quality monochrome; small display
94	16	160K	50Hz	no	Small display
95	256	320K	50Hz	no	Small display; uses a lot of memory

If you have RISC OS 3, this has some extra screen modes that weren't available with RISC OS 2. Any screen modes that are already available on your machine and that clash with the Impression screen mode numbers will take precedence over the new modes, so you won't be able to try out or use the modes with the same numbers from the Impression disc.

If you didn't install the new modes supplied with Impression, you can experiment with them by putting disc 2 in the floppy drive, opening the directory Utils and double-clicking on NewModes. If you decide that you want to use the new modes, you don't have to reinstall Impression, you can just double-click on the directory NewModes when you want to use any of them. Chapter 20: *Making your own settings and customising Impression* tells you how to copy extra modules, such as NewModes, into the !Impress directory so that they are loaded automatically when you start up Impression.

If you decide to use a monochrome screen mode, you may like to use !SuperMono, also in Utils on Impression disc 2, to enhance the display. Double-click on this to load it and install its icon on the icon bar. When you are using a true monochrome mode (2 colours, not 4), it will improve the display. There is an icon bar menu for !SuperMono that offers halftoning. This is only available when you are using a monochrome screen mode. It gives better greyscale representation to improve the display. As it uses 16K of memory, use Quit from its icon bar menu to remove it if you don't want to use it.

Using the computer's memory efficiently

Impression uses quite a lot of memory and, especially in you have a 1Mb machine, you should try to make sure the memory is used as efficiently as possible so that you can run some other applications at the same time if you want to. Careful allocation of memory may mean that you can use another application, whereas if you leave your system as it is, you will have less memory available for other things.

You can save memory in each of these ways:

- choosing a memory-efficient screen mode

- setting the system sprite area to zero

- reducing the RMA and system allocations

- setting sensible values for the font cache parameters

- loading the spell checker from ROM (if you have the Spellmaster dictionary on ROM)

- using Impression's Minimise memory menu option to store parts of **large documents** on disc while working on them

- turning off the display of graphics.

Screen mode

The section above on screen modes will help you to choose a screen mode. However, it only describes the extra screen modes available. You can also choose from any of the standard screen modes. Mode 12 uses less memory than mode 15, but mode 11 is a usable monochrome mode that uses only half the memory that mode 12 uses; it takes only 40K. Mode 46 is a RISC OS 3 colour mode with slightly lower resolution than mode 12 and uses only 62.5K. If you have a VGA monitor, mode 25 gives a usable but not particularly elegant monochrome display and uses only 37.5K. Experiment with screen modes until you find one that works well for your screen, satisfying your requirements for redraw speed, screen resolution and memory use.

Configuration options

There are a few configuration options you can set to save memory all the time, not just when you are running Impression

You can set the system sprite area to zero without affecting the performance of the desktop or any RISC OS applications. In fact, Acorn recommends that you set it to zero for desktop use. You can also set the RMA size and system size to minimum values. To do this, press F12 (or choose *Commands from the system icon bar menu on RISC OS 3) to leave the desktop and use the command line at the bottom of the screen. (A cursor appears in a white strip below the icon bar.) Now type this text, pressing Return after each line:

```
co. spritesize 0K

co. rmasize 32K

co. systemsize 16K
```

Press Return again to go back to the desktop. These settings will be preserved even when you turn the machine off. If you want to set different values, you have to do it using these commands again.

Font cache

The font cache is an area of memory set aside for storing fonts. As you work, details of the fonts encountered or used in your document are stored in the font cache. The font cache starts at a given size and grows as necessary up to a maximum size. Fonts in the font cache can be redrawn on screen quickly as the computer doesn't need to refer to a hard or floppy disc for information about the fonts. A large font cache therefore means quicker screen redraws, but uses more memory. You will need to balance the speed of screen redraws with the amount of memory you are willing to tie up in the font cache. On a 1Mb machine, you will probably want to keep the font cache size fairly small. On a 4Mb or 8Mb machine, you could set it as large as 128K to get maximum screen redraw speed. The suggested values below are suitable for a 1Mb machine.

The font cache is controlled by three settings:

- FONTSIZE is the size that the font cache is set at to start with. Try 64K on a 1Mb machine.

- FONTMAX is the largest size the font cache is allowed to grow to. It won't automatically take up this amount of memory, but you must be sure that you set it to a value you can afford to allocate to it if it is needed. 128K is the minimum you can set. Try this on a 1Mb machine, and increase it if you find that screen redrawing becomes slow. Whether or not it does will depend on how many fonts and sizes you to tend to use in your documents. If you use very few, you won't have any problems with 128K.

- FONTMAX3 controls the largest size of character that will be stored in the cache. Generally, large text is used fairly infrequently, so it doesn't matter if the computer has to refer to the disc to draw large text because the increase in redrawing speed will be fairly small.

Setting a large value for FONTMAX3 so that even large font sizes can be cached uses a lot of memory for little return in redrawing speed. For a 1Mb machine, set it to 30; this means that characters larger than 30 pixels won't be cached (i.e. they will be retrieved from disc as necessary).

If your computer runs RISC OS 2, you will need to make these settings from the command line. Press F12 and then type:

```
co. fontsize 64K

co. fontmax 128K

co. fontmax3 30
```

Press Return at the end of each line, and then press it again to return to the desktop.

If your computer runs RISC OS 3, you can make the settings with !Configure. !Configure is stored in the ROM. Open a directory display for Apps (on the icon bar) and double-click on !Configure to open this directory display:

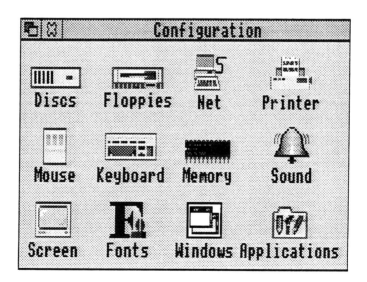

Double-click on Fonts to open this dialogue box:

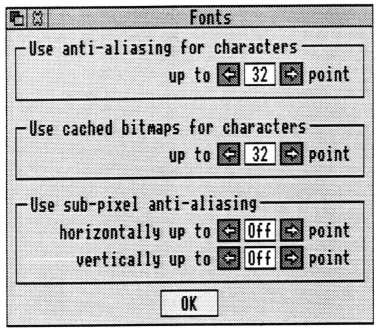

The second setting controls the size of characters that will be cached (FontMax3 described above). Increase or decrease the number using the arrow icons and then click on OK to save and use the setting. In RISC OS 3, the character size is set in points rather than pixels.

Double-click on Memory in the directory display to open this dialogue box:

Set the value for the font cache (equivalent to FontSize described above) and Font cache limit (equivalent to FontMax) using the arrow icons. If you set Font cache limit to 0k, there will be no limit to how large the cache can grow. This setting is not suitable for a 1MB machine. When you have made the settings you want, click on the close icon to remove the dialogue box.

Spell checker

When you load the spell checking dictionary, this takes up extra memory beyond the normal amount Impression takes to run. You can save about 90K if you have Spell-Master, a dictionary on ROM (a hardware chip that can be fitted into your computer). Spell-Master is available from Computer Concepts. If you order it, make sure you tell them what computer you have and whether it is running RISC OS 2 or RISC OS 3. You will also need an expansion card to hold the extra ROM, so if you are considering buying Spell-Master on ROM just to save memory, you might find that it is cheaper to upgrade your computer by adding an extra 1MB of memory. Your dealer can do this for you.

Minimise memory

There is an option on the Impression icon bar menu that enables you to make the most of the computer's memory while running Impression by keeping only a small portion of a document in memory at a time. The option **Minimise memory** tells Impression to read a short chunk of a document into memory and retrieve other sections from disc as necessary. Your document will be saved to disc as you move from one area to another. This means there will be more disc accessing, and processing a document will therefore be a little slower. However, if you have a

1MB computer and want to handle long documents, this provides a memory-efficient way of doing so.

Minimise memory can only work if the document has already been saved to disc or loaded from disc, as otherwise Impression won't know where to store the document. Impression always keeps the whole of the current chapter and any selected picture in the computer's memory (RAM). **Minimise memory** will therefore save you memory only if your document is more than one chapter long. Any frames that contain text saved to disc will be crossed out when visible on screen. You will be able to see that the frames are there, but not what they contain. If you want to load the contents of a frame, click in it. Impression may have to save some other part of the document to free enough memory to display the contents of the frame you have clicked on.

Hiding graphics

Pictures take up much more memory than text. To save memory, you can turn off the display of graphics. This also increases the screen redraw speed, as it is slow for the computer to redraw graphics, particularly complex pictures. You can hide all the pictures in your document using **Hide graphics** in the Misc menu. Pictures will appear as empty frames in your document, both on screen and in printouts. To re-display graphics or print them, use **Show graphics** in the Misc menu.

You can also hide a single picture. This can be useful if you have one particularly large and complex picture, but others that are small or quick to redraw, or that you need to be able to see. To hide a single picture, use the Hide graphic button in the Alter graphic dialogue box. Turn it back on by turning the button off again.

Hidden graphics are not printed, whether they are turned off individually or with all other graphics. You will need to turn one or all pictures back on before printing if you want to print any graphics.

Enhanced graphics

You may find that Impression's graphics handling is perfectly adequate for your requirements, especially if you generally use Draw files rather than sprites. However, if you want a better representation of the graphics, or if you want to be able to rotate sprites you have imported, you can use the Enhanced graphics option from the Preferences dialogue box to improve the appearance of monochrome graphics on screen and to enable you to rotate sprites in RISC OS 2. Enhanced graphics is described in chapter 11: *Graphics*.

The enhanced graphics option loads an extra module which takes up 20K of memory. Unless you want to rotate sprites in RISC OS 2, you may feel it isn't worth the memory overhead.

Adding extra fonts

At some point, you may decide that you want to add extra fonts to your system. Maybe you didn't add all the fonts supplied with Impression when you installed it, or maybe you have bought some extra fonts. In either case, you can copy them into your !Fonts directory and use them with Impression or any other application that uses text fonts. You will be able to print the fonts, but if you have a PostScript printer you may have to take a few extra steps before you can print them. You should only have one !Fonts directory on your system. As you get new fonts, follow the procedure described here to add them to a single !Fonts directory.

To add extra fonts, open the directory called !Fonts on a hard or floppy disc by holding down the Shift key and double-clicking on the directory icon. Inside is a directory for each font. Put the disc holding the new fonts into the floppy disc drive and open a directory display for the directory holding the new font(s) you want to add. Drag the directories for each font you want into your own !Fonts directory. When you have finished, close the directory and then click on the !Fonts icon once. This enables the computer to 'see' all the fonts so that it knows where to find them when you want to use them. The new fonts won't be available in any applications you had already loaded before copying the fonts as they will already have taken the information about fonts from the !Fonts directory before you added the new fonts. Save your work, then quit the applications and start them up again so that the fonts become available. You will be able to use your new fonts in Impression as soon as you load it after copying the fonts; you don't need to make any other settings. (Although most applications will be able to load fonts that you have copied, some require you to make extra settings; Acorn Desktop Publisher is an example. If you find that your new fonts aren't available in any applications, look at the user guide for the application to see if you need to make any changes.)

The fonts supplied with Impression are:

- Character

- Corpus

- Dingbats

- Greek

- Homerton

- Pembroke

- Trinity.

Corpus, Homerton and Trinity are supplied with all RISC OS computers and you will already have them in the !Fonts directory supplied on your hard disc or the Applications discs. If you have a RISC OS 3 computer, these fonts are stored in ROM (read-only memory) to save memory for you to use for applications and programs. **DO NOT** load the Impression versions of these fonts into your !Fonts directory if you are using RISC OS 3; it is unnecessary, as they are already available and are accessed more quickly from ROM and without using the memory available for programs. Loading the software versions of the fonts will confuse the computer.

PostScript printers

If you have a PostScript laser printer, you may have to do a little extra before you can print your new fonts. PostScript printers have a limited number of resident fonts; if you want to use any more fonts, you must either buy the fonts and install them in your printer or download them from the computer.

If you are using RISC OS 2 and your new fonts don't match any already resident in the printer, you will need to check whether you have been given PostScript versions of the fonts and whether you need to buy a font for the printer.

If you are using RISC OS 3, you can download any screen font to use with the printer. The procedure is described in chapter 16: *Printing Impression documents.*

What next?

The next chapter explains how to make some settings to customise Impression for your own use. This can involve setting preferences, altering the default document loaded when you open a new document and changing the choices you made when you installed Impression.

20 Making your own settings and customising Impression

There are several settings you can make so that Impression behaves as you want it to. These involve setting preferences from the icon bar menu. You can also make changes to the default document that Impression loads when you start it up and open a new document. You can change the settings you made when you originally installed Impression, too. This chapter describes how to:

- set the units Impression uses for measurements

- set the default view sizes used for document and master pages

- set display option defaults

- set defaults for spell checking and abbreviations

- make new frames snap to existing frames

- use 'smart quotes' for imported text

- turn hyphenation on or off for all documents and styles

- alter the default document loaded when you open a new document

- change the installation by adding or removing modules.

To change any except the last two of these, you need to use the **Preferences** option on the icon bar menu. It displays a dialogue box like this:

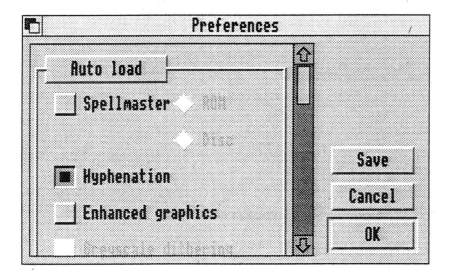

Your changes will take effect when you click on OK.

Units of measurement

Impression can use up to three different units of measurement for different things. You can choose from a wide range of units. By default, Impression uses:

- millimetres to measure distances relating to the page, such as page size and frame size (Page units on the dialogue box)

- points to measure text size, line spacing, and so on (Style units)

- centimetres for the ruler (Ruler units).

To set the units, scroll through the preferences dialogue box until this section is visible:

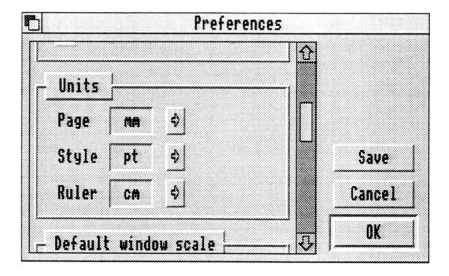

There is a menu button beside each setting. Click on this to display the units available, and then click on the unit you want to use. The units are:

- millimetres

- centimetres

- metres

- inches

- feet

- yards

- points

- picas.

It is difficult to envisage circumstances in which you would want to set feet, yards or metres as your units for anything, let along for text, but they are all available if you want them.

Whichever units you pick will be used to report measurements shown on the screen. This includes the active display of a frame's size as you are defining it, the space and font size show in the Style dialogue box and the positions of ruler items. However, you can input sizes in any of the units Impression recognises as long as you use its standard abbreviations (mm, cm, m, in, ft, yd, pt, pi).

View sizes

When you open a new window, it is scaled at 100%, so the document appears at its actual size. Depending on the page size your document uses and the screen mode you want to use, this may mean that not all of your document is visible on screen at once, even if you make the window large enough to fill the screen. You can alter the default size at which pages of your document will be displayed, and the size at which the master pages will be displayed.

Scroll through the Preferences dialogue box until you get to the Default window scale section:

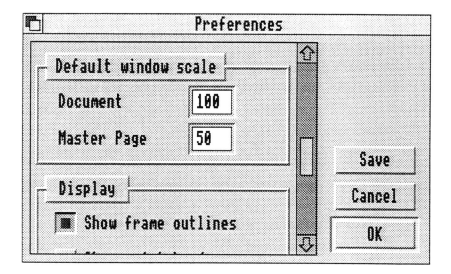

The sizes shown are scales given as percentages (so 100% in the document field means that the document pages will be shown at full size). Type the scale you want to use in each field. You must use the same format (i.e. a percentage) and not a scale such as 2:1.

Setting display option defaults

As well as setting the default view scale, you can set four other viewing options:

*   whether to show the outlines of frames

*   whether to show the margins in which the printer can't print

*   whether to show page rulers all the time

*   whether to make the cursor flash on and off.

These are all set from the Display section of the Preferences dialogue box:

```
┌──────────────────────────────────────────────────┐
│ ▣        Preferences                               │
│  ┌─ Display ─────────────────────┐  ⬆             │
│  │  ▣  Show frame outlines        │                │
│  │                                │                │
│  │  ⬜  Show print borders         │                │
│  │                                │    ┌─────────┐ │
│  │  ⬜  Show page rulers           │    │  Save   │ │
│  │                                │    └─────────┘ │
│  │  ▣  Flashing cursor            │    ┌─────────┐ │
│  │                                │    │ Cancel  │ │
│  └────────────────────────────────┘    └─────────┘ │
│                                       ┌─────────┐  │
│     Micn                              │   OK    │  │
│                                   ⬇   └─────────┘  │
└──────────────────────────────────────────────────┘
```

If you turn off Frame outlines, you will be able to see the contents of the frames (text and graphics) but the edges of the frames won't be shown. Any printing borders you have added to frames will be shown. The currently active frame will have a visible border, too.

If you turn on Show print borders, a pale grey border around the page will appear showing the area that the currently loaded printer driver can't print in. If there is no printer driver loaded, a default limit is shown.

If you turn on Show page rulers, rulers are shown along the top and the lefthand edge of the page. These are not the same as the rulers that you use to define attributes of a style, but can help you to position frames and graphics.

If you turn off Flashing cursor, the cursor remains on screen all the time. In monochrome screen modes in particular, it is easier to see the cursor if it is flashing.

Spell checking and abbreviations

If you want to use spell checking and/or expansion of abbreviations, you can set these on in the Preferences dialogue box so that they will be started up automatically for each document you open and you won't need to use the Spelling and Abbreviation options from the Misc menu each time. Move to the bottom of the Preferences dialogue box to display the Misc section:

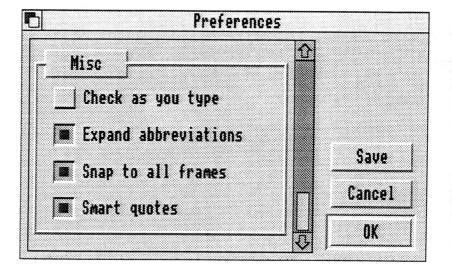

If you turn on the button beside Expand abbreviations, your abbreviation default dictionary will be loaded when you start Impression and will be used to expand the abbreviations you type.

If you turn on Check as you type, you will also need to load a dictionary automatically. To do this, move to the top of the Preferences dialogue box to the Auto load section:

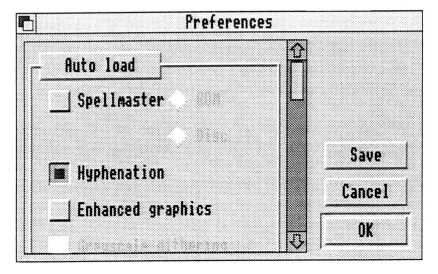

Turn on Spell-Master. If you have bought Spell-master on ROM, turn on the button beside ROM. If you haven't, turn on the button beside Disc to load the dictionary from disc when you start Impression. This will cost you an overhead in memory (more if you use Spell-Master from disc than from ROM), so if you have a 1MB computer, think carefully before setting this on as a default.

Snapping frames

When you create a new frame, it will automatically snap to any guide frames you are creating it over or near. This makes it easy to align frames in regular columns. However, you can also make frames snap to any nearby frames. To use this, move to the Misc section at the end of the Preferences dialogue box and turn on Snap to all frames.

Smart quotes

The quotation marks available from the typewriter keys on the keyboard are straight marks that don't distinguish between opening and closing : " and '. If you want to use different opening and closing marks, ', ', " and ", you need to get these using !Chars or the Alt key in combination with these codes:

- Alt-144: '

- Alt-145: '

- Alt-148: "

- Alt-149: "

However, when you import text from another file (perhaps one you have created with 1st Word Plus or Edit), you can instruct Impression to use these 'smart' quotes automatically. To do so, turn on the button beside Smart quotes in the Misc section at the end of the Preferences dialogue box.

The opening and closing quotation marks are called 'smart' because Impression has to look at each instance of ' or " and decide whether it is an opening or closing quotation mark and substitute the appropriate mark accordingly. It is best to check through your file after importing it to make sure that Impression has got it right everywhere.

Remember that any quotation marks you type into the document yourself as you edit it will be straight marks unless you remember to use the Alt combinations instead. Your document will look untidy if you mix smart and straight quotation marks.

The smart quotes option also interprets any double dashes typed with the hyphen key (-) as a long dash—, called an em dash, that is commonly used as a punctuation mark. For example, if you read in a file containing this text:

He said: "No - I don't think so".

It would appear in Impression as:

He said:"No — I don't think so".

(The Alt key combination for an em dash is Alt-152.)

If you are importing a program listing, don't use the smart quotes option as the computer will not recognise smart quotes and em dashes in a program: you must use straight quotation marks and hyphens.

Hyphenation

You can set hyphenation on or off for each style individually, but unless you turn on hyphenation with the Preferences dialogue box (or from the dictionary dialogue box), the hyphenation module won't be loaded and hyphenation won't work for any styles. To auto-load the hyphenation module, turn on the button beside Hyphenation in the first section of the Preferences dialogue box.

If you don't auto-load the hyphenation module, you will only be able to use hyphenation in any individual style if you load the hyphenation module from the Dictionary dialogue box. To do this, use **Dictionary** from the Spelling submenu (from Misc) and then use the menu button beside the field saying Main dictionary and click on Exception. A warning dialogue box will appear telling you that the hyphenation module is not loaded. This dialogue box has a Load button; click on it to load the hyphenation module. Hyphenation will then be available.

Changing the default document

When you open a new Impression document, it is copied from a master document held inside the !Impress directory. This sets up the master pages and styles that appear by default. If you create a large number of documents that use the same layout, or if you always want your BaseStyle to be different from the 14pt Trinity of a default new document, you can alter the default document. Indeed, if you like you can customise this document considerably, perhaps putting master pages for all your common documents into it and removing master page formats you never use. If you use Impression for business, for example, you could create master pages for your letterhead, invoices, statements, orders, credit notes and so on. You can then call up whichever you want to use by using **Alter chapter** and giving the master page number you want.

Don't change the default document on the original Impression discs. Always leave this so that you can reinstate the default if you change your mind or do anything wrong. Change just your working copy of Impression.

To open the default document, hold down the Shift key and double-click on the !Impress icon in the directory display. This will open a directory display like this:

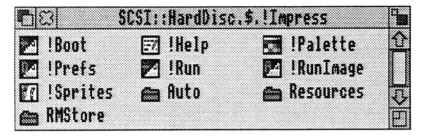

Now open the directory called Auto; this contains an Impression document called !Default. !Default is the default new document. You can open it by double-clicking on its icon. Make any changes you want to the master pages and styles, and then save the document with the same name. Alternatively, create the document you want to use as the default and save this in the !Impress directory as !Default. Rename, delete or move the original !Default first. Save any other documents you have loaded and remove Impression from the icon bar using **Quit** in its icon bar menu. When you reload Impression it will use your new default document each time you click on the Impression icon to open a new document.

Changing the installation settings

When you originally installed Impression you made some choices about which loader modules and draft printing modules to use, and whether to use NewModes. You can change the installation you chose without reinstalling Impression if your requirements later change.

If you installed Impression using the !Install program, any loader modules and draft printing modules, and NewModes if you chose to use it, will have been copied into a directory inside !Impress. If you occasionally want to use some modules that you haven't installed, you can load them when you need them by putting the disc holding them into the floppy disc drive and double-clicking on their icons in the directory display. However, if you want to install a module for frequent use, you can copy it to the appropriate place in !Impress and it will be loaded each time you start Impression just as if you had installed it at the beginning.

To copy loader or printer modules or NewModes into your installed version of Impression, open a directory display for !Impress, then hold down the Shift key and double-click on !Impress. In the directory display that appears, double-click on the directory Auto. Now copy in any modules you want to load each time you start up Impression. You can use this procedure to copy in the extra modules supplied with Impression Business Supplement, too.

What next?

The next chapter shows a few examples of layouts you can achieve with Impression and explains how to do them. The files described are all provided on the disc that accompanies this book.

21 Examples

This chapter shows you a few designs that might give you inspiration for your own work. The chapter is rather different from the others in that it shows you examples of pages and then explains briefly how to recreate them. All the documents illustrated are on the disc that accompanies this book. The styles used in each are not described fully here. To see details of a style, select some text in the document on the disc and use **Edit style** to display the style dialogue box.

Document 1: Business letterhead

This is a simple business letterhead:-

GREY STRIPE PUBLISHING LTD

143 Grosvenor Road, Houghton, Derbyshire, DB12 6RT
Tel. 0774 719940 Fax. 0774 719818

VAT No. 513 2883 20
Regd No. 1234567890 Regd Office: 143 Grosvenor Road, Houghton, Derbyshire DB12 6RT
Directors: K G Barry, P L Phillipps

It uses two master pages: the first creates the headed page but the next page does not have the letterhead so that it forms a continuation page. If you wanted to have several continuation pages you could create a page 3, then a page 4 and delete the page 3, so getting another continuation sheet. Alternatively, you could delete the frames holding the letterhead, logo and company details on page 3. As we have made the main text frame on master page 1 as large as the frame on the continuation sheet, but put it behind the frames holding the letterhead and logo, the text frame will already be the right size when you delete the letterhead on page 3.

The logo was created in Draw and dragged into a frame on the master page.

Document 2: Domestic letterhead

This is a letterhead for a domestic address:-.

Sylvia Bunch
125 Beechwood Close
Cambridge CB3 1TH
Tel. 0223 68119

This uses two master pages again, with the address details on the first page and the next page blank for a continuation sheet. Follow the instructions for document 1 to get extra continuation sheets. If you want to change this letterhead to use for your own address, change the address details on the master page.

Document 3: Labels template

This is a template for the sheets of sticky labels available for feeding into laser printers.

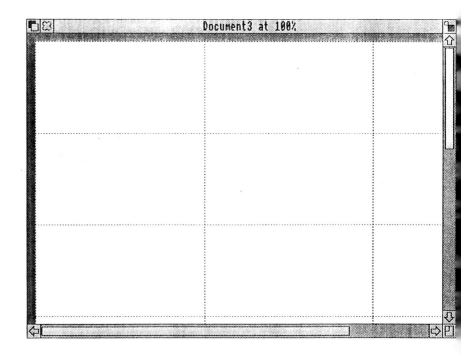

It has a single master page holding 24 frames, one for each label. The master page was originally created with three guide frames using no margins and no gaps between columns. A single frame was created on the master page, then **Alter frame** was used to set its size exactly, to set text repel outside the frame off, and to set internal repelling margins of 5mm vertical and 7mm horizontal. These margins keep the text away from the very edge of the label. If there is a slight error in how the paper is fed, the text will not be able to run from one label onto the next because there is a clear margin of 5mm top and bottom and 7mm left and right on each label. The frame was copied 23 times and the copies positioned with snap to all frames set on. The frame was copied 23 times and the copies positioned with snap to all frames set on. The frames were then linked in sequence from left to right across the rows and top to bottom down the page. Because the frames are linked, you can drag in your existing mailing list to the top lefthand frame on page 1 and the list will flow through all the labels, creating new pages if necessary. You may need to add extra Returns so that a new address always begins on a new label. There is room for six lines of text on a label this size. If all your addresses are shorter than this, you could increase the point size of BaseStyle to 11pt to make the labels more easily legible and to avoid having to add so many Returns to move the first line of each new address onto a new label.

Document 4: Newsletter

This is the first page of a newsletter layout.

Beeston Toddlers' Group NEWSLETTER

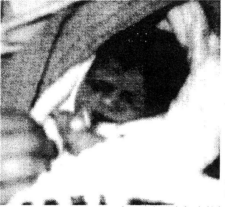

Lauren in hospital after the birth

BABY LAUREN BORN AT PLAYGROUP

Baby Lauren Sumner was so keen to join Beeston Toddlers Group she arrived early – Lauren was born at the playgroup while her mother was there with older brother Todd.

After a lightening-quick labour of 35 minutes, which didn't allow mum time to get to hospital, Lauren was born at 12.17 weighing 2.85kg – a healthy 6lb 5oz.

Her mother said : 'I won't need to put her name down early for the Toddlers Group; she's already made it clear she wants to join!'

Rebecca wins championship

Rebecca Nevis, the five-year-old gymnast who attended Beeston Toddlers Group until she started school in September has won a regional gymnasts' championship for under-10s.

Rebecca has been practising gymnastics for two years and now her brother Paul, three, wants to start.

On winning the champtionship, Rebecca said: 'It's great. I tried really hard and I won. I'm very happy.'

Her prize was £100 for her school to spend on sports equipment and the chance to compete in the national finals next month. Rebecca's mother will accompany her on the trip to London to compete in the finals.

Rain spoils fete

Beeston Toddlers' Group and the Beeston City Football Club had organised a fete for last Sunday. However, weather-forecasts warned of rain and the fete was called off at the last minute. Organiser Sally Lord said 'We were obviously all very disappointed. Everyone had worked very hard to make things for the fete and to collect jumble and organise games but in the end nothing came of it. We hope to reorganise it for a weekend next month, perhaps after the school holidays have started and there are fewer school activities to compete with it for parents' time, attention and money.'

If you would like to help by providing anything for sale or for use as a raffle prize, or if you would like to run a stall or game, contact Sally Lord on Beeston 879310.

Bring and buy sale raises £98

Beeston Toddlers' Group annual bring and buy sale raised £98 last month. The most successful stall was Mrs Sanjit's cake and chutney stall, which raised £47.60. Hers was the most successful stall last year, too. Mrs Sanjit says her secret family recipes are so good that no one can resist them – it looks as though she's right!

Inside this issue

The pair of master pages have only guide frames, which form the basic layout for the three columns. The header and footer text is in frames on the master page. The masthead was created by writing the word NEWSLETTER in a Draw file in grey 45pt Homerton bold with the font height set to 70pt. This was imported into a frame on the page, and another frame was then superimposed to hold the rest of the title. This second frame was adjusted with **Alter frame** to give it a transparent background.

The photograph of the baby was scanned in and imported into a frame, then scaled to fit the frame. The frame size was adjusted to get rid of blank space.

The BaseStyle was edited to give it a first line margin of 4mm to create the indented paragraphs. 'Inside this issue' is in a centred style in a transparent frame laid over a grey frame. The grey frame was created on top of the text to start with, and then sent to the back of the stack with **Put to back** in the Frame menu. The items in the contents list have a right tab set at 5.7cm with the leading string '. . ' (fullstop-space-fullstop-space).

If you have the disc that accompanies this book, you will be able to see that the second page has been left blank to show the guide frames.

Document 5: Pamphlet

This is a simple pamphlet advertising the menu of a pizza delivery company.

Phone 0916 71934 for pizza deliveries night and day.

Catering for parties by arrangement.

ANTONIO'S GOLDEN PIZZA PARLOUR

14 FRIDAY STREET, WEYBURY
Tel: 0916 71934 for 24 hour delivery service

DRINKS

Fresh fruit salad with Greek yoghurt	2.20
Coffee cream cake	2.30
Ice cream (vanilla/chocolate/strawberry)	1.80
Italian beer (0.3ltr)	1.40
Frascati (75cl)	5.00
Valpolicella (75cl)	6.00
Fruit juice (apple, orange, pineapple)	0.80
Soft drinks (cola, lemonade, orangeade)	0.80
Mineral water (still or sparkling)	0.80
Capuccino	1.10
Espresso	0.90
Cafe latte	1.10
Hot chocolate with cream	1.30

Price include VAT.

Please be sure you give your address and credit card details when ordering by phone.

PIZZAS

Tomato and cheese	2.75
Mushrooms, garlic and cheese (no tomato)	3.15
Sausage, onion, tomato and cheese	3.80
Pepperoni, basil, tomato and cheese	3.80
Capers, red pepper, tomato and cheese	3.60
Spinach, egg, tomato and cheese	3.50
Prawn, pine nuts, courgette and cheese (no tomato)	4.80
Anchovies, onions, tomato and cheese	3.80
Red pepper, green pepper, tomato and capers (no cheese)	3.60

PASTA

Tagliatelle, smoked ham and mushroom in a cream sauce	4.50
Spaghetti, minced beef and onions in a tomato and herb sauce	4.50
Cheese and spinach ravioli in a creamy cheese sauce	4.25
Paglia e fieno, prawns, courgettes in a creamy cheese sauce	5.50
Lasagna with mixed vegetables and tomato and cream sauces	4.30

SIDE ORDERS

Garlic bread	1.10
Garlic bread with herbs	1.20
Garlic bread with cheese	1.40
Mixed seasonal side salad	1.70
Green side salad	1.50
Italian bread	1.10
Grated parmesan cheese	0.60

DESSERTS

Zabaglione	2.10
Tiramisu	2.10
Chocolate fudge cake	1.90
Strawberry cheesecake	1.90

The first and last pages have frames with borders (using border 10). The frame on the last page was made local with the Alter frame dialogue box and changed in size. **Force to next** in the Frame menu was used to force items of text onto the next page when necessary, as at the start of page 2.

The subheadings for the different categories of food have a coloured text background set with the Style dialogue box. The prices are given after a decimal tab.

The document is intended for printing as a pamphlet, with the scale set to 66%, and with the Fit lots and Sideways options chosen.

Document 6: Report

The document uses a single master page which holds the main text frame and the footer frame and text (a page number added with Insert Current page number):-

REPORT TO STANDING COMMITTEE

A J Kegan

27 September 1992

Mainheading

This is some text that could be a report. The text doesn't say anything useful but it is a convenient way of showing the layout of the text and the styles that can be used. This is some text that could be a report. The text doesn't say anything useful but it is a convenient way of showing the layout of the text and the styles that can be used. This is some text that could be a report. The text doesn't say anything useful but it is a convenient way of showing the layout of the text and the styles that can be used. This is some text that could be a report. The text doesn't say anything useful but it is a convenient way of showing the layout of the text and the styles that can be used.

This is some text that could be a report. The text doesn't say anything useful but it is a convenient way of showing the layout of the text and the styles that can be used. This is some text that could be a report. The text doesn't say anything useful but it is a convenient way of showing the layout of the text and the styles that can be used.

SubheadingA

This is some text that could be a report. The text doesn't say anything useful but it is a convenient way of showing the layout of the text and the styles that can be used. This is some text that could be a report. The text doesn't say anything useful but it is a convenient way of showing the layout of the text and the styles that can be used. This is some text that could be a report. The text doesn't say anything useful but it is a convenient way of showing the layout of the text and the styles that can be used. This is some text that could be a report. The text doesn't say anything useful but it is a convenient way of showing the layout of the text and the styles that can be used.

SubheadingB

This is some text that could be a report. The text doesn't say anything useful but it is a convenient way of showing the layout of the text and the styles that can be used.

This is some text that could be a report. The text doesn't say anything useful but it is a convenient way of showing the layout of the text and the styles that can be used. This is some text that could be a report. The text doesn't say anything useful but it is a convenient way of showing the layout of the text and the styles that can be used. This is some text that could be a report. The text doesn't say anything useful but it is a convenient way of showing the layout of the text and the styles that can be used.

2

SubheadingA

This is some text that could be a report. The text doesn't say anything useful but it is a convenient way of showing the layout of the text and the styles that can be used. This is some text that could be a report. The text doesn't say anything useful but it is a convenient way of showing the layout of the text and the styles that can be used.

SubheadingB

This is some text that could be a report. The text doesn't say anything useful but it is a convenient way of showing the layout of the text and the styles that can be used.

SubheadingB

This is some text that could be a report. The text doesn't say anything useful but it is a convenient way of showing the layout of the text and the styles that can be used.

SubheadingB

This is some text that could be a report. The text doesn't say anything useful but it is a convenient way of showing the layout of the text and the styles that can be used.

This is some text that could be a report. The text doesn't say anything useful but it is a convenient way of showing the layout of the text and the styles that can be used.

This is some text that could be a report. The text doesn't say anything useful but it is a convenient way of showing the layout of the text and the styles that can be used.

SubheadingA

This is some text that could be a report. The text doesn't say anything useful but it is a convenient way of showing the layout of the text and the styles that can be used.

Mainheading

This is some text that could be a report. The text doesn't say anything useful but it is a convenient way of showing the layout of the text and the styles that can be used. This is some text that could be a report. The text doesn't say anything useful but it is a convenient way of showing the layout of the text and the styles that can be used. This is some text that could be a report. The text doesn't say anything useful but it is a convenient way of showing the layout of the text and the styles that can be used.

This is some text that could be a report. The text doesn't say anything useful but it is a convenient way of showing the layout of the text and the styles that can be used. This is some text that could be a report. The text doesn't say anything useful but it is a convenient way of showing the layout of the text and the styles that can be used.

SubheadingA

This is some text that could be a report. The text doesn't say anything useful but it is a convenient way of showing the layout of the text and the styles that can be used. This is some text that could be a report. The text doesn't say anything useful but it is a convenient way of showing the layout of the text and the styles that can be used. This is some text that could be a report. The text doesn't say anything useful but it is a convenient way of showing the layout of the text and the styles that can be used.

PART 2

4

345

Pages 2 and 3 have a repeating grey frame containing text rotated in Draw using RISC OS 3, but it could have been created with !FontDraw using RISC OS 2. Page 4 has a grey repeating frame, again with rotated text, but in a different position.

The BaseStyle has a left margin and first line left margin of 25 mm. All the heading styles that centre text or set it to the left of the BaseStyle margin (outdented headings) have these two margins set to 0mm. If centred styles did not have this margin set the text would be centred between 25mm and the righthand margin. Text on page 2 has been forced to the top of this page by using **Force to next** from the Frame menu; it could have been done by making this a new chapter. Text on page 4 does begin a new chapter.

The frame on page 1 has been made local and its size has been adjusted.

Document 7: Business set

This document has master pages defined for some of the documents a business might want to use:-

AARDVARK EARTH-MOVING EQUIPMENT

Tandy Industrial Estate
Willington
Cambs CB6 8TR
Tel. 0734 51946

VAT Reg No 914 2396 45

Proprietor: Jake Mills

AARDVARK EARTH-MOVING EQUIPMENT

Tandy Industrial Estate
Willington
Cambs CB6 8TR
Tel. 0734 51946

VAT Reg No 914 2396 45

INVOICE

Date & tax point:

Qty	Description	Unit price	Extension
		Sub-total	
		VAT	
		Total	

E&OE: Terms 30 days nett.

Proprietor: Jake Mills

AARDVARK EARTH-MOVING EQUIPMENT

Tandy Industrial Estate
Willington
Cambs CB6 8TR
Tel. 0734 51946

VAT Reg No 914 2396 45

STATEMENT

Date & tax point:

Date	Ref	Debit	Credit	Balance

Proprietor: Jake Mills

name here

job title here

AARDVARK EARTH-MOVING EQUIPMENT

Tandy Industrial Estate
Willington
Cambs CB6 8TR
Tel. 0734 51946

There is a master page for ordinary letters, one for invoices, one for statements and one for business cards. The first three master pages are A4; the final master page is very small. This would be suitable for generating a file to take to an imagesetter when the individual's name and job title had been filled in.

The first three master pages are all single A4 pages. Each page in the document is a different chapter, and uses a different master page. The people working for this business could save this document with the name !Default inside the Auto directory in the !Impress directory and it would be opened automatically each time they started a new Impression document. They could then use **Alter chapter** in the Edit menu to select the master page they wanted to use according to which type of document they wanted to create. For example, someone wanting to create an invoice would open a new document, then use Alter chapter and set the master page to 2; the invoice template would then be used for the page.

The frames that make up the forms for the invoice and statement are all transparent so that the borders are fully visible. There is only one border on each edge. This means that where two frames abut each other, only one has a border set for the side touching the other frame. This is necessary to keep the borders the right width. The borders are always added to the same side of two frames that line up, too, to keep the lines of the form aligned properly. In the two pairs of adjoining frames below, the border in the top pair of frames has been set in the lefthand frame and in the bottom pair it has been set in the righthand frame. You can see that the lines don't match up properly.

This is because the border is added to the outside of the frame, so in the top pair it has been added to the right of the shared edge and in the lower pair it has been added to the left of the shared edge.

It isn't possible to build up these forms on the master page using styles with vertical and horizontal rules set, as this then becomes text on the master page which can't be altered on a body page. This means that the details of the invoice can't be added. Because you can't mix text from a master page and text you are adding to body pages in the same frame, the label 'Date & tax point:' is in a frame of its own, with another frame for the information to be added in each letter.

Document 8: Quiz

This document uses a pair of master pages so that there can be a large inner margin for double-sided copying and binding.

QUIZ

This quiz will help you to discover whether you have a healthy lifestyle. Answer the questions honestly. Tick a box to indicate the response that it most accurate for you.

1.   How much alcohol do you drink?

     0–2 units a week

     3–10 units a week

     10–20 units a week

     more than 20 units a week

2.   How often do you exercise?

     less than 20 minutes a week

     21–60 minutes a week

     1–3 hours a week

     more than 3 hours a week

3.   How much do you smoke?

     not at all, and have never smoked

     1–5 a day

     6–20 a day

     more than 20 a day

     used to smoke, but have given up

4.   Which of these do you eat regularly?

Chips and other fried foods

Chocolates and sweets

Puddings and cakes

Fresh fruit and vegetables

5.   How much tea and coffee do you drink?

None

1–3 cups a day

4–7 cups a day

8 or more cups a day

6.   How much do you sleep each night?

fewer than 6 hours

6–8 hours

more than 8 hours

The document has a style set, called Options, for drawing tick boxes. The boxes are made up from vertical and horizontal rules. The style has two vertical rules set, at 11 and 13 cm. It has a rule-off set above the text with 0pt offset, and one set below with -2pt offset. The rule-off left margin is 11 cm and the rule-off right margin is 13 cm. This means that both rules are drawn between 11 and 13 cm, which matches the positions for the vertical rules that make up the sides of the boxes. Vertical and horizontal rules have thickness 1pt. There is no need to press Tab after the text in a line using the Options style; the box is completed when Return is pressed, as this is when the final rule is added.

You can use horizontal and vertical rules in this way to construct tables, tick-boxes, and anything else that requires boxed text.

What next?

The next chapter explains what you get if you buy Impression Business Supplement and how to use it. You may want to buy this if you plan to use Impression professionally. It provides some extra loader modules, facilities for imagesetting at a print bureau, and a mail-merge program.

22 Impression Business Supplement

If you use Impression professionally you may want the extended facilities offered by the Business Supplement. The Business Supplement gives you:

- a mail-merge program, allowing you to produce batches of personalised letters

- facilities for preparing files for imagesetting, including colour separations

- extra loader modules.

This chapter outlines these features to help you decide whether you need the Business Supplement.

It also explains briefly how to use the items that make up the Business Supplement.

Mail-merge

A mail-merge system enables you to produce a series of similar documents in which a few details differ from one copy to another. You are probably familiar with the junk mail offers that appear to be addressed to you personally and yet obviously present the same offer to everyone. These are generated with a mail-merge program. However, there are some useful things you can do with mail-merge, too, such as sending personalised letters to all your customers advising them of new products.

A mail-merge system needs two types of file: a master letter, which contains the main text and references to data to be retrieved from the second file, which is a data file holding names, addresses and other details. To use Impression's mail-merge facility, you need to create your master letter as an Impression document, but your data file as a plain text (Edit) file. You can then use the application !Importer to produce your merged letters. You can sort the letters into alphabetical order and remove any duplicates, if you like, using the !Sorter program. These two programs are supplied as Impression Business Supplement's mail-merge facility.

Creating your data file

The data file must be saved as a plain text file. You can create it in Edit, or you can create it in Impression and use the **Save text story** option without saving the styles.

The data for each letter forms a *record*. A record may contain several *fields*. Each field must be on a separate line and you need to leave a blank line between each record. In the master document, you will need to refer to the information in the data file by giving the number of the field. You must put the data in the same order for each record so that an instruction to retrieve the data from field 2, for example, always retrieves the same item (the recipient's name, perhaps).

You will probably want to include addresses in your data file. As an address may have as few as two lines or as many as six or seven, you will need to allow for the longest address when writing the master document. The address details should come last in each record as it doesn't then matter how many lines there are in the address. If you put the address details before the end, a short address will result in data from the next field being hijacked for the final line(s) of an address. For example, if you give three address lines in your master document and your data file gives the address followed by the person's car registration number, a person with just a two-line address will get the car registration appended as line 3 of the address.

In the example shown below and included on the disc that accompanies this book, the letter informs customers that their car insurance premium has been increased. The variable items of data that are included in the data file are the names and addresses of customers, their car registration numbers and the amount they will each have to pay.

In this example, each record has seven fields, the first giving the customer's name, the second giving the car registration number, the third field giving the price of the premium and the last four fields giving the address:

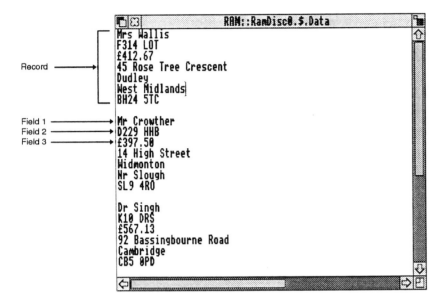

Dr Singh has only three lines in her address, so it is important that the address comes at the end of each record in this data file.

Make sure you press Return at the end of the last line in the data file and then save it as a text file.

Creating your master document

Your master letter must have the layout, styles and text that you want to appear in your final letters. The only difference between it and your final letters is that in place of all the customised information that will change between letters, you need to include an instruction to the Importer program to find the appropriate data. When you want to add an instruction, use the **Merge command** option from the Misc menu. A dialogue box like this appears:

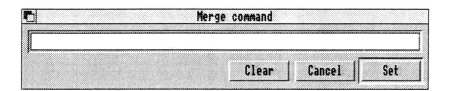

You will need to refer to your data items by the field number. The instruction you need to type to tell Importer to retrieve data from a field in the text file has the format

    :Importer GetField <n>

where <n> is replaced with the field number. The field number represents the data item that will be inserted, such as :Importer GetField 4 to substitute the data from field 4 in the position of the merge command. The commands are not case-sensitive, so you can use any combination of upper and lower case in the merge command field.

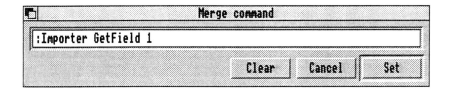

You can also add the current time and/or date using the special instruction

    :Importer GetTimeDate

You can specify the format for the time/date if you like using the formats recognised by RISC OS. These are described in your RISC OS *User Guide*.

Use the **Merge command** option when the cursor is at the position at which you want to insert the command. For example, you may begin your letter by giving the recipient's name and address, so you would need to put the cursor at the top of the page (the default position) and then use the **Merge command**. To retrieve the recipient's name from the first field in the data file, type `:Importer GetField 1` in the writable icon and then click on Set. In the document, the command is shown like this: `<Merge>`. You would then press Return to move the cursor to the next line and use the **Merge command** again to add the command `:Importer GetField 2`, which again will appear in the document as `<Merge>`.

Eventually, you will have a document that looks something like this:-

See following page

J Shark & Co

14 Radley Court Road
Bassingbourne
Cambs CB3 5ED
Tel: 0318 63015; Fax: 0318 63234
VAT Reg No 891 2310 56

<Merge>
<Merge>
<Merge>
<Merge>

<Merge>

Dear <Merge>

I regret that since your claim earlier this year, the premium for insuring your vehicle registration number <Merge> has been increased to <Merge>.

A revised direct debit has been enclosed; please complete it and send it to your bank. If you fail to do so before the end of the month, your insurance will lapse.

Yours sincerely,

J Shark

Registered office: 14 Radley Court Road Bassingbourne Cambs CB3 5ED

Save the master document as a normal Impression document and close it down using **Remove document** from the icon bar or document menu. (If you don't remove it, the merge operation will still work, but a warning dialogue box will appear telling you the document is already loaded when you try to use it. If this happens, just click on OK.)

Running the merge program

Once you have a master document and a data file, you are ready to run a mail-merge job. Open a directory display for the Business Supplement disc, open the directory MailMerge and double-click on the !Importer icon. This doesn't load onto the icon bar, but appears as a window like this on the desktop:

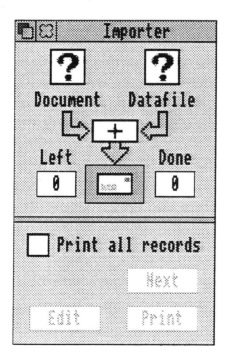

The program doesn't create files for all the merged documents; you are intended to send them directly to the printer. You can edit a merged file, but the merge job is abandoned as soon as you decide to edit a document. It is important to load a printer driver and make sure the printer is ready before you begin the merge operation. Close any other Impression document windows you have open as Impression may print the wrong document if you leave others open.

When you are ready, drag the icon for your data file (the text file) onto the window. Its icon appears in place of the ? icon on the right. Now drag the icon for your master document onto the window. Its icon appears in place of the ? on the left and Importer begins to process your files. The window reports how many files have been processed (Done) and how many remain (Left). The processed document is visible on screen, but the pointer changes to a cross if you move it over the document, showing that you can't make any changes, place the cursor or even display the menu. After the first document has been processed, click on Print to print it out, or Next to process the next one. If you click on Next, the first will be lost as the next one writes over it. You can click on Print all to process and print all the documents without pausing. You can also click on Edit to look at the last document processed and make changes to it. If you do this, though, your original master document is overwritten by the processed one; you are unlikely to want to do this as you won't then be able to complete the merge job or re-use the master document.

To process and print all the documents in turn, use Next and Print in sequence until a message appears telling you all the files have been completed. If you want to stop processing the merge at any point, close the Importer window.

Sorting records

The mail-merge system includes a program called !Sorter which sorts text into alphabetic order. It is claimed that it is useful for sorting the data file into order, and can also remove any duplicate entries, but in fact it is only useful if the first letter of the first field in each record is significant, as it sorts on this (or on single lines). For example, if your data file has in the first line the name of a company, such as Firebrand Firelighters, the sort program may be useful to you as the first letter is significant. However, if you have names like 'Mr Charles', or 'A J Hillsden', then the program won't sort the data meaningfully — the first of these would appear under M and the second under A, whereas you would want them under C and H respectively. You may find that Sorter is quite useful for other things, but it's not very useful with mail-merge.

When you double-click on the !Sorter icon, Sorter loads and its icon appears on the icon bar:

There is an icon bar menu that lets you control how text is sorted:

You can sort on single lines, so that the first character of each line is examined and the lines put into order on this basis. You can sort on records, in which case text between blank lines is considered as a single item. Records are put into order on the basis of the first letter of the first line. You can discard duplicate entries, which means any duplicates will be deleted. Any slight variation in duplicate entries, such as different punctuation or different use of capitals, will prevent the program recognising that the entries are duplicates, so they will be left intact. The Discard duplicate option works only with single line sorting. The final menu option allows you to quit the sorter program and free the memory it was using.

Click on the menu items you want to use and then drag a text file to the icon. A sorted file will be produced with the default name Sorted. You can rename it if you like. Drag the text file icon to a directory display to save it.

Extra loader modules

The Business Supplement supplies some extra loader modules which you may find useful if you want to load text you have created in another system. The loader modules supplied on the disc are:

- LoadASCII. This is for loading plain ASCII text (such as Edit files). You need it only if you have other loaders automatically started up when you start Impression. If you do have other loaders and don't load this module, each of the other loaders will volunteer to load plain text; you may find the spacing of a text file loaded with a specialist module needs altering. Keep LoadASCII in the Auto directory if you are auto-loading any other loader modules and you sometimes want to load plain text. Don't rename any of the modules so that this one is no longer first alphabetically, as this is the means Impression uses to check whether a loader can handle the text in the file you are dragging in. LoadASCII must see the file before the other loaders do.

- LoadC. This reads in and correctly formats C language files. If you don't use this loader for C files, the curly brackets will confuse Impression as Impression also uses curly brackets in its internal text formatting descriptions.

- LoadCSV. This is the latest version of the Standard CSV loader supplied with Impression. It converts the commas used to separate data fields in CSV (comma - separated value) files to tab characters and creates any rulers needed to format the text. You must have opened a directory display for !System or !Scrap before using a CSV loader.

- LoadCSV+. This is a more advanced CSV loader that can handle and correctly convert CSV files that contain boxes or tables. It uses rules to build up the tables in Impression. The placing of Returns is important, as rules are only drawn when the text is followed by a Return; make sure there is a Return at the end of the file. You must have opened a directory display for !System or !Scrap before using a CSV loader.

- LoadJunRTF. This loader is for loading RTF (rich text format) files into Impression Junior. See the description of LoadRTF.

- LoadPDream. This loads PipeDream files, translating them as well as possible. It does not cope with graphics, printer driver constructs, colour constructs, option constructs (%O%parameter value), or leading and trailing character format. Formulae and @slot reference@ are not calculated. To load a document without tables from PipeDream, you will need some extra space on your work disc as you may need to create a temporary file. Load the LoadPDream module and drag the PipeDream file into an Impression window. The file may be double-spaced, in which case, save the text story as a temporary file. Quit Impression to get rid of the PipeDream loader and load LoadReturn (described below). Import the temporary file using this loader to strip out all the extra Return characters between the lines. Because calculations aren't carried out, and the spacing may be odd, tables don't translate well like this. The best approach is to load the PipeDream text in the way just described, then to save the tables from PipeDream as CSV files and use the CSV loader. If you use this method for the whole document, styles will be lost, but you can generally achieve reasonable results using the first method for the text and the second for the tables, then dropping the tables into the first document. It is best not to use multiple text columns in PipeDream and then use the PipeDream loader module as Impression will try to copy the column layout but using tabs rather than real text columns. This makes later editing of the text virtually impossible. You must have opened a directory display for

!System or !Scrap before using either the PipeDream or CSV loaders.

- LoadReturn. This is a simple loader to strip out extra Return characters between lines. Some packages may use linefeeds and Returns in such a way that when a file is loaded into Impression it becomes double-spaced, with an extra Return between each pair of lines. The LoadReturn loader can handle many types of text. If you are going to import text that is correctly formatted after using this loader, save your work and quit then reload Impression to get rid of LoadReturn, as it could otherwise wreck the format of the next file you import.

- LoadRTF. This loads RTF (rich text format) files preserving a lot of layout information. Many Macintosh and PC programs can save text in RTF files. With the RTF loader you can keep character set and font information, style definitions, and some document information. Colours, pictures, page information such as margins, headers and footers and page numbers are not preserved. RTF styles are converted, but not RTF effects. To transfer RTF files from Word (for DOS, Windows or Macintosh) you will need to use the mapping utility !MapUtil described later in this section.

- LoadWP42. This loads WordPerfect 4.2 (or earlier) files. Most effects are preserved, but not calculations, footnotes, red lining, hyphenation hot zone, page numbers, headers and footers, text columns, printer commands, changes of font or pitch and date and time functions. There is an Impression document called !CharMap in the same directory as the

loader modules which shows the character
mapping for WordPerfect character sets. This
will help you to identify any wrongly
converted characters.

- LoadWP51. This loads WordPerfect 5.1 files
which have a data or PC - data filetype. Again,
look at !CharMap for help with character
mapping. MapUtil recognises the 13 character
sets available with WordPerfect 5.0 and 5.1 so
that you can set up character mapping if
necessary.

- LoadWStar. This is a loader for WordStar files
of version 2.2x to 4.0 inclusive. To import
WordStar 5.0 or WordStar Professional files,
use the WordPerfect option in Star exchange
to output your work as a WordPerfect file and
then use a WordPerfect loader.

You can use one of these loaders by double-clicking
on its icon to load it before dragging your text file
into an Impression document. If you know you will
want to use one of them repeatedly and want it to
load when you start up Impression, follow the
instructions in chapter 20: *Making your own settings
and customising Impression* for copying the module
into the Auto directory inside !Impress.

If you are importing files from PC discs onto a
computer running RISC OS 2, you will need to use
PC-Access, the PC Emulator, MultiFS or PCDir to
read the files from the disc. If you use PCDir to read
files created with WordStar or WordPerfect, rename
any files that have one of these suffixes: .TXT, .DXF,
.C, .H, .SCR, .DOC, .ME, .PAS. These suffixes can
cause problems. Remove the suffix by renaming the
file from DOS using the Rename command.

MapUtil

The utility MapUtil is a font and character mapping program to help you match fonts used in RTF files with RISC OS fonts and to make sure that special characters (such as accented characters) are converted to their equivalents on your RISC OS computer.

Install MapUtil onto a floppy or hard disc by copying !MapUtil and !MapInfo from the Loaders directory. Don't use the original copy to run MapUtil as setting it up involves writing to some of the files that make up the program. Keep the original disc safely in case you ever need to reinstall it. Double-click on the copy of MapUtil you have made. The computer will take a while to load it, as it copies into MapUtil details about the fonts you have available. This delay occurs only the first time you load MapUtil. The icon looks like this:

MapUtil offers several facilities. You can use it to:

• insert special characters into a file

• map alien fonts to fonts available on your computer

• map characters between an alien font and a RISC OS font.

You can save the settings you make so that you can use them again next time you load MapUtil.

When you click on the MapUtil icon, a window appears showing the characters available.

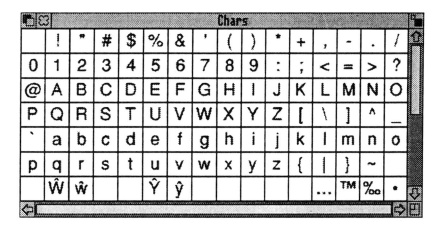

You can change the font in which they are displayed. Click the Menu button to show a menu listing the fonts available on your system, and then choose the font you want to use for the display.

Position the cursor at the point in your document where you want a character to appear and either drag the character from the Chars window or click on it with Adjust to copy it into your document.

If you want to set up font mappings to map fonts from the RTF file to RISC OS fonts, display the icon bar menu for MapUtil and choose **Font Mapping**. This displays a window for you to choose an alien font and map it to a RISC OS font:

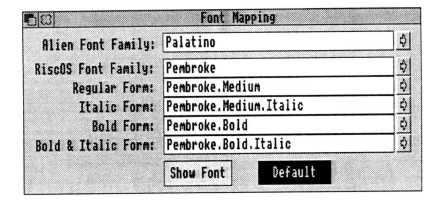

Click on the menu icon to the right of the first field to display a menu listing the non-RISC OS fonts known to MapUtil. Click on the one you want to map so that its name appears in the field. Now use the menu icon to the right of the next field to display a menu listing RISC OS fonts available on your system and choose the font you want to map the alien font to. The next four fields will be filled in with default values; these will be the fonts in the RISC OS family that are suitable matches for the regular, italic, bold and bold italic forms of the alien font. You should not need to alter these, but if you do you can pick a font from the menu displayed when you click on the arrow icon to the right of each of the fields.

The regular characters in a font (0-9, A-Z, a-z) are likely to be the same for a RISC OS font, a PC font and a Macintosh font, but if you have any symbols or other special characters these may have different character numbers in the alien font and the RISC OS font. You can use MapUtil's character mapping facility to correct the character mapping for a font if necessary.

If you find that characters are not translating properly when you import your RTF file into Impression, choose **Char Mapping** from the MapUtil icon bar menu to correct the mapping. It displays two windows, one superimposed over the other. The window at the back is the same as the Chars window used to insert a character in a document. It shows the character set for a RISC OS font. The front window shows a conversion table. The default conversion table which comes up when you first select character mapping shows the mapping for the Archimedes Latin1 character set. Display the menu to see a list of the other character sets available. These are:

- *mac* for Macintosh files

- *ansi* for files created from a program running under Windows on a PC

- *pc* for files created from a program running directly under DOS on a PC

- *WP 0-12* for files created with WordPerfect using character sets 0-12.

Click on the name of the character set conversion table you want to use. It will replace the Latin1 set. You can now map characters by dragging a character from the RISC OS window behind and dropping them onto the appropriate character squares on the front window.

If you like, you can set MapUtil to use each font when displaying its name in a menu (displaying Homerton.medium using Homerton, Trinity.bold using Trinity bold, etc). To do this, make sure the option **Show Fonts** is ticked in the icon bar menu.

If there are any blank lines in a font list, this is because the sprite needed to display the font in that position isn't available. To add it, click on **Gen. Sprites** in the icon bar menu. This is necessary because menu items can only be text in system font or sprites; to display text in a font other than system, the items must be displayed as sprites. To display all font names in the same default font (system font), turn off Show Fonts.

Imagesetting from Impression

You can produce PostScript files suitable for taking to an imagesetting bureau using just Impression with a PostScript printer driver. This is explained in chapter 16: *Printing Impression documents*. However, if you want to produce high-quality output with grey tints, spot colour or full colour, if you want to use page sizes other than A4 or have A4 pages with crop marks, you will need to use the extra imagesetting facilities provided with Impression Business Supplement. The following subsections explain how to use Expression-PS to prepare files for imagesetting using monochrome, spot colour and full colour. The instructions for monochrome files include material you will need to prepare spot colour or full-colour separations, too.

Using an imagesetting bureau

If you want to get a document you have produced with Impression professionally printed for publication and distribution, you will probably need to use an imagesetting bureau to prepare bromides or film for you. An imagesetting bureau can produce very high quality output using resolutions much higher than a laser printer can manage. The standard resolution of a Linotype imagesetter is 1270 dpi (dots per inch), whereas standard laser printer resolution is 300 dpi. If you have work printed from laser printed output, it will have a noticeably rougher appearance than if you use image-set output.

An imagesetter can print on bromide, which is a special glossy paper with a very smooth surface, or output directly onto film. The printer will need to make up a film anyway, so output on bromides will be photographed by the printer; you might decide to ask the imagesetting bureau to output direct to film. Although it costs more per page than setting on bromide, it will give you a better quality final output and will save money on the printer's bill. Talk to your printers before you decide to find out whether they want you to provide bromide or film and, if they want film, whether they want a positive or negative image.

Unless you find an imagesetter who can handle RISC OS discs, you will need to prepare PostScript files on a PC disc. If your computer runs RISC OS 3, it can format, write to and read PC discs. (Use the **Format, Other formats, DOS 720k** option from the disc drive icon bar menu to format a disc to PC format.)If your computer runs RISC OS 2, you will need a program such as PCAccess, PCDir, MultiFS or the PC Emulator to format and use PC discs.

If you want to produce a document that uses just one colour ink (monochrome) you won't need to use any of the colour options with Expression-PS, even if the ink you want to use isn't black. If you want isolated blocks of colour, such as some text in a different colour, or some coloured frames, you need to use *spot colour*. If you want full colour pictures such as colour photographs, you will need to use *colour separations*. Full-colour printing is quite complex and you may need to ask for quite a bit of help from the imagesetter and printer you intend to use.

Questions to ask before you start

Once you have chosen an imagesetting bureau and a printer, there are a few things you need to ask them before you prepare your PostScript files.

Ask the imagesetting bureau

- what resolutions they have available. You need to decide whether you want standard resolution (usually 1270 dpi) or a high resolution (perhaps 2540 dpi). This will depend on the content of your file and what you finally intend to do with it. If you have lots of greyscale pictures you may want to use a higher resolution, for example.

- whether they have all the fonts you intend to use. If you use fonts that the imagesetter doesn't have, text in those fonts will probably be printed in Courier (Corpus).

Ask the printer

- whether to prepare bromide or film and, if you are preparing film, whether it should be positive or negative.

- what screen density, measured in lines per inch (lpi), is suitable for the job you are asking them to do and the press they intend to use.

- whether you should choose a dot shape other than round for halftones.

  whether you should choose a screen angle other than 45° for a monochrome job involving halftones.

Generating monochrome files for imagesetting

Before you prepare your PostScript file, make sure you have checked your document very thoroughly. Print it out and check it to make sure all the headers and footers appear where you want them to, the margins are correct, the page breaks are in sensible places, and so on.

Load a PostScript printer driver and set output to file. There is an explanation of how to do this in chapter 16: *Printing Impression documents*. Now open a directory display for Impression Business Supplement, open the directory TypeSett'g and double-click on !ExpressPS. Its icon appears on the icon bar:

Click on this to display the Expression-PS window:

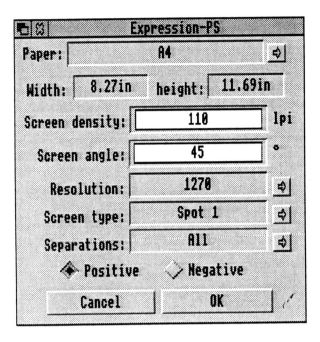

Many of the settings you can make from this window apply to monochrome, spot colour and/full colour jobs. (If you are using RISC OS 2, there will be two extra buttons on the dialogue box allowing you to match font names and add PostScript font names; these are described later in the section *Using different fonts.*)

The first field lets you set the paper size. The default size is A4, but the menu on the button to the right of the field offers these alternatives:

•   A4 (210 x 297 mm)

•   A4 extra (235.5 x 322 mm)

•   A3 (297 x 420 mm)

•   A3 extra (304 x 444.5 mm)

•   Letter (8.5 x 11 in)

- Letter extra (9.5 x 12 in)

- Legal (8.5 x 15.38 in)

- Legal extra (9.5 x 15 in)

- A3 Long 18 (11.97 x 18 in)

- A3 Long 20 (11.97 x 20.01 in)

- A3 Long 23 (11.97 x 22.75 in)

- Tabloid (11 x 17 in)

- Tabloid extra (11.69 x 18 in)

- Letter transverse (11 x 8.5 in)

- A4 transverse (297 x 210 mm)

The sizes with 'extra' after them allow additional space around the page size so that crop marks can be added. If you want to use crop marks, choose one of these sizes.

The exact size of the page in inches is shown in the fields below the name of the page size.

The screen density is a measure of the density of print in lines per inch. This doesn't refer to the computer screen, but to an engraved glass screen that printers used to use. Although the screen isn't used for electronic imagesetting, the measure is retained. The default value of 110 should be suitable for most jobs; if your printer asks you to use a different density, put the cursor in this field and change the value. Don't change it without advice from your printer unless you know what you are doing.

The screen angle again refers to a printing screen that isn't actually used in electronic imagesetting. Halftones are printed not by using grey ink, but by using different densities of black ink against white paper to render different levels of grey. The dots are not printed directly up and down or across the page as the rows of dots would be too obvious. Usually, the screen would be turned through 45° so that the dots don't obviously form rows. With electronic imagesetting, the rows of dots are still positioned at an angle for the same reason. You can't change this angle if you are producing colour separations because different colours are printed with different screen angles, but if you are producing a monochrome image, you can alter the screen angle if you need to. Again, don't change the angle without professional advice unless you know what you are doing.

The resolution is the number of dots per inch the imagesetting machine will print to build up the image. Ask the bureau what value to choose from the menu. The default value is a standard resolution used by most bureaux.

The screen type setting controls the shape of the dots used to build up halftones. There is a menu offering the options:

- Spot 1

- Spot 2

- Triple spot 1

- Triple spot 2

- Elliptical spot

- Line

- Crosshatch

- Mezzotint.

Again, don't change the spot shape unless you have been advised to or you know what you are doing.

For a monochrome image, leave Separations set at All, the default setting.

You will probably want a positive image if you are setting on bromide, but a negative image if you are setting on film. Ask your printer for advice if you are in any doubt. Click to turn on the button beside the setting you want.

When you have finished making the settings with this window, click on OK. You can save your settings for future use with Save choices in the Expression-PS icon bar menu. Don't make any further settings from the printer driver as these will override settings you have made with Expression-PS. When you have made the settings, you can use the Print dialogue box from Impression to set the scale, orientation and so on and start the print job. You may need to print pages in batches to prevent the PostScript file becoming too large, especially if you have graphics in the document.

When you are ready to take your files to the bureau, transfer them to a PC disc. A DOS filename can only contain eight characters, so you may need to rename your files before transferring them.

Spot colour jobs

If you want to use spot colour in your file, you will have to set the colour or colours you are using to be pure cyan, magenta or yellow and use the CMYK method of defining colours. You will need to do this for coloured text or frames. You can set tints for halftones in your spot colour, but must always use pure colour (that is, don't mix proportions of cyan, magenta, yellow and black). This doesn't mean that your final printed document must have only these three colours in it, but that you need to use these to get the separations. The printer can use the separations to print any colour you like. For example, you could use a style like that shown below, with the rule in blue:

This style has a rule below set.

Leave the text colour black, but set the rule-off colour, using the CMYK method, to be pure cyan, magenta or yellow. You can set the tint density by altering the percentage for your chosen colour, but don't mix colours. 100% is the darkest tint, and gives solid colour. You might set this rule to be 70% magenta. When you come to prepare the file for the imagesetter, you will need to prepare black and magenta separations. The rule will be printed in a 70% grey tint on a separate page from the black text; the text will appear on the black separation without its rule. When you take this to the printers, you can ask them to print it in any colour you like; magenta has been used only to distinguish it from the black elements. You can use up to three spot colours, as you can use cyan, magenta and yellow.

When you are ready to prepare the files for a spot colour job, display the menu for separations and choose a colour you have used. You will need to print all the separations separately, so make the other settings you need and then send the document to the printer with your first colour chosen from the Separation menu. If you haven't used the spot colour on every page, send only the pages on which it is used when you make up the file for the colour separation, otherwise you will be paying to set blank pages. You will need to send all pages for the black separation, as this will have your text on. Change the name of the file the printer driver is sending output to after sending the first separation. If you don't change the name of the file, the printer will send output for the second separation (or batch of pages) to the same file, overwriting the first one. Instead you can change the name of the file that has been created after the first separation has been completed instead of changing the filename from the printer driver menu (with RISC OS 2) or dialogue box (with RISC OS 3). All but one of your files will then have a data file icon rather than a PostScript file icon. This doesn't matter, and makes no difference to the files.

Full-colour printing

If you want full-colour illustrations in your document, you will need to use full- (or four-) colour printing. This is much more expensive than using spot colour, so don't use it unless you are sure you want it. It is expensive because it is difficult; the colour separations have to be overlaid exactly so that the colour appears in the right place. The printers will use your four separations to print each colour component in turn. If the separations aren't aligned exactly the colours won't appear where they should — they will be *out of register*.

You can use tints and colours that are any combination of cyan, magenta, yellow and black if you are going to use full-colour printing. You don't need to use the CMYK method to define colours in your document, and obviously any sprites you have imported won't use this method of colour definition.

You need to produce the four colour separations separately, sending each to a different file. Make the other settings you want with the Expression-PS window and then choose a separation from the menu. You will need to use all of them except the All option, and it doesn't matter which order you do them in. After you have printed one, change the name of the file the printer driver is using to receive output and then print another colour separation. If you don't change the filename, your first separation will be overwritten by the next. Again, you don't need to send all the separations for pages that don't have colour graphics. Send just the black separation to the printer driver for pages that only have black text and no colour.

Using different fonts

If you want to use fonts other than those that are given font mappings in the printer driver you are using, you will need to add font mappings to the PostScript files you produce. You can do this either using FontPrint if you have RISC OS 3, or using the Match font and Add PostScript font buttons on the Expression-PS window if you are using RISC OS 2.

Before you can use extra fonts, you will need to know their real PostScript names. For example, the font distributed as Clare is actually a version of AvantGarde, and must be mapped to this before a PostScript printer or imagesetter can recognise and use it. The method you will need to use to add extra font mappings will depend on whether you are running RISC OS 2 or RISC OS 3.

RISC OS 3

If you are using RISC OS 3, you will need version 2.11 or higher of Expression-PS; earlier versions don't run with the RISC OS 3 printer drivers. The Match names and Add PostScript names buttons are not available from Expression-PS if you are running RISC OS 3, so you can't map extra fonts from Expression-PS. However, FontPrint in directory App1 allows you to set up mappings which will be stored inside the PostScript printer driver.

Load and make active the PostScript printer driver you want to use to produce your PostScript files for the imagesetting bureau. This may be an Apple printer driver, or a Linotype printer driver. Now load FontPrint by double-clicking on its icon. You can see which fonts are already mapped by clicking on the FontPrint icon on the icon bar to display its window. For the Apple LW+ printer driver, the window looks like this:

Printer: 'Apple LW+'		
Printer type:	Apple LaserWriter Plus	
Clare.Medium	Map to	AvantGarde-Book
Clare.Medium.Oblique	Map to	AvantGarde-BookOblique
Clare.Demi	Map to	AvantGarde-Demi
Clare.Demi.Oblique	Map to	AvantGarde-DemiOblique
Robinson.Demi	Map to	Bookman-Demi
Robinson.Demi.Italic	Map to	Bookman-DemiItalic
Robinson.Light	Map to	Bookman-Light
Robinson.Light.Italic	Map to	Bookman-LightItalic
Corpus.Medium	Map to	Courier
Corpus.Bold	Map to	Courier-Bold
Corpus.Bold.Oblique	Map to	Courier-BoldOblique

Defaults   Save

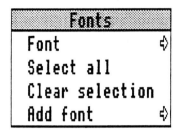

You can use any fonts that already have a mapping without doing anything further. However, if you have a font which is not listed, you will need to add it to the list and map it to a PostScript font. You can only add a font which already exists on your system and is in your !Fonts directory. (You should only have one !Fonts directory on your system.) If you have just bought a new font, you will need to copy it into !Fonts before you can set up a mapping for it.

Let's assume you have bought a version of Garamond called GraysInn. To add this to the list in the FontPrint window, move the pointer over the window and display the menu:

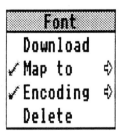

Move the pointer over Add font and off to the right to display a submenu listing all the fonts available on your system. Click on the name of the font you want to add (GraysInn). It will be added to the bottom of the list in the window (you may need to scroll through the window to see it) with the caption Download. You don't want to download the font, so now you need to map it to a PostScript font. You need to know the proper PostScript name of the font you are going to use in a form the imagesetting machine will recognise; you may need to ask your bureau for the proper form of the name. Click on the name of the font you have just added to the window to highlight it, then display the menu again. This time, move the pointer over Font to the right to display the submenu for this option:

Move the pointer over the second option, Map to, to display a list of fonts. These are fonts that are already recognised. At the bottom of the list is a space in which you can type the name of font not listed. If you wanted to map GraysInn.medium to Garamond Roman, you would need to type Garamond-Roman at the bottom of the menu and then press Return. If you also had GraysInn.Medium.Italic, you would need to add this too, and map it to Garamond-Italic.

If you had bought a copy of Palatino that was called something other than Pembroke, you would need to add the name of your version of the font, but map it to Palatino chosen from the menu. It doesn't matter if you have more than one font mapped to the same PostScript name.

This procedure maps fonts to the Adobe standard fonts. This is the most likely requirement. Ask your imagesetting bureau whether it is suitable if you have any doubts; you will need to tell them which fonts you intend to use. If necessary, you can change the encoding to Adobe special using the Encoding submenu from the Font submenu shown above.

When you have finished adding fonts, click on Save to keep your settings. A dialogue box will appear for you to give the password for the PostScript device. The default password is zero, and this is in the field already. Click on OK to use this. If you are using a computer attached to a network and the password is rejected, this is probably because there is a PostScript printer on the network and someone has set a password for the printer. You will need to ask the system manager for advice. S/he may ask you to use a different printer driver, in which case you will need to set up your mapping again with that printer driver loaded. Whatever password you use, you may need to use it each time you load the printer driver in future.

RISC OS 2

If you are using RISC OS 2, Expression-PS has the Match names and Add PostScript name buttons, enabling you to add new font mappings quite easily to your PostScript files. Expression-PS will make the necessary changes to the PostScript file once you have told it the font mappings you want to make.

If you suspect that there is no mapping for a font you want to use, click on Match names on the Expression-PS window. A new window will appear listing Acorn font names on the left and PostScript names on the right. There will be an entry for each font available on your system. As long as there is a name on the right, you can use the font and it will be correctly mapped. If there is 'none' beside any font names, those are not mapped. You may be able to map them to a font the computer already knows about, or might have to give the name. You will need to know the correct form of the PostScript name; you may need to ask your imagesetting bureau.

To see if you can map the font to a name the system already knows, move the pointer over the line containing the name of the font you want to use and click the Menu button on the mouse. A menu showing a list of PostScript font names is displayed. If the one you want is included, click on it to map it to the font you highlighted and then on OK. If not, click outside the menu to remove it. If you need to add a font name because it isn't included in the list, click on the button Add PostScript name. This displays a small window for you to type the PostScript name. After you have typed it, click on Add name or press Return; the name will be added to the list held by Expression-PS and you will then be able to use it in mappings.

New mappings and font names are stored inside Expression-PS. You don't need to repeat the mappings as they are saved from one session to the next. However, they are only used with Expression-PS, so you must load it each time you want to use the fonts mappings you have added.

Communicating with a PostScript printer

If you have a PostScript device attached to the serial port of your computer and you know how to use the PostScript language, you can send commands directly to the printer. To do this, load TalkPS by double-clicking on its icon. It doesn't load onto the icon bar but opens a window like this:

You can type PostScript commands in the window, and responses from the printer will also appear in the window. Only use this if you already know how to use the PostScript language. When you have finished using it, click on the close icon to remove it and close down TalkPS.

What next?

The next chapter gives a brief summary of the menu options available in Impression. If you want to know in detail what a menu option does, look it up in the index to find the reference to a full explanation.

23 | Impression menu checklist

This chapter summarises the options available from the Impression menus.

Main menu

The main Impression menu gives access to the submenus. It looks like this:

```
Impression
  Document  ⇨
  Edit      ⇨
  Effect    ⇨
  Style     ⇨
  Frame     ⇨
  Misc      ⇨
```

Some options in the submenus may be greyed out; this is because they are not currently available. To use some of the options, you have to have the cursor positioned in a frame, have a frame selected or have some text selected. Some options are not available if there is no text in your document.

Some of the menu options change according to what you are doing. For example, if you have some text selected, the fifth item in the Document menu is Save selected text. If you don't have any text selected, but have the cursor in a text story, the item is Save text story.

Document menu

Info displays information about the current document and chapter. The keyboard shortcut is Ctrl-F1.

Load new document displays a reminder telling you how to load an Impression document.

Load to cursor displays a reminder telling you how to load text into your current document.

Save document displays a Save as icon for you to save your document. The keyboard shortcut is Ctrl-F3.

Save selected text or **Save text story** lets you save part or all of a text story as ASCII text, with or without linefeeds, Returns and Impression styling information. The keyboard shortcut is Shift-Ctrl-T.

Remove document deletes the current document from Impression's memory, but not from the disc. If you have unsaved changes it displays a warning giving you the chance to cancel the operation. The keyboard shortcut is Shift-Ctrl-Z.

Print displays a dialogue box for you to set printing options and send a document to the printer. To save the print settings without sending the document to the printer, click on Print with the Adjust button. You can also use the Print button (to the right of F12) to display this dialogue box.

Scale view displays a dialogue box for you to choose a scale at which the document window will be displayed. The keyboard shortcut is Ctrl-F9.

Preferences displays a dialogue box for you to turn on or off auto-saving and set an interval for auto-saving the document.

Edit menu

Cut frame or **Cut text** removes the selected text or frame and stores it on the clipboard. The keyboard shortcut is Ctrl-X.

Copy frame or **Copy text** makes a copy of the selected text or frame and stores it on the clipboard. The keyboard shortcut is Ctrl-C.

Paste frame or **Paste text** pastes the frame or text on the clipboard into the document. You will need to click in the document to give the position for a frame to be pasted; text will be pasted in at the cursor position. The keyboard shortcut is Ctrl-V.

Delete frame or **Delete text** removes the selected text or frame, but does not store it on the clipboard. The keyboard shortcut is Ctrl-K.

Select text story selects the whole text story that the cursor is in. The keyboard shortcut is Ctrl-T.

New chapter displays a dialogue box for you to make settings for a new chapter. The keyboard shortcut is Ctrl-F7.

Alter chapter lets you make changes to the definition of the current chapter. The keyboard shortcut is Shift-Ctrl-A.

Delete chapter removes the current chapter; it is not stored on a clipboard.

Insert new page adds a new page after the current page.

Delete page deletes the current page.

View master pages opens a window showing the master pages for the current document. The keyboard shortcut is Ctrl-F2.

Effect menu

All effects are applied to the currently selected text, or from the cursor to new text you type if there is no text selected.

Clear all effects cancels any effects being used at the cursor position or removes all effects from selected text.

Text font leads to a submenu offering all the fonts available on your system.

Text size leads to a submenu offering different text sizes and the option to specify a custom size. The keyboard shortcut is Ctrl-Shift-S.

Line spacing leads to a dialogue box for you to set the line spacing. The keyboard shortcut is Ctrl-Shift-L.

Text colour leads to a colour picker dialogue box for you to set the text colour using one of the three methods RGB, CMYK or HSV.

Underline turns underlining on. If it is already ticked, clicking on this option turns underlining off. The keyboard shortcut is Ctrl-Shift-U.

Subscript turns on subscript text. It if is already ticked, clicking on it turns it off. The keyboard shortcut is Ctrl-Shift-K.

Superscript turns on superscript text. It if is already ticked, clicking on it turns it off. The keyboard shortcut is Ctrl-Shift-J.

Left align sets text flush with the left margin but leaves the ends of lines ragged. If it is already ticked, clicking on **Left align** returns text to the justification option set by its style. The keyboard shortcut is F5.

Centre centres text between the margins set for its style. If it is already ticked, clicking on **Centre** returns text to the justification option set by its style. The keyboard shortcut is F6.

Right align sets text flush with the right margin, leaving the beginnings of the lines ragged. If it is already ticked, clicking on **Right align** returns text to the justification option set by its style. The keyboard shortcut is F7.

Fully justify justifies text so that it is set between the margins, aligned with both. If it is already ticked, clicking on **Fully justify** returns text to the justification option set by its style. The keyboard shortcut is F8.

Style menu

New style lets you set up a definition for a new style. If there is some text selected when you choose this option, you can apply the style straight to that text by clicking on Apply when you have finished defining it. The keyboard shortcut is Ctrl-F5.

Edit style allows you to edit an existing style. By default, the style that will be editable will be the last style overlaid on selected text or applied at the cursor if no text is selected. However, you can use the menu button to the right of the field showing the style name to pick a different style to edit. You can also use this dialogue box to delete styles, merge styles or import styles from other documents. The keyboard shortcut is Ctrl-F6.

Clear all styles removes all styles except BaseStyle from the selected text (or the cursor position if there is no text selected). The keyboard shortcut is Ctrl-B.

New ruler lets you define a new ruler. It may apply from the cursor position or to selected text. The keyboard shortcut is Ctrl-Shift-N.

Edit ruler lets you edit a ruler that is already defined. Wherever the ruler is used in the document, it will be updated following your edits. The keyboard shortcut is Ctrl-Shift-E.

The next part of the menu lists all the styles that are defined in your document (except BaseStyle) and that you have chosen to show in the menu. To apply a style to selected text or at the cursor position, click on its name in the list. If you click on a ticked style name, that style will be removed from selected text or the cursor position. There may be keyboard shortcuts set up for some of the styles.

Frame menu

New frame leads to a submenu allowing you to create a new local frame, guide frame or repeating frame. Press and hold down the Select button at the position for the top lefthand corner of the new frame and drag to the position for the bottom righthand corner before releasing Select. If you create a frame on a master page it becomes a master page frame. You can't create a repeating frame on a master page. The keyboard shortcut is Ctrl-I.

Alter frame displays a dialogue box for you to make alterations to the selected frame. You can change the size, position, text repelling properties, colour and border(s) used. If a frame copied from a master page is selected, you can only alter its size and position if you first make it local. It is then dissociated from the master page and isn't changed if you alter the frame on the master page. A text story won't flow through a frame that has been made local unless you add it back into the flow. The keyboard shortcut is Ctrl-F10.

Alter graphic is available if the selected frame contains an imported picture. It leads to a dialogue box that lets you alter the position, scale, rotation and aspect ratio of the picture. You can also turn off and on the display of the picture. You can only rotate sprites if you have RISC OS 3 or have Enhanced graphics turned on (from the Impression icon bar menu). The keyboard shortcut is Ctrl-F11.

Snap to guides makes new frames snap to existing guide frames as they are created. It is ticked if it is turned on. It will only have an effect if you have defined any guide frames either locally or on the master page.

Snap to frames makes new frames snap to other frames on the page. It is ticked when it is turned on.

Borders set up displays a dialogue box for you to add and alter definitions of frame borders. You can add borders to a frame using **Alter frame**.

Group frames is available if you have more than one frame selected. It groups frames so that they can be moved or resized together. To select more than one frame, click in the first frame with Select as normal, and in the others with Select but with the Shift key held down.

Ungroup frames is available only if a group of frames is selected. It separates the frames again into single frames.

Force to next moves the text immediately in front of the cursor to the start of the next frame. The keyboard shortcut is Ctrl-G.

Put to back puts the selected frame to the back of the stack of frames. If there are no frames behind it, it has no effect. The keyboard shortcut is Ctrl-Shift-B.

Bring to front puts the selected frame on the top of the stack of frames so that it superimposes any others in the same area. If there are no frames in front of it, this has no effect.

Embed frame inserts a copy of the frame on the clipboard at the cursor position and fixes its place relative to the text. If the text moves, so will the frame. The keyboard shortcut is Ctrl-Shift-F.

Misc menu

Find displays a submenu allowing you to search for text, or go to a specified page or chapter. Pages and chapters are identified by number. Find text leads to a dialogue box allowing you control over searching for and replacing text. The keyboard shortcut is Ctrl-F4.

Spelling leads to a submenu offering spell checking facilities. You can check your work as you type, check spelling from the cursor position to the end of the story, or check the whole document. You can also load or edit a dictionary. If there is no dictionary loaded, you will be given the chance to load a dictionary when you choose one of the submenu options. The keyboard shortcut is Ctrl-F8.

Abbreviation leads to a submenu with two options. **Dictionary** leads to a dialogue box allowing you to set up and alter abbreviations; **Expand as you type** expands abbreviations using those in the currently loaded dictionary.

Kern leads to a dialogue box that allows you to set the horizontal and vertical kerning (inter-letter space) of the letter pair around the cursor. Position the cursor between the letters you want to kern before calling up this option.

Merge command the merge command is used with mail-merge programs such as that supplied with Impression Business Supplement. You may also be able to use the merge command with database programs; look in the documentation with your database program for advice on how to use it, as the requirements vary between programs.

Insert leads to a submenu allowing you to insert the current page number, chapter number, date or time. You can also choose the format for the page number or chapter number from submenus on these two options. The page and chapter numbers inserted are updated as you alter your document, but the time and date are fixed once they have been inserted.

Hide graphics turns off the display and printing of graphics. It is a useful way of saving memory.

Show graphics turns back on the display of graphics, including any pictures you have turned off individually using the Hide graphic button from the Alter graphic dialogue box.

Compile index displays a dialogue box for you to control the settings for and compile an index. The index will pick up all text in a style that has the index label set on.

Compile contents displays a dialogue box for you to control the settings for and compile a table of contents. The TOC will pick up all text in a style that has the contents label set on.

Impression icon bar menu

The icon bar menu looks like this:

Info leads to a dialogue box that gives the version number and copyright information about Impression.

New view leads to a submenu that lists all the documents currently loaded in Impression. Click on one to open a new window onto it.

Remove document leads to a submenu that lists all the documents currently loaded in Impression. Click on one to remove it from Impression (but not delete it from the disc). If you have made any changes to it since saving it, a warning dialogue box appears giving you the chance to save it first, cancel the operation or remove it without saving it.

Preferences leads to a dialogue box allowing you to set several options controlling how Impression behaves. You can set:

- automatic loading of the spell-checking dictionary from disc or ROM

- automatic loading of the hyphenation module

- turning on enhanced graphics (and greyscale dithering, if enhanced graphics is on)

- setting the default units Impression will use for measuring elements of the page, styles, and the ruler

- the default window sizes for document pages and master pages

- turning on the display of frame outlines, print borders and page rulers making the cursor flash or remain static

- automatically turning on spell checking as you type and abbreviation expansion as you type when you start up Impression

- making new frames snap to all existing frames

- using smart quotes for imported text.

Show flow displays arrows indicating how text flows from one frame to another. Clicking in the window will remove the arrows.

Minimise memory instructs Impression to store chunks of the document on disc rather than in RAM to save memory. This enables you to use large documents even if you have little memory free. There will be a slight decrease in running speed as Impression will need to retrieve other parts of the document from disc as necessary when you move around the document.

Quit closes down Impression, removing its icon from the icon bar and freeing the memory it was using for you to use for other things. If you have any unsaved work, a dialogue box will give you the chance to cancel so that you can save it before quitting.

What next?

The appendix lists the characters and the codes you need to use to get them with the Alt key.

Appendix: Character codes

The following table shows the decimal codes you need to use with the Alt key to obtain the characters and symbols that are not available from the typewriter keys. All these characters are also available from !Chars.

Decimal	Character code
160	no-break space
161	¡
162	¢
163	£
164	¤

Decimal	Character code
165	¥
166	¦
167	§
168	¨
169	©
170	ª
171	«
172	¬
173	-
174	®
175	¯
176	°
177	±
178	^{2}
179	^{3}
180	´
181	μ
182	¶
183	·
184	¸
185	^{1}
186	º
187	»
188	¼
189	½

190	¾
191	¿
192	À
193	Á
194	Â
195	Ã
196	Ä
197	Å
198	Æ
199	ç
200	È
201	É
202	Ê
203	Ë
204	Ì
205	Í
206	Î
207	Ï
208	Ð
209	Ñ
210	Ò
211	Ó
212	Ô
213	Õ
214	Ö
215	x
216	ø

217	Ù
218	Ú
219	Û
220	Ü
221	Ý
222	Þ
223	ß
224	à
225	á
226	â
227	ã
228	ä
229	å
230	æ
231	ç
232	è
233	é
234	ê
235	ë
236	ì
237	í
238	î
239	ï
240	ð
241	ñ
242	ò
243	ó

244	ô
245	õ
246	ö
247	÷
248	ø
249	ù
250	ú
251	û
252	ü
253	y
254	þ
255	ÿ
Alt-1	[1]
Alt-2	[2]

Dabhand guides

Dabhand Guide books

The following Dabhand Guides and software packs are **now available**. All quoted prices are inclusive of VAT on software, (books are zero-rated), and postage and packing.

Also by Anne Rooney

Mastering 1st Word Plus: A Dabhand Guide

By Anne Rooney

ISBN 1-870336-18-6

272 pages

Book: £13.95 3.5"Disc £7.95 Book and Disc together £21.90

A step-by-step guide that takes you through all the features of 1st Word Plus from installation to mail-merge, Mastering 1st Word Plus is comprehensive, thorough and easy to read.

Windows, A User's Guide: A Dabhand Guide

By Ian Sinclair

ISBN 1-870336-63-1

396 pages

Price: £14.95

A comprehensive guide to Microsoft Windows™ for the IBM PC and compatibles. This user's guide gives simple step by step instructions for new user's, and is packed with hints and tips that show even experienced users how to get top performance from their software. Also shows how to get your favourite non-Windows programs up and running under Windows.

Psion LZ, A User's Guide to OPL: A Dabhand Guide

By Ian Sinclair

ISBN 1-870336-92-5

224 pages

Price: £12.95

Enjoy better understanding and complete command of your Psion LZ with this guide. Includes a comprehensive guide to all the built in programs as well as the OPL programming language.

Ability & Ability Plus: A Dabhand Guide

By Geoff Cox

ISBN 1-870336-51-8

415 pages

Price: £16.95

A comprehensive guide to the popular Ability software by Migent. The six software modules are introduced in a logical easy-to-understand manner. Copious examples and useful tips are provided throughout, and the differences between Ability, and the upgraded version Ability Plus, are explained in detail. There are dozens of illustrations throughout the book to show exactly what appears on the screen at various stages.

Basic on the PC: A Dabhand Guide

By Geoff Cox

ISBN 1-870336-96-8

752 pages

Book: £16.95. 3.5" disc, £6.95. 5.25" disc £4.95. Book and 3.5" disc together, £21.95 Book and 5.25" disc together, £20.95

A comprehensive.tutorial and reference to the programming language provided free with most IBM-compatible computers. As well as a friendly and helpful tutorial in BASIC programming, the book contains a complete command reference, detailing every command in BASIC on the PC with examples of its use.

Windows 3.1: A Dabhand Guide

By Jon Mountfort

ISBN 1-870336-66-6

Over 500 pages

Price: £16.95

A comprehensive guide to Microsoft Windows 3.1. Ideal for beginners and invaluable for experts. Easy to understand, packed with illustrations, helpful hints & tips.

Wordstar 6: A Dabhand Guide

By Geoff Cox

ISBN 1-870336-88-7

448 pages

Price: £16.95

Aimed at all users from the beginner to the experienced word-processor operator. Expert tips demonstrate how to use Wordstar's many features including how to use Wordstar as invoicing program.

Amstrad PCW Series: A Dabhand Guide

By F. John Atherton

ISBN 1-870336-50-X

368 pages

Price: £13.95

Assuming no previous knowledge of word-processors or computers, the first aim is to get you up and running, and producing attractive documents. The book then explores and explains every major feature available in LocoScript 2, LocoFile, LocoSpell and LocoMail.

AmigaDOS: A Dabhand Guide

By Mark Burgess

ISBN 1-870336-47-X

270 pages

Price: £14.95

The complete and comprehensive guide to AmigaDOS for the user of the Commodore Amiga. This book provides a unique perspective on the Amiga's powerful operating system in a way which will be welcomed by the beginner and experienced user alike. Rather than simply reiterating the Amiga manual, this book is a genuinely different approach to understanding and using the Amiga.

Just some of the topics covered include: filing with and without the workbench, the hierarchical filing system, pathnames and device names, multi-tasking and its capabilities, The AmigaDOS screen editor, AmigaDOS commands, batch processing, error codes and descriptions, creating system discs, recovering damaged discs and using AmigaDOS with C.

Simply a *must* for all Amiga owners and users!

Amiga Basic: A Dabhand Guide

by Paul Fellows

ISBN 1-870336-87-9

560 pages

Price: £15.95

A fully structured tutorial to using AmigaBASIC on the whole range of Commodore Amiga computers. Many practical applications provide useful and informative programming techniques. No prior knowledge of BASIC required. A graphical theme is applied to the many examples in the book so that the techniques described are visually reinforced.

An *indispensable* reference to any AmigaBASIC programmer.

WordStar 1512: A Dabhand Guide

Including WordStar Express

by Bruce Smith

ISBN 1-870336-17-8

240 pages

Book: £12.95. Disc: 5.25in, £7.95; book and disc together, £17.95

A comprehensive tutorial and reference guide to WordStar 1512 and WordStar Express. The many features of this book include rulers, margins, copy, move, delete, dot commands, page layout, spelling checker, mail-merge, using printers, RAM discs, and Boost. Many screen dumps provide visual reinforcement.

VIEW: A Dabhand Guide

by Bruce Smith

ISBN 1-870336-00-3

248 pages

Book: £12.95. Disc: DFS 5.25in, £7.95 ADFS; 3.5in, £9.95. Book and disc together, £17.95 (ADFS £19.95)

The most comprehensive tutorial and reference guide written about using the VIEW wordprocessor. Both the beginner, and the more advanced user, will find it to be an invaluable companion whether writing a simple letter or undertaking a thesis. In addition, a suite of VIEW utility programs are provided, including: VIEW Manager, an easily extendible front end. Thorny subjects such as macros, page layout and printer drivers are revealed.

Mini Office II: A Dabhand Guide

By Bruce Smith & Robin Burton

ISBN 1-870336-55-0

256 pages

Price: £9.95

Official tutorial and reference guide to the award winning Mini Office II software. Covers everyday use of all modules. Featuring file management, the wordprocessor, mail merging, the label printer, the database, the spreadsheet, graphics, communication, and MiniDriver.

Master Operating System: A Dabhand Guide

by David Atherton

ISBN 1-870336-01-1

272 pages

Book: £12.95. Disc: DFS 5.25in, £7.95 ADFS; 3.5in, £9.95. Book and disc together, £17.95 (ADFS £19.95)

The definitive reference work for programmers of the BBC Model B+, Master 128 and Master Compact computers.

Archimedes Assembly Language: A Dabhand Guide

By Mike Ginns

ISBN 1-870336-20-8

368 pages

Book : £14.95. 3.5" disc, £9.95. Book and disc together, £21.95

Get the most from your Archimedes micro by programming directly in the machine's own language - machine code. This book covers all aspects of machine code/assembler programming for all Archimedes machines.

There is a beginner's section which takes the reader step by step through topics such as binary numbers, and logic operations.

To make the transition from BASIC to machine code as painless as possible, the book contains a section on implementing BASIC commands in machine code. All of the most useful BASIC statements are covered.

Archimedes Operating System: A Dabhand Guide

By Alex and Nick van Someren

ISBN: 1-870336-48-8

320 pages approx

Price: £14.95. 3.5in disc, £9.95. Book and disc together, £21.95

The book that is a must for every serious Archimedes owner. It describes how the Archimedes works and examines the ARTHUR operating system in microscopic detail, giving the programmer a real insight into getting the best from the Archimedes.

For the serious machine code, or BASIC, programmer included are sections on: the ARM instruction set, SWIs, graphics, Writing relocatable modules, vectors, compiled code, MEMC, VIDC, IOC and much more.

Basic V: A Dabhand Guide

By Mike Williams

ISBN 1-870336-75-5

128 pages

Price: £9.95

A practical guide to programming in BASIC V on the Acorn Archimedes. Assuming a familiarity with the BBC BASIC language in general, it describes the many new commands offered by BASIC V.

Archimedes First Steps: A Dabhand Guide

By Anne Rooney

ISBN 1-870336-73-9

240 pages

Price: £9.95

An introductory guide to the Archimedes, to guide you through those first few months of ownership. The Welcome Discs contain a wide range of useful programs which are fully documented. The book also goes further, to describe software and hardware additions to the Archimedes, how to choose and install them.

Budget DTP: A Dabhand Guide

by Roger Amos

ISBN 1-870336-11-9

222 pages

Price: £12.95

Every Archimedes and BBC A3000 owner receives copies of the !Draw and !Edit software, with RISC OS operating software. This book shows how these applications can be used to produce high-quality documents without the need for an expensive desktop publishing package.

SuperCalc 3: A Dabhand Guide

by Dr. A. A. Berk

ISBN 1-870336-65-8

240 pages

Price: £14.95

A complete tutorial and reference guide for one of the most popular pieces of software of all time - SuperCalc spreadsheet for the Amstrad PC1512, 1640 and other PC-compatibles. It will appeal to both the beginner and the more experienced user and covers every aspect of setting up, using and applying the spreadsheet.

Master 512 Technical Guide: A Dabhand Guide
by Robin Burton

ISBN 1-870336-80-1

417 pages

Price: £14.95

The definitive hardware and software reference for the dedicated users of the Master 512, Acorn's PC-compatible upgrade for BBC and Master computers.

Master 512 User Guide: A Dabhand Guide
by Chris Snee

ISBN 1-870336-14-3

224 pages

Book: £14.95 Disc £7.95. Book and disc £19.95 (£21.95 3.5")

The most significant tutorial and reference guide for the Master 512.

Here is a list of just some of the topics that are covered in the book: what you get on the discs, DOS Plus versions, explanation of the filing system, DOS Plus CLI commands (syntax, abbreviations and errors), transient commands, file types, reserved extensions, reserved words, I/O, the 512 memory map, how a PC works, 8086 registers, MS-DOS, 512 Tube, the 80186 monitor, differences between DOS Plus and MS-DOS, making software work on the 512, colour limitations, hard disc set-up, PC disc formats, software compatibility, public domain software...

C: A Dabhand Guide

1st and 2nd Edition

By Jon Mountfort

ISBN 1-870336-16-X

512 pages

Price: £14.95. 3.5" Disc £9.95. 5.25" Disc £7.95

This is the most comprehensive introductory guide to C yet written, giving clear, comprehensive explanations of this important programming language. The book is packed with example programs, making use of all C's facilities. Unique diagrams and illustrations help you visualise programs and to think in C.

Z88: A Dabhand Guide

By Trinity Concepts

ISBN 1-870336-60-7

296 pages

Price £14.95

An indispensable guide for all users of the Z88 portable computer. It covers all the standard built in application programs with clear explanations and easy to follow examples. No previous knowledge is assumed in this book which covers topics such as PipeDream, The Filer, printing, EPROM and RAM cartridges, machine expansion, file transfer, modem communications and an introduction to BBC BASIC.

Z88 Pipedream: A Dabhand Guide
By John Allen

ISBN 1-870336-61-5

240 pages

Price: £14.95

A definitive guide to PipeDream, the revolutionary integrated business software package on the Cambridge Computer Z88 portable computer. No prior knowledge is assumed.

Forthcoming Winter Books for 1992/3
RISC OS 3 First Steps

By Anne Rooney

ISBN 1 870336 83 6

Mastering EasiWord

By Anne Rooney

ISBN 1 870336 84 4

Wimp Programming Made Easy

By Alan Senior

ISBN 1 870336 53 4

**A Beginners Guide to Business Accounting
on the PC: A Dabhand Guide**

By Geoff Cox and John Brown

ISBN 1-870336-89-5

Graphics on the ARM: A Dabhand Guide

By Roger Amos

ISBN 1-870336-13-5

Basic Wimp Programming: A Dabhand Guide

By Alan Senior

ISBN 1-870336-53-4

Macintosh Graphic Design: A Dabhand Guide

By Nick Clarke

**Macintosh Professional Publishing:
A Dabhand Guide**

By Stuart Price

Psion Series 3: A Dabhand Guide

By Patrick Hall

ISBN 1-870336-97-6

Amstrad NC100 Notebook: A Dabhand Guide

By Ian Sinclair

ISBN 1-870336-68-2

Software available from Dabs Press

**FingerPrint by David Spencer for the BBC and
Master Micros**

Disc & manual, DFS version, £9.95, ADFS version, £11.95

A unique single-step machine code tracing program allowing you to step through any machine code program. FingerPrint will even trace code situated in Sideways RAM/ROM – learn how BASIC works!

MOS Plus by David Spencer for BBC Master 128

ROM, £12.9; Disc for Sideways RAM, £7.95 (3.5in, £9.95)

Provides ADFS *FORMAT, *VERIFY , *BACKUP, *CATALL and *EXALL in ROM and new * commands such as *FIND – which finds a file anywhere on an ADFS disc. A complete alarm system is present using the Master 128 alarm facility, as is an AMX mouse driver. The ROM also fixes the infamous DFS *CLOSE bug.

SideWriter by Mike Ginns for BBC and Master with Sideways RAM

5.25in DFS disc, £7.95, 3.5in ADFS disc, £9.95

A pop-up notepad which can be used from within any application from Sideways RAM. Simply press SHIFT-CTRL-TAB and your program is suspended, and you're in SideWriter ready to make a note. Press TAB and you're back with your application screen exactly as you left it. Notes taken in SideWriter can be saved to disc, transferred to a wordprocessor, or printed out.

Master Emulation ROM by David Spencer for BBC B/B+

ISBN 1-870336-23-2 Available Now

Software pack in ROM, £19.95 (disc for Sideways RAM, £14.95)

Provides model B and B+ owners with most of the features of the Master 128, such as the new * commands, the extended filing system operations including the temporary filing system, the *CONFIGURE system (using battery-backed Sideways RAM and/or a disc file), and if you have the hardware, Sideways or Shadow RAM. The only Master Operating System software not covered in this ROM is the extended graphics software. Works with all popular SRAM boards.

HyperDriver by Robin Burton for BBC and Master Micros

Software pack in ROM, £29.95. Sideways RAM version, only £24.95

HyperDriver isn't just another printer ROM – it's the ultimate one. And if you have a printer, then HyperDriver will be the most significant purchase you can make. It's absurdly easy to use and provides you with many of the facilities missing from your current software including: on-screen preview, CRT graphics, NLQ font and user-definable macros to name but a few. No matter what you use your printer for, wordprocessing, spreadsheets, databases, programming you will have in excess of 80, yes 80!, * commands available for instant use from within applications such as VIEW, InterWord and so on. Thus, commands can be embedded within text, spreadsheets etc.

HyperDriver provides a full preview facility so that you can see what will be printed on screen. The effects of all HyperDriver commands are displayed, for instance, italics, double height, bold, condensed, super and subscript, underlined and so on.

HyperDriver is fully Epson-compatible. HyperDriver's macro command facility allows you to add your own HyperDriver commands so that effects present on new releases of printer, eg. NLQ, double height and so on, can be added with the minimum of fuss.

The HyperDriver pack contains a 16k EPROM for permanent internal fitting to the micro, and a Sideways RAM image on disc. The disc also contains sample programs and files for ease of use and reference. A full and comprehensive 100-page manual and reference card complete this value for money package

The inbuilt NLQ font allows printers that do not have an inbuilt NLQ font to produce text of this standard, and provides printers that do have the capability with an extra NLQ typeface. CRT graphics handling and an integral VIEW driver are included.

HyperDriver is supplied in ROM format The accompanying disc contains a Sideways RAM version of HyperDriver plus numerous examples. The comprehensive 100-page manual ensures that you get the most from the product.

Please note:

All future publications are in an advanced state of preparation. We reserve the right to alter and adapt them without notification. If you would like more information about Dabs Press, books and software, then drop us a line to Dabhand Guides, PO Box 48, Prestwich, Manchester, M25 7HF.

INDEX

IMPRESSION II Disc

£2.00 inc. VAT

There is a disc to accompany this book which is available by sending £2.00 (to cover production costs and postage) to:

DABS PRESS

PO Box 48, Prestwich, Manchester. M25 7HN